Acclaim

"This sweet story is the perfect friends-to-lovers tale. Filled with authentic family dynamics, powerful themes, and the most wholesome of romances, Schaller kept me reading until the very end. If you're looking for a book that will make you grin like a fool and warm your heart, then *Riley + Sam* is the one for you!"

—ALISSA ZAVALIANOS, author of *Endlewood* and *Unearth the Tides*

"A cozy, feel-good story that will warm readers' hearts. Perfect for anyone seeking a sweet best friend romance, supportive family dynamics, and classic summer vibes."

—BECKY DEAN, author of *Love & Other Great Expectations*

"This is the perfect blend of swoony K-drama, best friends, family dynamics, and the quintessential American summer. Sheer perfection! One of the best books I've read this year!"

—AJ SKELLY, bestselling author of *Of Flame & Frost* and *Murder at Mistlethwaite Manor*

"Adorable. Sweet. Heartwarming. This book is the cutest and Ashley Schaller's story is sure to satisfy those wanting a clean read with a sweet romance!"

—BRITTANY EDEN, author of *Wishes*

"Faith, friendship, family and fame collide in this sweet YA romance about discovering who you are and having the courage to be that person, even through the doubts. From the first page, I was in love with this quirky family and the way they cared about each other. Add in the boy-next-door/first crush/second chance at love pop star hiding from his scores of teenaged (and not so teenaged) female fans, and what you get is a beautiful story which tugs at your heart, catches your breath, and leaves you smiling. Such a great read."

—HANNAH CURRIE, author of the Daughters of Peverell and Crown of Promise series

"Cheese and crackers! I didn't want to stop reading this clean and wholesome contemporary YA romance. Can this please be the start of a series? Readers will melt over the marshmallowy sweet childhood friends-to-first-love romance that develops between sensible Riley and boy-next-door-turned-overnight-pop-star, Sam.

A wise father, protective older sister, and two sidekicks (one of them furry) round out this lovable cast. Ashley Schaller delivers another trustworthy story loaded with faith that teens (and their parents) are sure to enjoy."

—STEPHANIE DANIELS, author of *The Uncertainty of Fire*

Riley + Sam

Riley + Sam

Quill & Flame
FIREBRAND

ASHLEY SCHALLER

Quill & Flame
PUBLISHING HOUSE

Riley + Sam

Cover background by Angela Lynum

Cover art by Julia Ruprecht

Chapter art by Angela Lynum

To Aly - Thank you for being my Lou-Lou.

Chapter 1

I stare down at the toilet bowl, tipping my head first one way and then the next as I size it up. Could it swallow me whole? It's not something I've given much thought since I was three years old, but now I hope it's possible.

A fist pounds on the other side of the locked door. "Riley Alyne, you open this door right now."

Great, Mackenzie's found me.

"Go away," I shout at my older sister as I pace away from the toilet in the little space allotted. I breathe deeply, taking in the scent of my hibiscus shampoo lingering from this morning's shower. If I can hold out for...I don't know...three more hours? I'll be in the clear.

"Get out here." *Thump.* The door rattles. Did she kick it? "It's your turn to deal with Aunt Augustine."

The thought turns my hands clammy. I clamp my lips shut. I'll play the silent game. Kenzie will get frustrated and leave. I lean against the sink counter and pick at my cuticles. Maybe I should paint my nails. It would buy me at least another fifteen minutes.

"R-i-i-i-i-l-e-y." She drags out my name and jiggles the door handle.

I massage the side of my neck. Pretend I don't recognize the desperation in her voice. Does that make me a terrible sister? Probably. I fluff my blonde hair and reapply some watermelon flavored lip gloss. Is there a smudge on my glasses? Yep, it's a smudge. I swipe them from my face and massage the fabric of my t-shirt over the lenses until they come clean.

"It's only fair." It's the silence following her words that sends a strike of guilt through my heart. Because I can picture her now, shoulders slumped in defeat, tears pricking her eyes, ready to give in if I refuse to open this door. My darling older sister is prepared to play the martyr if I can't get my act together.

Ugh.

She's right.

I'm a terrible sister.

With one last longing look at the toilet, I shove my glasses onto my nose and wrench the door open.

"Oh, thank goodness." Mackenzie spills into the cramped space and shoves the door closed once more. "Listen to me. Get out there and get your game face on. Aunt Auggie practically has me engaged to Joey McPherson." Her arms flail for emphasis. "I'm not ready to get married! And *Joey*? He still picks his nose."

"Woah, slow down. Aunt Auggie can't force you into an arranged marriage." I cross my arms over my t-shirt that says *today calls for an extra cup* with a coffee mug beneath. I had three cups this morning, something I won't admit to anyone, and it might account for the way my fingers tremble, but I needed the caffeine to hype myself up for this afternoon.

"She has the wedding colors picked out." Kenzie's voice rises toward a shriek.

"You're overthinking things, Kenzie."

"Easy for you to say. Two hours. I've had to deal with Aunt Auggie's cross examination for two hours. You owe me." She narrows her eyes and jams her extended finger in front of my nose as if I didn't hear her.

I push up my glasses to remind her I'm wearing them and can see her just fine without needing to study her fingerprints.

She pulls back, but her hand settles on her hip, signaling she's still prepared to do battle. "It's your turn and I refuse to hear otherwise. You will *not* get out of this."

I heave a sigh, but she's right. Duty calls. "But what do I say?" I haven't figured out what I want to do with my life, and Aunt Auggie can smell an unplanned life a mile away. With my high school graduation coming next year, she's sure to be sniffing out my ten-year plan.

Mackenzie throws her hands in the air. "I don't know. Make something up."

Okay, she's officially had it. My beautiful sister with her long chestnut hair is about to have a complete meltdown which hasn't happened since I-don't-know-when. Time for an intervention.

I grab Kenzie's shoulders and lean closer until our faces are inches apart. "Breathe. In and out. No worries. I'll deal with Aunt Augustine. You take a few minutes to collect yourself, and then you can get back to enjoying your party." After all, this is her day. One of those once in a lifetime things. And considering we never threw a party for her high school graduation, she doubly deserves to enjoy her graduation from college, party included.

"Right." She inhales and shakes out her hands. "Yeah, okay."

I pat her back before taking a few deep breaths of my own. Too bad they don't make vests for verbal jabs like those that can stop bullets. But that's okay. I've got this. Fair is fair. Except I still haven't opened the door.

"Riley." Kenzie's voice is full of warning and payback if I balk now. "Lou-Lou is running interference and it's not fair to leave her out there alone."

"Would it be so bad?" I shove my hands into the back pockets of my jeans. Kenzie and I can camp out here for the next couple hours. No one needs to know.

Mackenzie gives me a look.

Because it would be a horrible thing to do. Our twelve-year-old cousin isn't even related to Aunt Auggie.

"Go." Kenzie flicks her wrist, banishing me to my fate.

"Fine." I make sure she can see my eye roll, but then I obey and wrench the bathroom door open. The sound of chatter drifts from downstairs where people cram into almost every inch of the main floor and even spill onto the back deck and into the lawn. Aunt Auggie insisted on a large party to mark Kenzie's college graduation. Something about the oldest child flying the nest even though Kenzie plans to continue living here while working nearby.

The scent of something sweet wafts up the staircase. Well, at least I can enjoy a cupcake while Aunt Auggie grills me. I mean if my mouth is full of sugary carbs, I can't do much more than grunt, and then she's free to come to her own conclusions.

Oh, Lord, give me strength, because I really don't want to do this. I offer up the prayer as I clench the banister and prepare to meet my fate.

As soon as I trudge down the last step, Lou-Lou springs off the couch where Aunt Auggie has her cornered. "Oh, look Riley's here."

Traitor.

I shoot up another prayer for strength, peace, and a whole extra dose of love before I paint on a happy face and allow Lou-Lou to drag me over to my relative.

"Oh, thank you, Olivia. I've been wanting to speak to Riley all afternoon." Aunt Augustine squeezes Lou-Lou's arm and rises to blow an air kiss past each of my cheeks while clasping my hands long enough that it gets awkward.

"No problem." Lou-Lou slaps my back before scampering off to hide out in some dark corner.

Double traitor.

The least she could have done was stick around to facilitate peace during our little chat.

"How are you dear?" Aunt Augustine releases one of my hands to fluff her hair which is almost crispy from too many trips to the hair salon to replace her grays with a vibrant amber hue.

I tuck my free hand in the back pocket of my jeans while I have the freedom to do so. "Oh, you know, I've been busy. Lots of clients this month."

"Are you still doing those little scribbles of yours?" She raises one penciled eyebrow.

"Digital art," I correct, working hard to keep any offense out of my tone.

"That's right." She releases my second hand to bat hers around in a dramatic fashion. "I can never keep up with the terms kids use these days."

Okay. Enough about me. "How are you? How was your trip to Paris?" If there's nothing else I've learned, you have to keep her talking about herself if you don't want your life choices ripped to shreds.

"Lovely as always, though I need to remember to hire someone to clean my villa before I arrive next time. The dust!" She shakes her head in disgust.

Yeah. She has a villa. In Paris. A dusty one, but a villa all the same.

"Ooh, yeah, that's a shame." I rub my arm because I don't know what else to do with my hands. "Did—"

"So dear, your own graduation isn't too far down the line. Please tell me you've made plans." She leans in close like we're a pair of conspirators and fusses with her pearl necklace.

And here we are. "Um, no, not really." I inwardly cringe and tuck my hair behind my ear. "I was actually thinking of taking a gap year." Yep. I said it.

Her eyes narrow and she leans forward, pointing one painted nail in front of my eyes. "Gap years are for lazy children who want to live in their parents' basements rent free for the rest of their lives."

I clamp my teeth together. Hard. I could list articles, studies, the works, but when her mind is made up, it's made up, and there's not much point in arguing against her.

Aunt Auggie plants her hands on her hips. "Surely your father has something to say about such a foolhardy idea?"

Actually, he's had a lot to say. Like how he might take time off of work so we can travel somewhere together. Maybe a few well-placed words and resources wouldn't be amiss. Just enough to show I've thought this through. "Well, actually, I've done a little research and have been saving up with the commission money I make, and—"

"Oh, Riley darling, when are you going to get a *real* job?" She leans in close.

Again.

Umm...personal space? I tilt backward. And a real job? As if hours bent over my tablet don't count. Just because it's fun and I love it, doesn't mean it's not work. Not like she'll ever believe I have a shot at turning it into a viable career. "You know, I think I hear Kenzie calling me." I jab a thumb over my shoulder. "It was great catching up with you." I pat her arm and scurry away before she can stop me. I duck behind a group of Mackenzie's friends and work my way to the refreshment table and snag a cupcake with tons of sugary blue icing as a reward for surviving.

"That lasted five minutes."

I jump and find Lou-Lou standing beside me, arms crossed.

"Only five?" I ask around a mouthful of junk food.

"Really, Riley?" She cocks an eyebrow. "I held my own for a good fifteen minutes if not more. We won't even talk about the record Kenzie *still* holds."

"Okay, okay," I concede as I grab a napkin from the table and swipe frosting from my fingers. "I'm a wimp."

"You can say that again. I'm disappointed in you Riley Alyne Anderson."

How on earth does she manage to rattle off my full name like she's a century older than me? I can't even defend myself.

Kenzie saves me by stepping in front of the fireplace with a microphone. "Hi, I'd like to say a few words. Most importantly, thank you all for coming. Each one of you has truly been a blessing in my life..."

If I were to draw this moment, I would focus on Kenzie's beaming smile, Dad's hand on her shoulder, being—well—a proud dad. I'd blur the crowd. A splash of color, a bit of light. Enough details to convey they were here, but not enough to take away from the centerpiece.

I laugh with the others as she tells a joke about Dad and he bashfully waves her off. Rub the lump in my throat and move up front to give her a side-hug when she mentions how much she wishes Mom could have been here to see this momentous life-step. We all do. But as she goes on to thank influential teachers and friends, I wander away from the crowd and drift to a stop in front of the window.

My gaze snags on activity at the empty yellow house next door. A figure with a hoodie pulled over his head fumbles with the front door. Uh-uh. No one messes with that house even if its owner hasn't been there in four years. I slide my phone from my pocket.

"What are you doing?"

I jump, free hand going to my chest where my heart thunders. "Mackenzie, you scared me." When did she finish her speech?

"Aunt Auggie's looking for you. She said something about finishing your conversation."

"She'll..."—I crane my neck, trying to get a view of the criminal's face—"have to wait. Besides, I'm calling the cops."

"What?"

I jerk my chin toward the guy who's now fussing with the welcome mat outside the neighbor's door. It's almost like he knows where they keep the spare key. Which yes, it's cliché and I tried to talk them out of it, but alas, they never listened. Now they'll wish they had.

"Put that away." Kenzie snags my phone and powers it off, as I'm about to dial.

"Mackenzie." I lunge, but she raises her arm over her head, using her extra two inches of height to her advantage. "You'll be arrested for aiding and abetting."

"Oh, please. You've been watching too many criminal dramas." She waves my phone in front of my face. "Think. He knows where the spare key is. The Hongs are probably renting the place out."

"One guy can afford that?" I cock an eyebrow even as a note of discomfort settles in my stomach. Why would the Hongs be renting the place after all this time? Sure, they moved away years ago, but still, it's theirs. Anyone else living there would just be wrong.

She crosses her arms, my phone still in her grip. "Riley, you have no idea what he does for a living or how old he is."

Young, based off the hoodie and skinny jeans, but I won't argue the point. "You're sure he's not breaking in?"

"Yep." She turns me to face the window once more. "There will probably be a moving van and a passel of roommates arriving tonight or tomorrow."

The guy has moved inside, shut the door behind him, and lights are flickering to life all around the house. All right, I admit if he's a criminal, he's not the smartest. I mean do you need a beacon to let people know you're there?

"I know you promised Sam you'd look after the place, but chill." Kenzie hands me the phone.

"Okay, okay. But if he comes out with his arms loaded with electronics, I'm blaming you."

"Sure thing, detective." She pats my shoulder.

"Riley"—Lou-Lou scampers over to me—"your aunt sent me to find you. And Uncle Gavin says it's time to pray before you cut the cake, Mackenzie."

"I'll be right there." Kenzie heads off to herd her friends toward the dining room table where a cake decked out in her college colors waits.

"But, but..." I stammer.

"You should have given her the full twenty minutes. At least." Lou-Lou shakes her head. "Just think, you could be eating cake right now." She shoves her purple glasses higher on her nose before flouncing off to join my sister at the cake cutting station.

So not fair.

"R-i-i-i-l-e-e-e-y," Aunt Auggie sing-songs as she makes her way over.

I paste on a smile even as my eyebrow twitches.

"Darling, I meant to ask..."

Chapter 2

I slump into my seat at the breakfast corner, glasses sitting low on my nose, hair thrown into a slanted messy bun.

"Wow, rough night, kiddo?" Dad sets down his tablet and studies me over the rim of his reading glasses.

I prop my chin on my hand and lean my weight on my elbow. "I stayed up way too late last night working on a project." I like to think of it as a reward for surviving Aunt Auggie. Bonus points, I get paid. Still, something isn't quite right with the art piece and I can't put my finger on what is missing.

"Whatcha working on?" Dad asks around a mouthful of cereal.

"A commission for an author. I guess she's going to use the art as a goodie for the pre-order campaign for her upcoming release." I'm not much of a reader, but when I searched up pre-orders a lot of information came up on how they help the authors. "I guess it's good for sales."

"That's cool." He bobs his chin. "Do you get a free copy of the book when it comes out?"

"Dad." I shake my head and laugh. "I get paid. That's enough."

"If you say so, kiddo." He lifts his tablet and returns to reading whatever had his attention before. I study him as his gaze bounces around the illuminated page. He's not looking great himself. But

I guess you don't get to become one of the head honchos at an up-and-coming marketing firm without working for it.

Our golden-retriever, Sarge, comes over and props his slobbery chin on my thigh, looking at me with pleading, chocolate-colored eyes. "After breakfast." I rub one of his soft ears between my fingers. He leans into my touch, but still grumbles his disappointment at my life choices. Walks come first, foremost, and always to him. Except when the temperature gets over seventy degrees.

"Oh, I wanted to talk to you about something." Dad jerks his attention from his screen to me.

I squirm on my chair. "I wanted to talk to you" can mean anything from *what do you think about ice cream for dinner?* to *Mom's dying.* I straighten the hem of my pajama shorts. "Yeah?"

He lays aside his reading glasses.

Uh-oh. This is serious. When the glasses come off, it always is. Please don't say you're sick, or Kenzie, or...no, not Sarge! I run a hand over my sweet dog's head as if it'll somehow undo what Dad's about to say.

"So, about this summer..."

It's big. Whatever it is, it's big. We're moving. Aunt Auggie's coming to live with us—

The front door bursts open.

Lou-Lou flounces inside, mismatched socks hitting her at knee level, a duffel bag slung over her shoulder, and a rolling suitcase at her side. "I'm here!"

"And that's what I wanted to talk to you about." Dad shakes his head and grins at my cousin.

"Can you believe it, Riley? I get to stay here for the *whole* summer." Lou-Lou dumps her luggage on the entryway rug and flings her arms around my neck.

"That's great." I pat her back and peek over her shoulder to raise my eyebrows at my dad.

He rubs his neck sheepishly.

"And to what do I owe this momentous occasion?" I pull Lou-Lou onto my lap. She may be twelve, but she's petite and a cuddler at heart.

She groans and rolls her eyes. "Business trip. To Hawaii of all places and they couldn't even bring me!"

"Not just Hawaii. China, India, Japan...and a few others I'm forgetting just now." Dad points his stylus at her.

Her parents travel all around the world, especially in the summer when they don't have to worry about Lou-Lou's school schedule. They take her along on their shorter trips. Sometimes. I love my aunt and uncle. A lot. But we're the designated 'dump Lou-Lou so we can travel the world' station. Sometimes I swear they had her to check off a box on their to-do-list. Fortunately, she's as dear to me as Kenzie.

"So, lucky you." Lou-Lou leans far enough away that she can flash me a cheeky grin. "You get me all summer."

"Lucky me." And while it may complicate some of my plans, it'll be a blast. "Go unpack your things."

She springs off my lap and zooms over to her discarded luggage. "Sleepover!"

Good thing I have a queen size bed. Kenzie's too much of a kicker for Lou-Lou to share with her, plus my sister will pull some oldest sibling privilege card. So, it'll be me, Lou-Lou, and Sarge. For the whole summer.

Yippee.

Dad's gaze connects with mine as Lou-Lou stampedes up the stairs and disappears into my bedroom. "I would have asked you. I know you planned to work on your art this summer and take on some extra commissions—"

I raise a hand, cutting him off. "It's fine, Dad."

"I got the text last night." He sighs. "You know my brother. Last minute is his thing."

"It's okay, Dad."

He rubs his neck. "Listen, if you don't want to do this, we'll work something out. Maybe my mom…"

I tilt my head to the side and give him a look. "Grandma Lois lives in a fifty-and-up neighborhood."

"I know, but she could take her for a week at least. Or there's Margery's sister." He snaps his fingers. "Lou-Lou could stay with her."

"She lives in a tiny studio apartment. Lou-Lou would be bored out of her mind." We cannot do that to her. Vanessa, I mean. No one wants a bored Lou-Lou on their hands.

He pinches the bridge of his nose. "I'm sorry, Ri."

"It's okay." I wave off his words. "I'll shuffle things around. Besides, Lou-Lou's not a little kid. It's not like I'll be babysitting her."

"Still, it doesn't seem fair. You wanted the quiet of the house all to yourself…"

I reach out and catch his hand. Squeeze. "It'll be fine. I promise."

He smiles, gratitude shining in his eyes. "Thanks, sweetie."

Lou-Lou skips down the stairs. "Okay, what's the first thing on our agenda?"

Dad stands and sweeps his breakfast things off the table and takes them to the sink. "I've got to head to work." He pops a kiss on my head and then does some serious six-step handshake with Lou-Lou. "You girls have fun."

"Have a good day," we call in unison as he steps into the garage.

"Sooo…" Lou-Lou props her hands on the table and waggles her eyebrows. "What are we going to do first?"

I massage my forehead. "Coffee. Coffee first. Always."

She sticks her tongue out. "You know my parents won't let me drink that stuff."

"Well, lucky for me, mine will." I tweak her nose and get up to pour myself a cup of black delightfulness and pull a jug of the good creamer out of the fridge as a special reward. I've had to hide it under a package of lettuce all week to keep Kenzie from drinking it all. I take a good long sip before turning to face my cousin once more. Ah, much better.

"Please, let's do something." She clasps her hands under her chin and bounces up and down. "I'm *so* bored."

"You've been here ten minutes."

"That's enough time to be bored."

"Fine. Let me finish my coffee, then you can help me take Sarge for a walk."

He wags his tail and trots to me like he expects me to drop everything and clip his leash into place right this second.

"Yes." Lou-Lou does a fist pump. And then her attention turns to the mug in my hand. "Chug, chug, chug!"

Sarge's tail slaps the floor to the beat of her chant. Great, they've joined forces.

I mock glare at Lou-Lou over the rim of my mug. "Olivia Anne, you be patient or I swear I'll make you study algebra all summer."

My cousin snaps her lips shut and sits on a barstool, hands folded daintily in her lap. "Well, let us know when you're ready. At your convenience, of course."

Right. Like she won't be chanting again if I'm not ready in the next five minutes. I gulp the rest of my coffee and place the mug in the sink. "All right, go get his leash."

Lou-Lou scans me from head to toe. "Not to be rude, cousin dearest, but maybe you'd like to get dressed first?"

I drop my gaze to take in my tie-dye sweater and matching shorts. "What's wrong with this?"

She leans back and shoots another judgmental look down my form. "Um...you're in your pjs."

"Listen, kid, if I can walk around a campground in my pajamas, then who decided it's inappropriate in a neighborhood?"

"The HOA?" Lou-Lou purses her lips.

"Funny. Let's go." I head to the front door, shove my feet in a pair of sandals, leash up Sarge, and jerk the door open.

Lou-Lou skips along beside me. "It's your reputation."

"Exactly."

We've barely gone past our mailbox when Sarge gives a sharp tug on the leash. I tighten my grip. "Easy, boy."

"You did let him out this morning, didn't you?" Lou-Lou's tone only holds a *small* note of judgment.

"Dad did. I—"

Sarge yanks again and the leash pulls free from my hand and he takes off.

"Was it a cat?" I yell over my shoulder. They're the bane of his existence.

Lou-Lou is fast on my heels. "I didn't see."

Sarge ducks through the neighbor's shrubs, leaving a burst of leaves and broken twigs in his path. Great. I race to the end of the hedge and slide around to— "No, Sarge! Sarge, sit!"

But it's too late. He's already knocked over the guy in shorts and a baseball cap. Right into a mud puddle.

No, no, no! How many lawsuits are going to come our way after this? I race to the pair only to have my feet shoot out from under me. I squeal. And land in the sticky wet goo. On my bum. Meanwhile, Sarge is all in the guy's face, his tail whipping in frantic glee.

"He's friendly?" I offer with a wince. Too bad this isn't quick sand. I'd be okay with being swallowed right about now.

"It's okay." The guy's laughing even as he tries to push Sarge backward.

I grab my dog's collar and haul him off as he gives one last giant kiss to the guy's face, knocking his baseball cap into the mud, revealing bubblegum pink hair.

"I'm *so* sorry..." I start to apologize, but then my eyes connect with his and my words trickle to an end. "Sam?" My grip goes slack and Sarge springs free once more, smothering my best friend in kisses.

Sam grins at me, roughing the fur on either side of Sarge's neck. "Hey, Riley."

All I can do is stare. "You're back."

"You didn't tell me you were coming home." I swipe at a loose hair falling free from my bun, leaving a streak of mud across my forehead. And I'm sitting here, covered in mud, in my pajamas. *A little warning next time, God?*

Sarge sits, tongue lolling out the side of his mouth, his work accomplished.

Sam sits straighter, one arm propped on a dirty knee. "I wanted to surprise you."

"I am surprised." Shocked. Dumbfounded. Flabbergasted. "But you should have said something. We could have had the whole place cleaned and waiting." I wave a hand to indicate the yellow house behind us.

Sam shakes his head. "It's okay."

"Look, one of my dad's friends probably knows of a cleaning service—"

"No, no." Sam snatches his ball cap, covering his vibrant hair once more. "No one can know I'm here."

"Oh." With him being all famous now, I should have expected as much. "Well, Kenzie and I could at least—"

He catches my flailing hand. "I know how to run a vacuum, Ri."

My gaze snags on his rich brown stare, and then we're both laughing.

"I'm glad you're back," I say.

He doesn't let go of my hand. "Riley, there's something I need to—"

"What are you two doing? You're acting like a bunch of pigs in a pen." I startle to find Lou-Lou standing behind us, hands propped on her hips.

I pull my hand from Sam's and try to stand, but my feet slip on the mud and I'm back on my bottom.

"Here, let me." Sam stands with far more grace and reaches to help me up.

"Thanks. Lou-Lou, you remember Sam, right?" I try to clean myself off, but it only streaks the mud further. Fabulous.

She gives me a look, clearly saying "duh" before she turns her studious gaze on Sam and bumps her glasses higher on her nose. "They use a lot of photoshop on your pictures, don't they?"

"Uh—" Pink streaks Sam's cheeks.

"Olivia," I squeak, reaching to adjust my own crooked glasses.

"And your roots are showing." Lou-Lou crosses her arms and shakes her head at Sam like she's scolding a child.

Sam jerks his hat lower.

"Lou-Lou," I hiss and stalk over to her. "You're being rude."

"He deserves it." She turns a glare on Sam.

Fire scalds my ears. Can the earth swallow us all now? "Lou—"

She holds up a hand, cutting me off. "Nope. Sam took off and dumped you here alone. Never to think of you again."

Oh. My. Goodness.

"Stop it." I make a grab for her arm, but she side-steps out of reach.

She focuses her ire on Sam and taps her foot. "What do you have to say for yourself, 'Sammy?' Hmm? I want to know."

"I..." He rubs at his neck and I wonder if he's realized he poured a handful of mud down his back.

"Lou-Lou, you were eight. I don't think you understand." I lean in close, hoping Sam can't hear. A few hymns and popular song covers posted online, and bam, my best friend turned into an overnight success. Of course, he had to leave. Opportunities to live your dreams don't come every day.

"Oh, I understand. 'Sammy' got all big and famous and left the little people behind."

Wasn't it this morning I told Dad she wasn't a little kid? If she keeps this up, she's headed for a serious time-out. "Lou-Lou, listen to me. Stop it. Right now."

"It's okay, Riley." Sam holds up a hand. "She's...she's right."

In that moment, all I can see is the pain in his eyes. My own heart cinches tight. "Sam—"

"Oh, no you don't." Lou-Lou snatches my hand and pulls me backward. "I watched you mope around for years. You're just getting over him. It's my responsibility to make sure you're not making a mistake."

"Lou-Lou." I fight her grip, but she is strong for a girl who barely reaches my chest. "Lou-Lou!"

"What?" She huffs after she's maneuvered me to the other side of the hedge.

"Sarge?" I wave a hand to the hedge and raise my eyebrows at her.

"I'll get him." Her eyes dare me to argue.

I could. I so could, but I won't. Because it'll be much easier to talk with Sam and get his story if she's not around. "Sam, ice cream night is still on Wednesday," I shout.

"I'll be there."

"Go to your room." Lou-Lou shoves me backward and points toward my house.

I can't help but laugh as I walk away.

Chapter 4

I've been grounded by a twelve-year-old. Classy. Except I'm in my room, door shut, earbuds in, and tablet laid across my lap. Am I supposed to be upset about this? I lay on my back, legs propped against the wall. My damp hair soaks the back of my clean t-shirt and I tap my electronic pencil against my screen. Except I can't concentrate on the commission I'm supposed to be working on. Instead, I open a clean page and start doodling.

The door opens.

I won't give her the satisfaction of looking.

A small foot taps in my peripheral vision. "You're *drawing* him?"

I startle and glance at my screen. Sure enough, a bubblegum pink-haired figure covers it. Oops.

Lou-Lou snatches my tablet. "He abandoned you."

"Hey." I roll to a sitting position. "He did *not* abandon me."

Her eyebrows shoot high.

"He just…" I comb a stray hair out of my eyes. "He got busy."

"The life of a star." She waves her hand dramatically. "Every celebrity's excuse to turn into a jerk."

"He is not a jerk." Or at least I hope not. How can I truly know when we haven't spoken in years?

Her nose wrinkles and she pinches her lips tight before turning her attention to my tablet. "This is good." She angles her gaze over the rim of her glasses. "Too good."

Ugh. So dramatic. "Give it back." I make a grab for it, but Lou-Lou dances out of reach.

"Delete." She jabs a finger against my tablet.

Brat. I scramble to my feet and snatch my device. But the screen is once again blank. "Olivia!"

She backs up, hands raised. "Listen. This is for your own good. Let's take a few deep breaths."

"You had no right." I toss my tablet onto my floral comforter and swivel on my cousin.

Her eyes round.

"Don't overreact." She retreats. "Riley!" She screeches as I charge for her. She's out the door, through the hallway, and scampering down the steps in a flash.

Curse her youth.

I scramble after her.

"Calm down." She slides behind the living room coffee table.

I hurtle the couch and face off with her. "What is your problem?"

"Nothing. I'm just trying to look out for you." She circles left.

I mirror her action. "Oh, so deleting my work is looking out for me?"

"That was *work*?" How does she drip so much condescension in one word?

"It could have been some fangirl's commission for all you know."

"You have more class than that." She sweeps me with a look. "Or so I thought."

That's it. I run at her.

She shrieks and races for the kitchen.

My foot catches on the leg of the coffee table. "Cheese and crackers!" I grab my throbbing foot and bounce around on my uninjured appendage. That's going to leave a bruise. "You are so dead," I shout at my cousin.

An eerie silence creeps over the house as I release my foot and slink toward the kitchen. The little sneak is no doubt hiding somewhere, ready to jump out at a moment's notice. I bypass the kitchen island, checking first one side, then the next to be sure she isn't crouching behind it. No Lou-Lou.

"Come out, come out, wherever you are." I speed toward the dining room table, but she's not there either.

Sarge trots over to me, shoving his nose into my behind like it'll somehow tell him if I've lost my mind.

"Hey." I nudge him back. Wait. An ally. I crouch at his eye-level. "Go find Lou-Lou."

He cocks his head.

"Lou-Lou. Find Lou-Lou."

He wags his tail.

Turncoat. Less than a day, and he likes her better.

I stand.

"R-i-i-i-l-e-y." Lou-Lou sings in a creepy voice. The freezer half of our fridge swings open. "Want an ice cream bar?"

I cross my arms and cock a hip. I will not be bought. "Nice try, kid."

A hand appears over the island, waving a package dotted with ice crystals. My favorite ice cream bar with peanuts and caramel swirl hangs in her grasp.

I. Will. Not. Be. Bought.

"It's the last one," she croons.

"Fine." I stalk forward.

The ice cream bar dips behind the counter. "You have to forgive me first."

I roll my eyes. "Whatever."

"Nope, you have to mean it."

"Fine. I forgive you." I hold out my hand.

She dutifully deposits the ice cream bar on my palm. I tear through the packaging and bite into the delectable goodness. A chilling blast of cold stings my teeth. Ouch.

The front door swings open and Kenzie enters. She stops abruptly, taking us in. Me with a half-eaten ice cream bar, Lou-Lou using the island as a shield.

"What's going on?" Kenzie deposits her backpack near the door and scratches Sarge behind the ears.

I straighten my shoulders.

Lou-Lou dashes out from behind the island. "Hold on, before you take her side, let me explain."

Kenzie crosses her arms. "I'm impartial."

Lou-Lou scoffs. "You're her sister."

"And you're practically one too."

Oh, forget this. "She deleted one of my pictures," I grumble around a mouthful of ice cream, but as the sweetness of the caramel sauce and the saltiness of the peanuts collide across my taste buds, it's hard to remember why I'm mad.

Kenzie's eyes go wide and she pins our cousin with one of her intimidating oldest-sibling looks. "Lou-Lou!"

Ha. Take that cuz.

"Wait." Lou-Lou backs away from Kenzie. "Let me explain."

"You should know better. Riley works hard on those. Lou-Lou...hours of work..." Kenzie waves her hand like she can't even fathom the thought.

I slide closer to her and shoot a smug look at my cousin.

Lou-Lou's eyes narrow. "I can assure you, it was for a good cause."

Kenzie pinches the bridge of her nose. "I don't think you understand—"

"She was drawing *him*," Lou-Lou cuts her off.

"Him?" Kenzie swivels to face me, frustration and possible anger overshadowed by curiosity and a sudden case of nosiness.

I push the rest of my ice cream bar into my mouth and dust my hands on my shorts to keep from answering.

"Him." Lou-Lou whips her phone out and shoves it in Kenzie's face.

"Sam?" Kenzie frowns at what must be a photo of our next-door neighbor. "Why were you drawing Sammy Hong?" An unspoken 'I thought you were over him' trails her words.

"Because—"

"He's here." Lou-Lou pulls her phone away from Kenzie and drags her over to the window.

"Here?" Kenzie stumbles to keep up with her.

Oh, no. I spring to block their view, but Sarge steps into my path, tail wagging.

They reach the window.

"Sammy Hong is living next door to us?" To her credit, Kenzie only squeals a tiny bit.

"You sound like a fan girl." I bump her aside with my hip, making room for myself at the windowsill.

"A fan of Sam? The kid can sing, but girl, I've known him since we were kids. I've seen him eat ants."

"Ew. Focus." Lou-Lou snaps her fingers in front of my sister's face. "He's back, and *she's* drawing *him*."

"Yeah, what's that about?" Kenzie eyes me.

Too late to blame it on some rabid fan's obsession? No, I can't lie to her. "I didn't mean to, but we ran into him today, and…" I offer a helpless shrug.

"You ran into him? What's he even doing here?"

I lift my hands. "I don't know. *Somebody* didn't let me find out."

Lou-Lou scoffs. "The guy broke your heart."

"I was thirteen and we were just friends. He did *not* break my heart."

"That's what you say."

Kenzie steps between us. "Okay, everybody simmer down. I'm sure we'll find out what Sam's doing here eventually."

"He's coming for ice cream tomorrow night," I say.

"Oh, he better not." Lou-Lou shoots a scathing look toward the window.

"Hey." Kenzie pokes our cousin's nose. "You be nice. And you"—her finger jabs toward me—"be careful."

These girls. "Of what?"

Kenzie steps close and touches my arm. "It's been four years, Ri. He's a world-famous superstar now. I'm just saying, things may be different. *He* might be different."

I cross my arms like a shield. "I'm different too."

"Just guard your heart, okay?"

Guard my heart? "Oh my goodness, Kenzie. It's not like I'm going to date the guy."

"Nope, you'd be ripped apart by his rabid fans," Lou-Lou drawls.

I stick my tongue out at her like the mature seventeen-year-old I am.

She sticks hers right back.

"Ri?"

I eye my sister. "What?" Haven't we blown this whole thing out of proportion enough by now?

"If he's coming for ice cream, you might want to think about restocking the freezer."

"What?" I swivel toward the freezer and yank the door open. Sure enough, the shelves are empty save for an ice cube tray, a bag of fruit, and a half-bag of peas.

"Yeah, that ice cream bar really was the last one." Lou-Lou grips the counter. "Bummer."

Oh, not so fast.

I snag the car keys from Kenzie's bag and shove them into her hand before grabbing Lou-Lou by the arm.

"Uh, what are we doing?" Lou-Lou drags her feet.

"We're all going to the store."

Chapter 5

Dad and I sit on the couch after dinner, sipping on our favorite loose-leaf caramel black tea. It's a tradition we started shortly after my mom died. When neither of us could sleep and we desperately needed a way to connect. Sometimes we watch movies, sometimes we read. Tonight, the news hums in the background while I get back on track with the art commission I was supposed to work on this afternoon and Dad catches up on the paperwork he brought home.

"Our beloved Sammy Hong has disappeared," a newsman announces in a dramatic voice.

I snap my head up, sending my tea splashing over my knee. "Ouch." I swipe at my leg. "Dad, turn it up."

He snags the remote and we both tilt forward as the middle-aged man on tv leans toward us.

"Eighteen-year-old Sammy Hong disappeared over the weekend after failing to take the stage at the sold-out final concert of his world tour. Fans are furious."

Footage from the concert plays. Band, crowd, stage. They are all there and ready to go. Except there's no Sam. Even when fans begin to chant his name nothing happens.

No Sam.

The band shares a confused look. Play the opening chords.

Something twists in my gut as the camera turns to Sam's manager who has taken the stage. She babbles a profuse apology, dismissing the crowd to a chorus of boos and swearing. A few outraged concert goers hurl water bottles at her. She darts off the stage, holding her clipboard as a shield.

"Oh, Sam…" What could have possibly driven him to leave? I think of how he looked this morning. There must have been pain I missed. Pain we've all missed.

The video ends and we return to the news anchor. "Sammy Hong's manager has refused to comment and we know this is not the first time Sammy has failed to show. Not only has he missed three big events in the last month, but he did not make his annual appearance at a charity for chronically ill children."

My mouth drops open. "Why wouldn't Sam sing? Something must have been wrong. He needs to call them and explain." I spring off the couch ready to march across the yard and knock on his door.

"Hold on." Dad catches my arm and pulls me back down.

"But Dad—"

"Shh." Dad's focus stays locked on the tv.

"Here's what fans have to say," the news anchor continues.

A teenage girl with an 'I heart Sammy Hong' t-shirt comes on screen.

"What would you like to tell Sammy Hong?" The interviewer extends a microphone in front of the girl.

"We love you, Sammy. Come home. Please," she begs.

A second girl in a different city holds a sign proclaiming her love of Sam. "We believe in Sammy Hong." She chants and the view expands to take in a group of girls behind her who all chorus the same thing.

The camera cuts to a different girl who is standing in the middle of the street, creating a bonfire. The camera pans out to take in the posters, albums, t-shirts, and various other memorabilia, most of which bear Sam's face from throughout the years.

"If you could say one thing to Sammy Hong, what would it be?" The interviewer probes.

The girl stalks toward the camera. "I trusted you, Sammy. I loved you. No more!" She screams and sets a poster on fire. "You promised to always be there for us. Where were you? Huh?"

I lean back, hoping my couch will save me from the girl's fury.

Thankfully, the news segment comes back to the original anchor. "Sammy Hong's manager asks that if any of his fans know where Sammy is, they call this number."

A phone number flashes across the screen and the news moves on to the next story. I mute the tv. And then sit there, the remote hanging from my fingers.

"Wow," Dad says.

I nod, too numb for words.

"Riley." Dad slips his glasses off and sets them aside.

Oh, no. "Dad, I'm sure Sam has some kind of explanation."

"It's not that, Ri. I'm not sure I want you to get tangled up with him. With this." He points his glasses at the tv. "The paparazzi are going to come crawling around sooner or later."

"But don't you think Sam needs a friend right about now?"

He steeples his fingers under his chin and props his elbows on his knees.

Something cold and dark slips through my stomach. "You're not...you're not going to forbid me from seeing him, are you?"

Dad blows out a breath. "No. For two reasons."

He locks eyes with me and I know this is serious.

"Reason one, I don't want to give you the opportunity to disobey me. Sam was your friend once and I don't want to put you in the position where you would have to choose between us."

I swallow hard and touch his arm. "Dad, I wouldn't."

"I know." He covers my hand with his. "Still, I don't want you to even be tempted by such a choice."

Warmth climbs my chest, but I push it back down. We're not done yet. "You said there was a second reason?"

He smiles. "The kid lives next door. The chances of you two actually avoiding each other are slim."

"Thank you." I lean my head on his shoulder, the fire draining from my body, the desire to march across the lawn to confront Sam fading with it.

"You're welcome, kiddo." He returns his glasses to their place and continues his perusal of his paperwork.

"Dad?" I whisper after several minutes.

"Hmm?"

"Do you think Sam's okay?"

"I hope so, Ri. I really hope so."

Chapter 6

I pace the living room, gnawing on my thumbnail and watching as the sky gets darker.

"What are you so worried about?" Kenzie asks.

"What if he's not Sam anymore?" I ask. What if he isn't *my* Sam?

"Not Sam?" She shoots me a questioning look before pulling five bowls from the cabinet.

I continue pacing. "The Sam I knew couldn't wait to step on stage and sing his heart out. Now he's a no-show?" Of course, he's sung, many, many concerts over the trajectory of his career. What's one more?

"Well, I hope he's a complete jerk and you never talk to him again." Lou-Lou slams a pile of spoons onto the counter. *Four* spoons.

"Lou-Lou, what a terrible thing to say." Kenzie nudges her aside and adds a fifth spoon to the mix.

Lou-Lou scowls at my sister's back.

"He's going to be here any minute. What do I do?" I turn to them, begging for some kind of help. Intervention. Something!

Kenzie blinks at me. "You act normal."

"No, you watch him and keep a knife in your back pocket." Lou-Lou pokes a finger at me.

"So, I can stab my booty when I go to sit down? No thanks, I think I'll pass on that one."

Kenzie steps around the kitchen island and grabs my shoulders. "Seriously though, breathe, Ri."

I inhale.

"If Sam's turned into a complete jerk, you'll know. But keep an open mind. You know how those news stories can be. Everything's probably been blown way out of proportion. I think what Sam needs right now is a friend."

A friend. Right. Heat washes through me and I duck my head. "Some sham of a friend I am."

"Riley, what matters is how you treat him tonight."

I lock eyes with her. When did my big sister get so wise?

God, please help me to be the friend Sam needs tonight.

Kenzie gives me one last squeeze and moves to wipe some dog hair off the counter.

"Wait, hold that pose." I snag my phone and snap a picture.

Kenzie raises her eyebrows.

"I want to draw it later." Even now I study the lines of her arms. The position of her fingers. I can already picture the strokes it will take to transfer the details to my tablet canvas.

"Weirdo," Lou-Lou says under her breath.

Kenzie snickers. But I know she doesn't mind. Or at least she's gotten used to it. After all, I am the baby of the family if you don't count Lou-Lou and I either do or don't depending on whichever has the most beneficial outcome. Point being, I can get away with anything short of murder.

The doorbell rings.

I shake out my hands. "What do I do?"

"Answer the door." Kenzie spins me around and shoves me into the foyer.

I swipe my palms down my cut off shorts. I can do this. I can have ice cream with Sam Hong like nothing has changed. Like we're still a pair of kids who don't know what's outside the little world of our school and neighborhood. I can do this.

I pull the door open. "H-hey." My voice catches as I take him in.

He's got his baseball cap yanked down, sunglasses on, and a hoodie pulled over his head even though it's got to be over eighty degrees outside.

I can't help but laugh. "What? Is this some kind of cheesy movie where you're a celebrity trying to hide?"

"That bad?" He cringes.

"Get in here." I grab his arm and tug him inside.

He trips over the door mat and just manages to catch his balance as I bump the door shut with my hip.

Sarge trots over and it's a miracle his tail doesn't stir up a tornado with how its wagging.

"Hi, boy." Sam greets him. "You've gotten so big. You were a puppy last I checked."

Kenzie steps forward and pulls our guest into a hug. "Hey, Sam."

"Hi, Kenz." He actually hugs her back. Hmm, I would have thought all the rabid fans would have made him wary of human contact by now.

"Sammy Hong." Lou-Lou stands behind the kitchen island, arms crossed, and offers a curt nod as Sam steps away from my sister.

"Olivia Anderson." Sam jerks his chin back at her.

Brr...frosty. I'm not sure what happened after I left Lou-Lou to collect Sarge, but it's clear the two aren't on any friendlier terms.

"O-k-a-y..." I shove my hands into the back pockets of my shorts.

Dad trots down the stairs, saving us all from an awkward silence. "Hey, Sam. Good to see you."

They shake hands and Dad claps Sam on the shoulder.

"Hey, Mr. Anderson." Sam ducks his head.

"Do your parents know where you are, son?"

Total Dad move. And yet Sam doesn't seem bothered by it. "Not yet, sir."

"Give them a call, all right? If I've learned anything in my years of parenting, it's that I always sleep better when I know where my kids are. If they've been watching the news, they'll be worried."

"Yes, sir."

"Good man." Dad pats his shoulder once more.

"But..." I sidestep closer to Sam. "If you're going to stay for ice cream, then we've got to have some ground rules."

"Ground rules?" Sam eyes me over his ridiculous sunglasses like he expects me to suggest he dye his hair blue. Which maybe isn't such a bad idea since he was last seen with the pink.

"We're ditching all of...this." I wave a hand at him in general. I snag his baseball cap, the sunglasses, and motion for him to lose the hoodie. He obeys. "Let's forget about Sammy Hong. Tonight, you're just Sam."

He ducks his head and grins the grin that makes the hearts of fangirls everywhere skip a beat.

Still, his hair is too perfect. While his head is ducked, minimizing our height difference, I pounce and run my fingers side to side, mussing his pink strands.

"Hey." He pulls back, but he's not mad. Nope, amusement dances in his eyes.

In an instant, things are back to how they used to be, the awkwardness of the silent years erased by the familiarity between us. Sam's still the boy I knew. Still my best friend.

I beam. "Come on, Ordinary Sam. Let's get some ice cream."

He shoves his hands into his pockets and trails me to the kitchen where Lou-Lou has grudgingly set out three different flavors.

I go for the caramel swirl, Kenzie aims for the mint chocolate chip, Sam chooses strawberry which has been his favorite ever since I've known him, and Lou-Lou does a predictable scoop of all three.

Dad leans his elbows on the counter.

"What are you going to have, Uncle Gavin?" Lou-Lou bounces on her toes, but she already knows the answer. When Lou-Lou's here, there's only one way Dad chooses his ice cream. It's a tradition they've had since she was three and she hasn't outgrown it.

Dad shuts his eyes and wags his finger between the ice cream cartons. "One two three, I like thee."

Lou-Lou shuffles the cartons around until he's repeated the chant three times. When Dad's finger lands in front of the mint chocolate chip, Lou-Lou giggles and proceeds to dish him a huge scoop.

"Which one?" Dad opens his mouth and Lou-Lou obligingly offers him a spoonful.

Dad peels his eyes open and glances at his bowl. "Shame, I was hoping for the caramel."

"Better luck next time, Uncle Gavin." Lou-Lou pats his shoulder and takes her ice cream to the couch.

We all laugh and Dad raises his bowl in a toast to the rest of us. "I'll be upstairs if anyone needs me."

I put the lids on the ice cream and start loading them into the freezer. Sam hands me the last one and our fingers brush. An electric sensation jolts up my arm. But that's ridiculous. I vowed long ago I would never fall for Sam Hong. I refuse to be like every other girl in America and beyond. Our eyes lock and stay connected. Stories and hurts, dreams and regrets, flash through Sam's eyes. Things he's never told me. Maybe never will.

"Let's watch a movie." Kenzie plops down on the couch beside Lou-Lou, breaking the moment.

"Sounds good to me." Lou-Lou aims the remote at the tv.

"Let's go." I snag my bowl and head for the living room.

Sam follows me and we sit on the floor in front of Lou-Lou and Kenzie's knees.

Lou-Lou picks some cute teenage rom-com I'm sure Sam will hate, but if he does, he doesn't complain. Instead, I catch him laughing a couple times. He even lets Sarge clean out his bowl when it's empty. Our knees brush. Once.

When the credits roll, I gather the discarded bowls and deposit them in the sink. Sam joins me, washing as I dry. Never mind we have a dishwasher. There's something peaceful about this rhythm. The swish of the scrub brush. The splash of the water. The whoosh of air as I take the next bowl from his hand.

"Ri—" Sam clears his throat. "Riley, can we...talk?" He shoots a look to where Lou-Lou has turned around on the couch to give him a steady stink-eye.

"Outside." I grab his wrist.

He resists my pull.

I stop in my tracks. "What?"

He scratches the back of his head. "It's...I don't...I don't want anyone to see me."

So much for the front porch. "It's fine, we'll sit on the back deck."

"Fine, but I better not get any mosquito bites." Lou-Lou stomps toward her discarded sandals.

"Uh-uh. Bed." I jab a finger toward the staircase.

"Riley." She folds her arms. "I'm twelve-years-old, not two."

"It's late. Bed."

She settles into her stance.

Great. Do I call for Dad or will that cause more of a fuss? Most likely the results will be Lou-Lou not being the only one acting like a toddler and I will not make a good impression on Sam if I lose it.

"Lou-Lou," Kenzie calls from the top of the stairs. "I picked up a couple of new face masks. You've got to try this one. It's amazing."

Oh, I owe her one, bless her heart.

Lou-Lou's eyes narrow, but she swivels on her heel and stomps up the stairs. "Don't think I don't know what you're doing. Bribery. I should resist, but alas I can't turn down a night of pampering." She turns and sticks her tongue out.

Sam sticks his right back.

"Come on." My sister slips an arm around our cousin's shoulders and ushers her toward the bedrooms, but not before she throws a wink my way.

I make a mental note to thank her later. "Come on." I tuck my hair behind my ear and lead the way to the deck, Sarge on my heels.

I sit and Sam folds himself beside me, Sarge wedges himself between us, head on his paws. I brush my fingers through his fur as I wait for Sam to speak.

Sam lifts his head and stares at the stars and gives a heavy sigh.

"I saw the news," I say, giving him an opening.

"And?"

"And what?"

"Do you think I'm some kind of flake?"

"Are you?"

"I don't know, Ri. I owe them a new album, or that's it. I'm done and everything I've worked for will be gone. But, the words don't come like they used to. It's like everything's dried up inside me. It's different. The thought of getting in front of all those people and singing...I panicked."

My heart breaks a little. How can something he's loved for so long make such fear pool in his eyes? "Do you still love it? The music I mean?"

"I think so, but sometimes, I just...I don't know."

"If it helps, I think everyone feels that way about their career at one point or another. And hey, God gave you a gift for a reason. That has to count for something, right?"

He stares at me for a second before laughing. "Why did I ever stop talking to you?"

I wave a hand. "Oh, you know, you got big and famous and moved away and—"

Sam catches my hand. "Riley, I'm sorry. I really am."

"I know." I hold his gaze. "I'm sorry too."

"I meant to stay in contact, I really did, but I got a new phone and lost your number, and by the time I had the downtime to track you down, well…" he shrugs. "I thought you'd have forgotten about me."

"Hey." I squeeze his hand. "I understand. I've always understood."

"But I wasn't there when you needed me." Pain reflects through his irises. "I'm sorry for your loss."

Mom. He's talking about Mom. I tug my fingers free from his and hug my knees to my chest. "I get it, Sam. I really do."

"That doesn't make it right."

"You're deflecting." I poke his bicep.

He drapes an arm over his knee and cranes his neck to view the stars once more. "You know, I'd give anything to go to a grocery store."

"Funny, most people would die for a personal shopper."

He laughs, but his posture remains rigid.

So, he doesn't want to talk about his career. All right. "Why don't you?"

"Why don't I what?"

"Go to a grocery store."

"Ri, are you crazy? If I take ten steps down the sidewalk, someone's going to recognize me and call the paparazzi."

"Ah, you think too highly of yourself." I lean close and stage whisper, "We live in a neighborhood where pretty much everybody is retired. They won't know who you are."

He snorts and ducks his head. "Yeah, I guess you're right."

"Seriously though, you should."

"Take ten steps down the sidewalk?"

"You already did that, you're here, aren't you? I mean go to the grocery store."

He gapes at me. "Seriously? Look at me, I'll stick out like a sore thumb." He runs one hand through his pink hair and tugs at his designer t-shirt.

"We can fix this." I muss his hair. "We fix this and lose the designer clothes, and you're good to go."

"You make it sound so easy." He plays with a ring on his right hand.

I lean in close. "It is that easy. No one is going to be looking for Sammy Hong at the local store. Trust me."

He shakes his head and rubs Sarge's ear. "What do you think, boy? Will you be my security guard when Riley's plan backfires?"

Sarge stares at us, eyes bemoaning the fact he isn't a certified police dog.

"He'll be here to chase off any crazies that try to follow us home, won't you, baby?" I croon.

Sarge's tongue swipes half my face in one giant lick.

"See, he agrees." I wipe my cheek.

"That's disgusting, that's what I see."

"Oh, live a little."

His face grows somber. "Thanks, Ri."

"For what?" I freeze at the intensity in his eyes.

"For letting me be Ordinary Sam tonight."

Chapter 7

I knock on Sam's door fifteen minutes before noon the next day.

Lou-Lou pouts behind me. "Give me one good reason I shouldn't call his manager right now."

"Because, Sam is our friend."

"*Our* friend?" She taps her foot.

"My friend."

"Whatever." But she doesn't whip out her phone, so that's a good sign.

I knock again.

"Are you sure he's home?"

"Where else would he be?" I tip up on my toes and crane my neck in an effort to peek through the high window built into the door.

"Partying. Ditching everyone in his life for fame and money."

"Sam isn't like that."

She huffs. "And how do you know, hmm?"

"Just trust me, will you? Here, hold this." I shove one of my bags into her arms and use the freedom to bang on the door once more.

It creaks open and Sam appears, wearing a t-shirt and baggy pajama bottoms. His hair stands on end in a style which takes bedhead to a whole new level.

"Riley?" He rubs at his eyes.

"Please tell me you weren't sleeping."

"Fine, I won't tell you." He covers a yawn.

"Well, you'd better wake up fast. You've got a big day ahead of you." I plant a hand on his chest and nudge him farther into the house.

"A big day?" He stumbles over a pair of his shoes left discarded in the entryway. Never mind they're designer. Maybe even custom.

I turn and take my bag from Lou-Lou who is glaring at Sam. "We're going out."

"Out?"

"Do you lip-sync?" Lou-Lou folds her arms.

Sam scoffs. "You insult me."

"I'm going to need proof." She cocks an eyebrow. "It seems to me that you only know how to copy others."

"Lou-Lou." I nudge her leg with my foot.

"He's mimicking everything you're saying. It's like he doesn't have anything up here." She taps her temple.

"Olivia!" I squeak.

But Sam chuckles. "You'll have to forgive me, minion, but I just woke up. If you want to blame someone, your cousin appears to be the culprit."

Lou-Lou makes a grumbling sound in her throat.

"Like I said, we're going out." I close the front door with my foot.

Sam shifts his weight. "I can't."

"Sammy Hong can't, but Ordinary Sam? That's a different story." I hold my bags high.

"I don't know." He scratches the back of his head, making his hair stick up in an even more dramatic way.

"Have a little faith." I bounce on my toes and put on my best begging face.

He hesitates.

I sigh and lower my arms. "Look, you can't be a captive in this house forever. What's the worst that can happen?"

"I get kidnapped by some super fan?"

"Puh-lease. Dude, you need to take a humble pill. Besides, Lou-Lou and I will act as your loyal body guards." Speaking of, where are his bodyguards? But I don't ask, because it might scare him out of the whole thing.

"Really? Because I feel like her loyalty is easily bought." He jerks his chin toward Lou-Lou.

"Excuse me?" Lou-Lou touches a hand to her chest. "My loyalty is to Riley. And I can't be bought."

He shoves his hands in his pockets and blinks at her.

"Okay, okay." I step between the pair before Lou-Lou can whip out her verbal claws. "Let's just try this, and if you're not sure, we'll do something else. Deal?"

Sam sighs. "Okay, it's worth a try. Give me a second to get dressed, and I'll grab my sunglasses."

"The same 'disguise' as last night?" I share a look with Lou-Lou. "That's so cliché."

"It was bad," Lou-Lou agrees.

"Let me guess, you have something else in mind?" His lips quirk into the beginning of a smile.

"Yep." I lift my bags once again. "Let's go upstairs."

Sam leads the way to his bedroom with its connected bathroom.

"First, put on something you don't care about," I instruct.

He snags a pair of shorts and a t-shirt from his dresser and disappears for a moment before coming back dressed in trashy clothes he must have once worn for a painting project.

"Sit." I jab a finger at the old towel I've spread on the floor.

Sam folds himself onto the towel as commanded.

"This is not going to work." Lou-Lou plops onto the bed.

"I thought you were loyal." I fumble through my bags.

"Loyalty doesn't mean I don't question your life choices."

"Good to know." I pull a box of black hair dye from my supplies and catch Sam's eyes. "Do you trust me?"

He looks from the box to me. "I trust you."

"Good." I snag a hairbrush from Sam's dresser, leftover from when he went through a long hair phase. It also served as his first microphone once upon a time. Proverbs 3:5-6 is scrawled across the back in tween Sam's nearly illegible handwriting. I toss the makeshift mic to Sam to get rid of any tangles before I go back to rummaging through my bags. I come up empty. "I forgot gloves."

"My mom used to keep some in the kitchen drawer by the fridge," Sam says. "I think they kept pretty much everything here when they moved."

"Okay. I'll be right back. Stay right there." I jog down the stairs and check the kitchen drawer. Sure enough, there's a box of disposable gloves with a few pairs left inside. Perfect. I make my way upstairs before Sam can change his mind or Lou-Lou has time to do anything too devious.

"Find them?" Sam asks.

I stop in my tracks. The guy has 'I heart Riley' scrawled across his cheek. "Uh…"

"What? What did she do?" Sam rubs at his face, but the action does nothing to erase the marker ink. "She said she was helping with the disguise."

Lou-Lou blinks innocently. "My mom made me promise to work on my penmanship this summer."

My ears are too warm, and I don't know what to do except laugh.

Sam raises an eyebrow and hurries to the bathroom to check the mirror. When he returns, twin blossoms of red mar his cheeks.

"Here." I lick my thumb and try to scrub away the impromptu tattoo. The ink doesn't even smudge.

"Sorry. I thought this was washable." Lou-Lou twirls the marker between her fingers.

Sure, she did. "Don't worry. I have a makeup wipe in my purse. But first." I waggle the box of hair dye in front of Sam.

He sinks onto the raggedy towel spread over the floor. It doesn't take long to pull on the plastic gloves and massage the black goop into Sam's strands.

"You're sure about this?" He squints at me.

"Boy, when I'm done, no one will even recognize you."

"I'm counting on it."

"Yeah, right." Lou-Lou mutters as she scrolls through her phone.

"Positive feedback only, please." I wag a finger at her, sending a drop of dye splattering onto Sam's ear. "Oops."

Sam flinches. "Focus, please? I don't want to go blind."

"Yeah, yeah." I massage his head until his pink strands are saturated with the black goop.

Once we've got the gunk well distributed, Lou-Lou helps me to wrap his head in plastic wrap. Around and around until everything is covered and Sam looks like some crazy alien who is due to return to his home planet any day.

"Ooh, nice look." Lou-Lou snaps a picture before I can stop her.

Oh, this girl has some nerve. "That better not appear on any social media."

"Nope. This is for pure blackmail purposes if necessary." She pockets her phone.

"Necessary?" Sam pokes at a droopy portion of plastic wrap.

Lou-Lou crosses her arms and stares him down. "Like if you break Riley's heart."

Oh. My. Goodness. Heat flares in my cheeks. I need to have a serious talk with her parents about teaching her tact. Maybe it'll be my summer project. That or teaching her how to dig nice deep holes, because I sure could use one right now.

Sam laughs. "You're sure this isn't your roundabout way of asking for an autograph?"

Her eyes narrow. "You would be the last celebrity on earth I would ask."

"Okay." I take my cousin by the shoulders and steer her out of the room. "Let's go find something to do while we wait for the dye to set."

Sam leads the way to his basement where he unearths an outdated game console. "Should we see if it still works?"

"I bet it would." I bend to take a closer look.

"Why not?" Lou-Lou flops onto one of the beanbag chairs distributed throughout the space.

Sam and I get the fossil hooked up, batteries replaced in the controllers with ones we find buried in a dusty drawer, and we settle in for half-an-hour of racing.

"Shove over," Lou-Lou growls as Sam passes her on the race-track. "Oh, you are so dead."

"No smack talk unless you have something to back it up with." He leans forward, racing more with his arms than with his controller.

"Shh," I scold as I putt, putt, putt behind the pair.

"I am winning this thing." Lou-Lou scooches closer to the tv like that might somehow help her Avatar car to cross the finish line faster.

"I don't think so." Sam takes a corner too fast and crashes against the guard rail.

"Loser." Lou-Lou cackles.

"Hey," Sam protests as I angle my car past his as he tries to maneuver back onto the track.

"Maybe if you focused on your driving—" And of course that's when I wipe out.

Sam smirks at me as he gets his car going in the right direction.

"Rude." I give his leg a gentle kick.

"Aw, come on now, Ri..." He jerks his controller sideways. "Don't be a sore loser."

"And...weep!" Lou-Lou crows as her car hurtles across the finish line.

"You cheated." Sam gapes at the screen.

"Who's the sore loser now?" I raise my eyebrows.

"Oh yeah! Who won? This girl." Lou-Lou parades around the room in a cocky victory dance.

"Rematch." Sam slaps his thigh. "I demand a rematch."

Lou-Lou shrugs. "It's not like it would change anything, but why not?"

We play two more rounds before the timer on my phone goes off. I pause the game.

"Hey!" Lou-Lou and Sam protest in unison.

I hold up my hands in defense in case they chuck their controllers at me. "Let's let Sam shower and rinse out the dye."

"I was about to win." Lou-Lou shakes her controller at me.

Sam scoffs. "No way. I so had you beat."

"Oh yeah? Let's find out." Lou-Lou hunkers deeper into her beanbag.

"Nope." I spring up, blocking the tv. "Shower." I jut a finger toward the stairs.

"Aw, come on, it'll only take a minute," Sam says.

"Uh-uh. You go shower right now. Don't you know leaving dye in for too long can damage your hair? I will not have your stylist coming after me, thank you very much."

He salutes. "You've got it boss. I'll get you next time, minion." He winks at Lou-Lou before setting aside his controller and jogging up the stairs.

"In your dreams, dude," Lou-Lou hollers after him.

"See, he's not so bad," I say once Sam is out of earshot.

"Yeah, I guess." She picks at a thread unraveling from the bottom of her t-shirt.

I run my fingers over the entertainment center, leaving a streak in the coating of dust. Sam either needs to bust out a duster or take my advice and hire a maid. This place is nasty. My fingers bump against a forgotten toy pony buried behind a tangle of cables. Left here by Sam's little sister. Hannah is a couple years younger and has managed to stay out of the media. I tried looking her up once to see how she's grown-up, but I couldn't find a single photo.

"What do you see in him?" Lou-Lou's voice is small. Quiet.

I turn my attention to her. "A boy who needs a friend. You promised me you were going to try."

"Yeah, yeah, I know."

"Then do it."

"I am trying."

There's not much left to say, and Sam will be down here any minute. I drop into the bean bag next to hers and nudge her foot with mine. "Thank you."

"You have to admit though, he's a terrible driver."

"How about you and I whoop him when he gets back?"

She holds out her fist. "Anderson girls rock."

"You bet we do." I bump my knuckles against hers.

Chapter 8

When Sam comes trotting down the stairs, my breath catches. Because he looks so different. So normal. Like...my Sam. Sure his face has aged, but the rest of him is the same. My Sam. The one with jet black hair which is delightfully opposite my own sunny strands. His designer clothes are exchanged for ones any normal person would be wearing. He's even ditched the thousand-something-dollar shoes for a pair of slip-on sandals.

"Wow." Lou-Lou whispers. "I didn't think it was possible, but wow."

"Yeah." All I can do is nod as my heart gives a funny little flip.

Pink stains Sam's cheeks and he rubs his neck. "Is it...am I okay?"

More like perfect. But I can't say that. I swipe my hands down my knees. "Yeah. Yeah, you're per—you look great."

"Let's go to the store." Lou-Lou pumps her fist.

It almost feels wrong when we pull into the grocery store parking lot.

Sam puts the car in park and we sit there.

"You're sure about this?" Lou-Lou leans between our seats. "Because I refuse to be mugged by a pack of rabid fan girls."

"Yeah, we'll be fine." I bob my head like it will make it so.

"Right. Totally fine," Sam says.

But neither of us make a move to exit the car. My palms turn slick and I'm breathing too fast. I lick my lips. Oh, what I wouldn't do for some lip balm right about now.

"Guys..." Lou-Lou groans. "Please somebody make a choice. Are we going in or not? We've been sitting here *forever*."

I turn to Sam. His eyes lock on mine.

"How about a little touch up?" I reach into the glove compartment and pull out Kenzie's emergency make-up kit. A few brush strokes are all it takes to add a smattering of freckles and a beauty mark to Sam's face.

"Riley, that's ridiculous." Lou-Lou shakes her head like we're the two biggest disappointments to walk this earth.

"Better not to take any chances?" I meet Sam's eyes. To see if he minds. My heart twinges. Because with a few strokes of makeup, I've erased my Sam and replaced him with a fake persona. And I regret it with every pulse of my heart. "Sam—" I reach to wipe away the gunk, but he catches my hand and squeezes.

"Leave it. You were right. Better not to take any chances."

Oh, but how I wish we could walk in and be the two of us. Sam and Riley, the kids who live on Deer Street. Best friends always and forever.

"Don't overthink this, Ri," Lou-Lou says. "I'm getting out. You two can join me if you wish, and if not, somebody text me the grocery list." She pops her door open.

I blow out a breath before slipping out of the car.

Sam rounds the vehicle and joins me.

"Ooh, look at you two being all brave." Lou-Lou slides between us and catches my hand. She may be twelve, but she hasn't outgrown hand-holding.

Please keep us safe, Lord.

Sam slips his hands into his pockets. "So, what is on the list?"

"Basics. Milk, eggs, coffee creamer." The wind throws my hair across my face and I tuck it behind my ear.

"Coffee creamer is a basic?" He laughs.

"It is for Riley." Lou-Lou fakes a shudder. "You do not want to see her in the morning before she's had her coffee. Trust me."

"I'll keep that in mind."

The automatic doors whoosh open, ushering us inside. Sam goes for a small cart, but Lou-Lou stops him. "Nuh-uh. Live a little. B-I-G."

"Okay, okay." He grabs a big one and Lou-Lou promptly positions herself on the back of the cart.

"Let's go." She jabs a finger toward the produce aisle.

I grab the handle, plant one foot on the cart, and push off with the other, launching us forward. Sam walks beside me.

"So, how is your fridge looking?" I ask him.

He winces. "Bare?"

"What have you been living off of?"

"I've been ordering take-out and having it delivered."

"Oh, I pity you," Lou-Lou says, resting her elbows on the cart handle. "You need a Kenzie in your life. Her cooking is..." She kisses her fingers before popping them open in an explosion.

"The best is when she does a slow cooker meal before she goes to work. The house smells divine all day long." I snag a bag of lemons.

"Stop, you're making me hungry."

"Do you cook?" Lou-Lou cranes her neck to look at Sam.

"I know how to heat something up in the microwave."

"Riley!" Lou-Lou half turns to face me.

I startle, almost dropping an avocado. "What?"

"How could you be friends with him for so long and not teach him how to cook?"

"I figured we'd get to it when it was important." Something inside of me stings for Sam. Because he was fourteen when he left. Before cooking mattered. Before he got rich and famous and had someone to take care of it for him. Before he bought his parents a mansion and they moved on. Sometimes I wonder if they even moved on from him.

"Well it is important." Lou-Lou angles a look at Sam, breaking me from my thoughts. "Don't you know cooking a meal for your girlfriend is like the most romantic thing ever? A girl wants a man who can cook."

"Oh, so I should start taking dating advice from you now?" He turns his head like maybe the conversation has made him feel awkward. "Besides, I don't have a girlfriend."

"Okay." I clap my hands. "Let's focus here, friends. What is the most important thing in this store?"

Lou-Lou perks up. "Candy aisle?"

"Nope."

"Meat?" Sam asks. "I'd love a good burger right now."

"No, but remind me to have Dad teach you how to grill." I snap my fingers. "Dairy. Keep up guys. We're not leaving this place before I get my hands on some creamer."

"Hey, we should go to the pet section too," Lou-Lou says as I steer us toward the back of the store where the walls of refrigerators reside.

"We don't need anything." I step away from the cart and scan the creamer selection. Some girls may spend hours trying to decide what dress to buy, but for me it's the coffee creamer that matters in life. Pick the wrong one, and the whole day is off to a bad start.

"Come on, Sarge deserves a new bone."

"He has three."

"Something squeaky then."

"He doesn't need anything."

Sam bumps me with his elbow. "Come on, Ri. Don't deprive your dog of the simple joys in life."

"Fine." I snag my favorite brand of caramel creamer and toss it into the cart. "We'll get him something. *One* thing."

"Yes," Lou-Lou crows.

This girl. You'd think she was Sarge's mother or something with how she spoils him. But it's innocent enough, so why not?

"Your turn." I push the cart to Sam who takes over steering.

On our way to the pet aisle, we snag some lunch meat, cereal, bread, and a few frozen dinners for Sam so he at least has *something* on hand at home.

"Ooh, that one!" Lou-Lou points to a rubber pig which makes an obnoxious sound when Sam squeezes its middle.

"Seriously?" I ask.

"Sarge will love it." Lou-Lou demonstrates her own puppy dog eyes. "Come on, Ri."

"Yeah, Ri. Sarge will love it," Sam says.

And I will rue the day I bought this until he breaks the squeaker, but I don't have a *#dogmom* sweatshirt hanging in my closet for nothing. "Okay, fine. You win. The pig comes with us."

"Yes." Sam and Lou-Lou exchange a high-five.

"Are we done here?" I raise an eyebrow, daring either one to protest.

They exchange a look. When did they go from barely tolerating each other to being in cahoots?

"I think so. What do you say, minion?" Sam looks to Lou-Lou.

She pretends to examine her nails. "Unless someone plans to buy me some gum, I think we can depart." She looks at me through her eyelashes.

"You'll get a cavity."

She huffs. "You sound like my dentist."

"Well, maybe he's right."

"You're no fun, Riley." Lou-Lou huffs and crosses her arms.

"Yeah, no fun," Sam parrots.

I pretend not to notice when he slips a pack of gum onto the conveyor belt when we reach the cashier.

A group of giggling girls wait behind us, a couple bottles of soda in hand. As I reach for one of the dividers to put behind our groceries, my attention snags on the magazines lining the shelves.

Superstar Sammy Hong Disappears reads one headline, sporting a picture of a pink haired Sam. *Rumors Fly as Sammy Hong Continues Silence Over Disappearance* another boasts. *Is Sammy Hong Running from the Law?* one outrageous gossip rag asks.

"He's kind of cute," one of the girls waiting in line whispers behind her hand, pointing at Sam's back.

Cheese and crackers! As discreetly as I can, I shuffle the magazines, moving health and home décor ones in front of the ones about Sam and plant myself behind him. "Here you go," I say, louder than necessary as I place the divider behind our groceries.

"Oh, thanks," the girl drooling over Sam says, blinking in a half-surprised, half-guilty look. Maybe she thinks I'm his girlfriend.

I offer a sugary sweet smile. "No problem." I slide half a step to the side, blocking her view as Sam pulls out his wallet to pay for the groceries. Last thing I need is for these girls to catch a glimpse of his driver's license or something.

"Hey, look what Tammy posted." One of the other girls holds out her phone, catching the nosy one's attention.

S.O.S, I mouth to Lou-Lou. She catches the hint and starts piling the groceries into the cart. Oh, I hope she doesn't crack the eggs. Still, I can't move to help her, or I risk exposing Sam's profile and I don't know if these girls are fans or not, but even with the freckles and false beauty marks, Sam looks too much like his celebrity persona and it doesn't help he's already drawn their attention.

"Have a nice day, hon." The cashier passes Sam the receipt.

"You too." He pockets his wallet and turns away, getting the cart moving again.

Please don't let these girls recognize his voice, I pray. What if they're super fans who've watched every single interview he's ever had?

One of the girls shuffles through the magazines. One more and she'll find Sam's.

No, no, no.

"Come on, we're going to be late." I plant a hand on Sam's back, urging him to step on the gas.

"Late for what?" Sam tries to turn to look at me, but I push him harder.

By now the girl will have seen his picture, and we cannot give her time to put two and two together.

"You're no genius, huh?" Lou-Lou grabs the front of the cart and adds her momentum, getting us through the doors and into the parking lot.

"What is going on?" Sam asks.

"Just get in the car," I say. "We'll load the groceries."

His lips form a wordless *oh* and his eyes go wide. The surprise is soon overshadowed by what can only be described as a deep sadness.

Oh, Sam.

"You're still fine, I think, but I don't want to risk it." I try to smile so he won't see the panic settling on my shoulders. This was way too close of a call. Who am I to think I can keep this boy safe when it takes a team of security guards to keep him alive?

Sam doesn't argue. He climbs into the driver's seat and slumps low while Lou-Lou and I load the bags into the trunk. She shoots me a worried look. I shrug and slam the trunk closed.

That's when my gaze connects with the girl from the checkout line. She's pointing at us, talking rapidly with her friends. They're laughing, shaking their heads like they don't believe her. But this girl recognized Sam. I know it to the depths of my soul. Now I can only hope her friends can convince her she's crazy.

"Get in," I say to Lou-Lou.

To her credit, she springs to obey.

I scramble into the passenger seat and lock the doors.

"Everything okay?" Sam asks.

"Yeah." I brush my hair behind my ears and find the girls again. The others are dragging the one away, still laughing and shaking their heads. "Yeah, I think we're good."

Sam expels a breath and falls against his seat. "This was a bad idea."

"No." A pang shoots through my heart. "No, Sam. You deserve this. You should be able to go to a grocery store if you want to."

"Didn't I forfeit that when I chose my career?" He puts the car into drive and maneuvers us through the parking lot.

Is it actually possible for a heart to break? Because I think mine is.

I place a hand on Sam's knee, the only assurance I can offer, because I don't have the words to fix this. I don't know how. *Please, God*, I pray. But that's all I have.

It's a quiet drive home.

"How much do I owe you?" I ask when Sam pulls into my driveway.

"Ri, the groceries are on me." He slings an arm over the steering wheel and offers an easy smile.

"Oh, no, I couldn't—"

"I can afford it, trust me." He grimaces and throws his door open.

"Really, Sam, I—"

He catches my arms as I join him at the trunk. "Let me do this for you, Riley. I had fun today."

"Even with how it ended?" I shouldn't feel guilty. I had no control over any of it, and yet my heart pricks with remorse.

"Even with how it ended." He catches my gaze. "I haven't had so much fun in a long time. Thank you."

Lou-Lou clears her throat and its then I realize Sam is still holding my arms. A flash of electricity dances beneath my skin.

He smiles sheepishly and steps back.

I force myself to blink and tuck my hands into the back pockets of my shorts. He's here temporarily, I remind myself. Besides, I vowed never to fall for Sammy Hong, and I intend to keep my promise.

"Well, I should get going." Sam jerks his thumb toward his house and backs away.

"Sam, wait."

His eyebrows raise and he pauses.

"Just...wait." I hold up a hand to enforce the command and jog around to the front of the car and yank open the glove box. I snag a makeup wipe and return.

"Everything okay?" Sam rocks on his heels.

"No." Not at all. Everything is a jumble of confusion, but this one thing I can fix. "Bend down."

The bewilderment doesn't clear from his eyes, but he ducks his head all the same. I run the makeup wipe across his face, erasing the freckles, the falsehood, and unearth the boy beneath. For the moment at least, my Sam is back. I pull away. "Just be Sam tonight."

His dark stare snags on mine. Intense. "Riley..." But he doesn't finish.

I twist the makeup wipe around and around my pointer finger. "And while you're at it, why don't you stay for dinner?"

"Ah." He rubs the back of his neck and scuffs his sandal against the driveway. "I wouldn't want to impose."

"Please? You wouldn't be imposing." Please don't say no.

He shakes his head. "I've taken up enough of your day."

"Listen, buddy." Lou-Lou steps around me. "The only problem we're going to have is if the two of you make me carry these in by myself." She gestures to the trunkful of grocery bags.

"And by the time you help us put everything away, you might as well stay," I say.

"Okay. Dinner it is."

He runs his portion of the groceries over to his house while Lou-Lou and I start unloading our haul in the kitchen.

Sarge's pleased bark announces Sam's return.

"What can I help with?" He deposits the last of the groceries on the counter and washes his hands.

"Uncle Gavin left me a chore list. You can get started on that." Lou-Lou points to the refrigerator where the only item on her list checked off is making the bed.

"I don't think so." I pinch her arm.

She yelps and darts away.

The rumble of the garage door signals Kenzie's arrival.

"And there's our head chef. Just do what she says and I don't think you can mess anything up too badly." I wink and bump Sam with my hip so he knows I'm joking.

"Let's let Sam cook, so when he messes up, we can order pizza." Lou-Lou bounces on her toes.

"And that is a solid no." Kenzie tosses her purse on the couch. "While you're at my house, you eat a nice home-cooked meal. It's good for you."

"Boring." Lou-Lou rolls her eyes.

Please. The girl loves Kenzie's cooking more than anything, but I'd have to tickle her to death before she'll admit it to my sister's face.

"Rice cooker. Now." Kenzie snaps her fingers and points to the cabinet where we keep the thing. "I'm going to take a shower, and when I get back, I expect everything to be prepped for some fried rice." The girl is addicted and manages to sneak the dish onto the menu at least once a week. Sometimes I think she'd eat it every day if she lived alone.

Lou-Lou obeys and scoops rice into the machine.

Sam gets the luxurious job of defrosting a bag of frozen veggies, and I pop a tray of bacon into the oven.

When Kenzie jogs down the stairs, wet hair piled high in a bun, she gives a nod of approval. "Very good. Now make yourselves scarce while I whip this up and it should be done by the time Dad gets home."

Lou-Lou scampers into the living room where she sets up with a ball of yarn and a crochet hook. She'd look like a little old lady if not for the fact she still thinks stripes and plaid match. But man, the girl can craft tons of cute things on a whim.

"She's good, huh?" Sam leans his shoulder against the wall, jerking his chin at the half-finished dinosaur she's working on.

"Yeah. I've tried to talk her into opening an online shop more than once, but she 'doesn't work well under pressure.'"

Kenzie's playlist of dramatic break up songs revs to life as she bangs dishes around in the kitchen, wailing her heart out along to the music.

"Is she okay?" Sam throws a look over his shoulder.

"She's fine. She's never even dated, let alone been broken up with." Which is such a shame. The men of the world are missing out on the gem who is my sister. But I guess that's what happens when you take work and studying so seriously. Plus, she's always felt like she needed to fill Mom's empty shoes, causing her social life to suffer. But I don't complain. After all, the circumstances have turned her into my best friend.

"What about you?" Sam's focus locks on Lou-Lou's blurred fingers.

I take up residence against the wall next to him. "What about me?"

"You know..." He shrugs. "Have you dated anyone?"

I laugh and fold my arms, but then I look at him. Oh. He's serious. I lift my shoulders like it'll alleviate the weight settling over this conversation. "There's been a boy here or there, but I don't know, none of them have felt...right."

"Right?"

I scratch my head. "Yeah. I guess I've always thought when I found the right guy, it would feel right. Don't get me wrong, he'll have to be someone who I can weather highs and lows with, but we'll just fit."

His jaw tightens and his gaze becomes distant, like he's seeing something far beyond Lou-Lou's crochet project.

I laugh again, airy and awkward. "Maybe it's stupid. I don't know. But that's how Dad always described his relationship with Mom. They just...fit."

He looks at me then. Long and intense. "It's not stupid, Riley."

Kenzie belts out a round of lyrics, wailing her heartbreak on time with the music.

Sam cringes, pressing his ear to his shoulder. "You're sure she's okay in there?"

I poke his side. "Oh, you think you could do better?"

His eyebrows raise. A challenge. "I know I could."

"Let's hear it then."

"Nah, wouldn't want to upstage your sister."

I plant a hand on my hip. "Oh, come on now, don't chicken out. Let's hear it."

"Really?" He cocks an eyebrow.

The scent of cooking bacon wafts through the house, making my stomach grumble. "I dare you to try."

He does. And yes. He can. He can do so much better. Not that I'll ever tell Kenzie, but man, this song should have been written for the boy next to me.

He ends with a flourishing bow.

I bet the girls go crazy for that one.

"And?" He peeks at me.

"Okay, yeah, you're good."

"Duh. It's what he does for a living," Lou-Lou chimes in from the couch.

I cock my chin high. "How was I supposed to know they didn't pull some funny business in the recording studio?"

Sam clutches his chest. "I am deeply offended."

"I would be too," Dad says.

Guess I didn't hear him come home over Sam and Kenzie's duet, combined with the pounding beat of her music. We're all lucky it's Dad and not some serial killer breaking into the house.

"Hey, how was work?" I ask.

Tired lines form around his eyes and mouth, but he smiles and says, "Fine."

I wish Mom were here on days like this. Because Dad always tries to shield us from any difficulties he experiences at the office. If she were here, he'd have someone to confide in. As it is, Sarge trots over, tail wagging up a storm. Dad grins as he rubs the golden fluff's head.

Kenzie's music shuts off. "Okay, come eat."

"I hope you have an appetite," Dad claps Sam on the shoulder. "Mackenzie knows her way around the kitchen."

"Yes, sir." Sam trails Dad to the table.

Lou-Lou pulls an armful of bowls from a cabinet and I get the forks. Kenzie dishes, and then we all grab hands, ducking our heads as Dad says grace. A part of me warms when Sam's hand settles in mine without hesitation. He remembers. I squeeze his hand so he'll know I noticed. He squeezes back.

"Amen," Dad says, and it's a free for all as we start shoveling the fried rice into our mouths. It's still very warm and I cup a hand around my lips, blowing to release some heat. I let my gaze travel around the table, thankful for each face here. Especially Sam's. *Thank you, Lord for bringing him back.*

"Pass the hot sauce," Lou-Lou cranes her neck, searching the table.

"This?" Sam holds up the bottle.

She makes a beckoning gesture. "Yup, pass it over."

Sam grimaces. "Who puts hot sauce on fried rice?"

"This girl." She jabs a finger at herself before dousing her rice in a crazy spray of sauce.

Sam whistles. "Respect."

"This is great hon, thanks," Dad says to Kenzie.

She pauses in lifting a forkful of rice to her mouth. "Of course."

"Kenzie," Lou-Lou sing-songs, "how's Alex?"

Crimson circles my sister's cheeks and her wide, panicked gaze goes to me. Like I've ever been able to silence our cousin.

"Who's Alex?" Sam perks up, looking between the pair.

Mackenzie swipes her hands down her jeans. Grabs her napkin. Twists the innocent piece of cloth into a knotted mess. "No one."

"Her coworker," Lou-Lou supplies, "and she *likes* him."

Kenzie dives for her water glass and guzzles the liquid like maybe she's trying to drown herself.

"Olivia," I hiss and reach to kick her under the table.

"Ouch!" She shrieks, slamming her knee into the table, rattling every dish on the surface. Good grief, subtlety is not her strong suit.

"Girls," Dad's voice is thick with warning.

"Hey, I'm just saying maybe if Kenzie actually talked to the guy, he might ask her on a date." Lou-Lou sighs like she is the victim in this situation.

"Lou-Lou." Kenzie coughs, choking on her next mouthful of water. "I don't even know if he's interested," she finally manages.

"Well, you won't know unless you talk to him," Lou-Lou huffs. "Maybe ask him to give you the occasional ride to work instead of that Jenny girl."

Kenzie squirms in her chair, ears a blistering shade of red.

Sam clears his throat and reaches for his own water.

I guess he's not used to this level of family drama at the dinner table even though he has a younger sister. Something twists in my chest. How long has it been since his family were all together for a meal?

Kenzie rubs her fork between fidgety fingers. "Lou-Lou—"

"I'm just saying—"

"It's none of your business." I give Lou-Lou a long look.

"But—"

I pinch her leg with my toes.

Her fork clatters to the table and she gives me a serious glare.

"Girls, if you intend to brawl, please relocate to the back yard." Dad plants his elbows on the table and stares each of us down. "Honestly, I think Sarge has better manners than the two of you."

Yeah. Sarge. The dog who currently has his chin planted in Sam's lap like he thinks our guest is going to magically drop a piece of bacon into his waiting jowls. And maybe it's not too far-fetched of an idea, because I think I've seen Sam sneak him a few of the peas from his bowl. He's still not gotten over his phobia of the little green orbs.

"Sam, have you talked to your parents?" Dad manages to casually throw out the question in between helping himself to another scoop of dinner.

Sam squirms, dislodging Sarge from his perch. "Yes, sir."

Oh? I perk up and turn my full attention on the boy beside me.

"That's good." Dad's eyebrows raise, hopeful.

Sam grunts and pokes at the last few grains of rice sitting in his bowl. "Mom's glad I'm alive. Dad thinks I should call my manager. Act like an adult." He rubs at the side of his neck. "He's right, I guess."

Pain cuts through my middle. Sam's eighteen. Sure, a legal adult, but how adult can you be when you've spent an important piece of your life with a manager dictating your schedule and parents who took the mansion you bought them and then stopped caring? Not like I've been keeping tabs or anything...

I reach under the table and find Sam's hand. Squeeze.

He shoots me a glance from the side of his eye and a smile pulls at his lips.

God, please bring healing to his family.

"We're here for you, son. I hope you know that." My dad gives Sam a deep nod.

"Thank you, sir, I appreciate it." Sam sits a little taller in his chair.

He doesn't let go of my hand.

Chapter 9

"Let's go for a walk after this." Sam swipes a towel over the bowl in his hand.

I glance up, elbow deep in bubbly sink water. "I thought you were worried about being recognized?"

"Yeah, but the grocery store went well today, and like you said, almost everybody around here is retired, and that's not exactly my target audience. I think we'll be fine."

"Okay, yeah. Sounds good." I lift a shoulder, trying to rub a stray hair out of my eyes without using my soap covered hands.

Sam steps close, swiping the tendril behind my ear.

"Thanks," I say.

Neither one of us moves.

"You know you guys could use the dishwasher, right?" Lou-Lou raises her eyebrows from the kitchen entrance.

Sam steps away. "Where's the fun in that?"

"Fun?" She looks from the sink to the pile of dishes waiting to be dried, and then she shakes her head at Sam. "Dude, you really need to get out more. Tell him that's not healthy, Ri."

"Why don't you help us?" I point to the dishes. "We'll take Sarge for a w-a-l-k when we're done."

Sarge's nails clack against the wood floor as he prances over.

Sam laughs, flashing a dimple I forgot he had. "Riley, I think your dog knows how to spell."

How could I have forgotten? "He is crazy smart."

Lou-Lou holds up her hands and retreats. "Nuh-uh. You can't rope me into the manual labor you *chose* to do. You guys are on your own. I'm going upstairs to relax."

Sarge jams his cold nose against the back of my knee, urging me to finish as soon as possible.

"All right, all right." I nudge him back a bit.

Sam and I make quick work of finishing the kitchen clean up before we head out the door, Sarge charging ahead.

"Easy." I call him back to trot nicely beside me, the leash jingling against his tags.

"It's a beautiful evening." Sam pauses to throw his shoulders back, and close his eyes, face raised toward the gentle breeze chasing away the humidity.

"It really is." I join him as Sarge investigates a mailbox. Eyes closed, head lifted toward the sky. Just being. It's amazing and reminiscent of our childhood spent lying on the grass in Sam's backyard, watching the clouds.

"I didn't know how much I needed this," Sam says as Sarge pulls me into motion once more.

"This walk?"

"More than that. Just...a break." But then a shadow enters his eyes. Probably because this isn't exactly a vacation.

"Have you talked to anyone? From your label I mean?" I toe a piece of mulch strewn on the sidewalk.

"No." Sam's posture goes stiff and his jaw is tight enough I hope he releases it or he's going to feel pain tomorrow.

"Do you think you should?" I peek at him around a length of hair that has fallen across my face.

Sam keeps walking, his pace increasing until I have to jog to catch up. Sarge pants, tongue lolling from the side of his mouth.

"Sam?" Man, I sound breathless. I'm convinced some people have a running talent, but I am not one of them. In fact, it's downright embarrassing that a cramp pinches my side. "What about the album? Have you...written anything?"

"No. And I'm not sure I want to. If I were being honest," his nostrils flare as he inhales deeply, "I'm not sure if I ever want to go back."

My steps falter and I pause, not sure I've heard right. The Sam I knew would have traded everything for a career, and now he's ready to throw it all away? It's a delusional dream. He'll have to face whatever has happened eventually, especially considering there's sure to be contracts involved, but is it wrong of me to want to live out this fantasy? Just for a little longer.

"Yoohoo! Riley!" The call turns my head to the house across the street.

Cordelia Brown waves at me, flinging dirt from her gardening glove. "I have your money."

"Oh." I look both ways before crossing the street to the gray-haired woman. Sam trails me.

"Thank you so much for watching the dogs for me." Cordelia pulls off her gloves and pulls a folded fifty-dollar bill from her pocket.

"Of course. Did you have a good trip?"

"I have the sun tan to prove it, don't I?" She holds her hands out to either side, rotating slowly.

The lobster red color of her shoulders is sure to fade into a nice tan. Eventually.

"I do declare, Riley, the beach life agrees with me."

I laugh. "I can see that."

Her eyebrows raise when she comes around to face us. "I know you."

I laugh awkwardly, because of course she does, and maybe I should suggest she go see her doctor, but then I realize her attention is fixed on Sam.

"Oh, I don't think—" I start to say, but she bats my words aside.

"You're Sammy Hong."

Chapter 10

Cheese and crackers.

Sam and I both stand frozen, no doubt looking like a pair of deer trapped in the middle of the street with a semi-truck barreling toward us. Sarge wags his tail, looking up at me all confused and innocent.

"You must be—" Mistaken. But I can't lie, can I? Sweat collects beneath my shirt as my mind whirs, struggling to come up with a solution. *What do I do, God?*

"You are!" Cordelia beams like a pirate who's unearthed a hundred-year-old buried treasure. "My granddaughter and I saw your documentary in the theater last month." She leans in close.

Sam leans back.

"We even got matching t-shirts with your face on them," Cordelia whispers.

Sam's ears burn red.

"Mrs. Brown—" I step forward.

She holds up a hand, silencing me. "What are you doing all the way out here? Now mind you, I know you grew up just down the street and my granddaughter is right proud of that fact, thank you. *But...*" she draws the word out nice and long, "you haven't been home in years. Does this have anything to do with your disappearing act?"

Sam full on flinches.

"Listen, Mrs. Brown." I angle in front of Sam. "He's just here for a few days. To clear his head. No one knows, and we'd appreciate it if you could help us keep it that way."

Her eyes go big. "You're hiding out?"

"Oh, I don't think hiding is quite the right word." But what exactly is? "He's...laying low."

"Just for a few days," Sam clarifies.

I fold my hands in front of me, playing the part of humble beggar, because it's all that can save this situation. "Can you help us, Mrs. Brown?"

She squeezes my arm. "Why sure. Of course, I can." Then her eyes go all squinty and she angles close once more. I lean back, bumping into Sam's chest. "For a price."

Two signed t-shirts, a cd, and a wrist later, Sam and I scurry home in the descending twilight.

Cordelia's last whispered words as we were leaving ring in my ears, *"He's a keeper, Riley. Don't let that boy get away. I don't care what the news says. Most of that drama is fabricated anyway. But, you get the real story, and if he's as good and decent as I think he is, you don't let go of him for nothing, you hear?"*

All I could do was smile and pat her hand with a *thank you*.

Now, I'm walking briskly to put some distance between us and the older woman's house, Sarge lagging behind me, paws dragging to remind me he is not a fan of the heat and this walk has taken a whole lot longer than he expected.

"And here I thought your fans were all teenage girls," I say to lighten the mood.

"I thought you said no one around here would recognize me." There's a twinkle in Sam's eyes.

"Yeah, I was wrong."

Sam looks at me. I look at him. And then we're both cackling like a pair of hooligans.

I swipe tears from my eyes. "You're going to make one fangirl very happy on her birthday when Mrs. Brown gives her granddaughter all that stuff."

He laughs. "I think I made Mrs. Brown very happy."

"How long do you think the signature on her wrist will last?"

"Probably depends on if she truly 'never washes her hands aga in.'"

We crack up.

I pause at my front door. "Feel like watching some stars?" Maybe it's foolish, but I'm not ready to say goodnight. It also doesn't hurt that it was our regular summer tradition growing up. Summer nights were meant for staying up late, watching the stars, and dreaming of the future. On one of our many nights spent on a blanket, being chewed by mosquitos, Sam first told me of his dream of being a singer. I reciprocated by pouring out my heart for art. The two of us spent hours dreaming of our careers. The awards he'd win. The logos and memorabilia I'd design. Everything from the local bakery's next sign to hit Hollywood movie merch.

Sam pauses.

I bite my lip and finger the doorknob. Does he remember?

"Riley..." He rubs his neck.

Cheese and crackers! Heat crawls up my spine and settles on my face. I've over stepped. The guy has already spent the entire day with me, and now I'm assuming he'll want to stare up at the sky all night. Foolish. He's probably outgrown that by now.

"I'm not sure this is such a great idea."

Aim. Fire. The words pierce my heart and warm liquid washes across my vision. I reach to scratch Sarge behind the ears so I won't have to look at the boy on the sidewalk. "You're right. It's been a long day—"

"Us, I mean."

Us? I jerk my head up. "Oh?" Maybe he's decided our friendship isn't worth rekindling. Maybe—

"With everything going on, my career may be dragged through the gutter, and I won't drag you with me. I refuse, Riley. Other people in my life have already been hurt, and I won't do that to you." Sam's voice breaks.

"No, Sam." I reach out. Take his hand. "You don't get to make that choice for me."

His eyes lock on mine, a thousand thoughts darting through them.

I squeeze his hand. "Let me in."

His brow furrows. "Let you in?"

"I think it's been too long since you've allowed yourself to trust someone. You're safe with me...us, I mean." I jerk a thumb toward the house. "Let us in." *Please*, my heart pleads. All I can see is the hurting boy in front of me. How much worse off will he be if he shuts us all out? Then he truly will be alone. *Please let him say yes.*

Sam throws a look over his shoulder before turning his attention to me. "All right. One more night. But Riley, we both know this can't last forever."

We can try, I want to argue. But I don't. Because he's right. This will have to end. He'll have to go back and face all the drama. Sooner rather than later if he doesn't want things to escalate or be in some kind of breach of contract. "One more night," I say.

We head inside.

Lou-Lou hangs upside down on the couch, crocheting while some cheesy teen romance movie plays on the tv.

Soft music upstairs suggests Kenzie is reading, probably in a face mask and...I sniff. Yep, she's burning her vanilla candle. She swears there's no better way to unwind after a long day.

"Hey, guys." Dad peeks over the rim of his glasses from where he sits at the dining room table, going over more paperwork. Someone needs to remind him of the whole work-life balance concept.

"Hey, we're going to go do some star gazing." I unhook Sarge's leash and he trots over to his dog bed near the couch and flops down with a weary sigh. Man, the guy has such a hard life.

"Okay. Don't stay up too late. You have that commission due tomorrow."

"Oh, right." I snap my fingers. I was supposed to work on it today. My attention slides to Sam. Guess I got a little sidetracked. "Thanks, Dad." I snag my tablet and a throw blanket from the living room. I take a quick pitstop to drop the crisp fifty-dollar bill from dog sitting into an empty tea canister. Well, empty except for the little stash of green paper growing with every art commission or dog sitting gig. Europe here I come. In one more year.

"Ready?" Sam asks.

"Absolutely."

We head outside and I lay the blanket across the grass.

Sam lies on his back and I sit with my legs crisscrossed and power on my tablet while we wait for the stars to come out in all their glory.

"Riley," Sam tugs a chain out from under his shirt and twists the cross pendant back and forth.

"Hmm?" I add a few strokes of color to the heroine's hair, shading it in to look more realistic.

"You haven't…" He clears his throat. Tries again. "You haven't seen my documentary, have you?"

"Sam Hong, you're not asking me if I'm a secret fangirl, are you?"

He sits up and picks at the grass, but his lips quirk. "No."

I snort and continue adding the final touches to the commission. Just about done, and shaping up to be one of my best pieces yet.

"Have you seen it?"

"Does it matter?"

He shrugs. "Maybe."

"Sam, why would I pay money to go see a show about your origin story? I was there."

Except he doesn't laugh. He's dead serious.

I lower my stylus and watch him. "Why does it matter?"

"Because, if you want to know something, I'd rather have you ask, not watch some staged drama about my life, or worse, search it up on the internet."

Oh, Sam.

I hold out my pinky.

He stares at me.

I nudge him with my elbow. "Come on. Pinky promise. If there's something I want to know about you, I'll ask."

He extends his pinky and we lock fingers. Swing our hands.

"There, done." We break apart and I return to drawing.

"Let me see." Sam pokes my leg.

"No." I angle my screen away from him.

"Hey, that's not fair. I remember singing for you earlier today."

I wag my stylus at him. "That was a dare."

"Aw, come on, Ri." He pouts his bottom lip and blinks hard.

What harm can it do? The author is planning to print the drawing anyway and mail it out to about a hundred strangers. Maybe Sam deserves to be the first to see it. "Fine." I show him.

Sam releases a long whistle. "Wow, Riley."

"You think it's good?" I hold still. I don't know why, but for some reason his opinion matters.

"Amazing. You've come a long way since—"

I wrinkle my nose. "I was thirteen?"

"You were good back then, but this is...wow. You have a gift, Ri."

Heat creeps up my cheeks as I smile.

Sam tugs his phone from his pocket.

"What are you doing?" I pull my tablet close to my chest.

"Making a note."

"For?"

His thumbs fly across the screen. "To make sure you're hired for the next round of graphics when I go on tour again." His thumbs pause. "*If* I go on tour again."

"You will."

His gaze snags on mine. "How can you be so sure?"

"Because you're amazing, and you know what they say about publicity, it's all good, right?"

"Unless your own fans start hating you."

"They won't. If you get everything straightened out, then I'm sure—"

A shadow passes through his eyes. "I'm not ready."

And just like that, he erects a wall once more, refusing to let me in, or even truly explain what is going on. "You can't run forever."

"I know."

We both go quiet, him studying the darkening sky, me working my stylus across my screen.

"Sam..."

He turns to me. "Hmm?"

"Why did you stop writing your own music?"

He goes still for a long moment. "No one has ever asked that before. How did you know? That I stopped writing the songs I mean?"

Heat climbs my neck and settles in my cheeks. I fiddle with my stylus. "Sometimes I hear your songs play in the grocery store or on the radio and they don't sound like you." I would recognize his voice anywhere, but the songs and the messages they contain. It's not him. It took a quick internet search to confirm, but I'd already known.

Sam sighs. Deep and oh so tired. "They wanted songs that would sell. Hits. Songs to climb the charts. That's all anyone cares about anymore. I begged for this opportunity to write for myself again, and now the words won't come."

My heart breaks then. Shatters for the boy who could spend an entire day shut in his room, scribbling out lyrics that meant something. Songs that once pointed to the Savior he loved. Loves? I hate that I don't know.

Sam sighs. "It's all become so fake. Fake persona, fake hair, fake headlines. I've lost track of how many girlfriends I've supposedly had this year, when the truth is I haven't had time to go on a single date. Music...*life* used to mean something. I made choices I'm not proud of. And then, I couldn't take it anymore. So, I left. Walked out on every one of my obligations. All of it. Now I'm here."

I ache for words to help, but my churning heart comes up empty. *God, what do I say?*

"But hey," Sam breaks the silence, "they promised I would be a superstar. Looks like they meant it, huh?"

But at what cost?

Chapter 11

"R iley," Lou-Lou whispers.

I blink groggy eyes and shift, adjusting the blankets around me. My foot collides with her leg. "Hmm?"

"Are you asleep?"

"Yep." I squeeze my eyes shut and snuggle deeper into the covers. Who has a conversation in the middle of the night?

"You were right."

Oh, yeah. Lou-Lou does. I rub a hand over my face and shift until I can make her out through the moonlight trickling in from the window. Sarge shifts on the foot of the bed, signaling his displeasure with a deep sigh. "Right about what?"

"Sam." She fiddles with the edge of the comforter. "He's not so bad."

I roll onto my back and smile. Sam has done it. Lou-Lou's loyalty is not easily won, but now that he has, she's not likely to turn her back on him anytime soon. "Thank you."

"For?"

"Giving him a chance."

She wiggles closer, pulling the blankets to her chin. "It's going to be a great summer."

It's seven in the morning when Lou-Lou yanks me out of bed, makes me guzzle a cup of coffee, and drags me to Sam's doorstep.

"Lou-Lou, he's not even going to be awake," I groan as she hammers her fist against the door. Goodness, at this rate she's going to wake the entire neighborhood. "It's too early for this."

"Stop whining." She bangs on the door again.

After another round, it creaks open and Sam squints at us, his hair sticking up in a dozen different directions. Sleep marks cover one side of his face. "Riley?" He looks between the two of us. "Is everything okay?"

"What else?" Lou-Lou bounces on her toes and steps into Sam's house without being invited.

I follow her. It's that or stand awkwardly on the front porch. The smell of old perfume and dust has been replaced by a citrus cleaner. And is he diffusing something? I glance around and find an essential oil diffuser posted on a nearby side table. Lavender by the smell of it. My, his mother would be proud. I wonder what persuaded her to leave some of her precious stash behind.

"Good morning?" Sam closes the front door.

"What else?" Lou-Lou crosses her arms and taps her foot.

He blinks long and slow before rubbing at his eyes. "What else, what?"

Poor Sam, Lou-Lou needs to come with an after nine in the morning warning. Or at least after one cup of coffee. Maybe two, if I'm being honest.

"What else do you want to do before you have to leave? Throw a party? Go to the pool? A movie? Come on, the grocery store couldn't have been the only thing." Lou-Lou creeps closer with each word, and Sam steps back until he collides with the door.

"Woah now." I grab my cousin's shoulders and pull her away from him. "Let's let Sam breathe for a second."

Sam rubs his eyes. "What's happening?"

Lou-Lou props her hands on her hips. "What else do you want to do before you leave? There has to be something else you've been dreaming of. Come on, we've got to get a move on if we want to get everything done before you get caught."

"Get caught? That's reassuring, minion."

"It's the truth." She shrugs. "You can't keep up the charade forever."

Unfortunately, she's not wrong.

Sam pushes his fingers through his hair and blows out a breath. "Well..."

"*Well*?" Lou-Lou tips forward on her toes.

If I have to wrestle her back again...

"It's stupid." Sam shakes his head.

Lou-Lou and I cross our arms and share a look.

"We'll be the judge of that," I say.

Sam purses his lips and studies us for a moment. "All right. I want to go through a drive-thru."

Lou-Lou's mouth drops open. "That's just sad."

"A drive-thru?" Once more my heart sinks for the boy who has missed out on so much of what every other person considers normal.

"You promised not to judge." Sam narrows his eyes at us.

"No, we promised to judge. But," Lou-Lou snaps her fingers, "consider us your fairy godmothers, because your wish is our command."

"Yeah?"

"Yep." Lou-Lou gives a firm dip of her chin.

"Okay, make me breakfast."

Make him— "Wait, I thought we were going through a drive-thru?"

"And you're not that lucky," Lou-Lou adds.

Sam laughs. "Drive-thru is lunch. I believe in a home-cooked meal for breakfast."

"Oh, yeah?" I plant a hand on my hip. "Let's see it then."

"See what?"

"Your cooking skills." Because we all know he doesn't have any.

"What happened to fairy godmothers?"

"Key words *fairy godmothers* not slaves." Lou-Lou swivels on her heel and heads for the kitchen. "But, seeing as we haven't had breakfast either, let's put those groceries to use."

"I propose a list." I raise my fork all dramatic, careful not to let my bite of pancake slide from the tines.

"A list?" Sam looks up from his plate, syrup sticking to the corner of his mouth.

I sit on my free hand to keep myself from reaching out to swipe the stickiness away.

"Ooh, a list of all the things we need to do this summer." Lou-Lou bounces in her chair.

"Okay." Sam pulls off his baseball cap, runs his fingers through his hair, and replaces it backwards. "I can get behind that."

"But"—I free my hand from its prison and hold up a finger—"this list is going to have some rules."

"Rules?" Sam and Lou-Lou share a dubious look.

"Don't look at each other like that. Boundaries. That's it. Just a couple boundaries to see us through. Guidelines if it makes you feel better." I narrow my eyes, but my attempts at being serious are ruined as my piece of pancake slips off my fork and splatters into my pool of syrup.

"This is supposed to be fun, Riley," Lou-Lou drawls.

"This will help it be fun."

Lou-Lou opens her mouth, no doubt to argue, but Sam holds up a hand. "Hold on. Let's hear her out. There's no harm in that, and if we don't agree"—he shrugs—"there's two of us, so we hold vetoing power."

I sit straighter. "Excuse me? Vetoing power? Says who?"

Lou-Lou blinks at me long and slow. "It's only fair."

"For who?"

The pair share another one of those looks. Oh, no fair. They're ganging up on me!

Sam folds his arms on top of the table. "All right, let's hear them."

Lou-Lou gives an affirmative dip of her chin and copies his posture.

Fine. They want to make this all official? Bring it on. "One, we need a timeline." I hold up a finger and eye Sam. "We can't keep this up forever. You have to go home eventually."

His gaze darts away, but he nods anyway.

"Aw." Lou-Lou throws her head back and groans.

"She's right, minion. I have to go back eventually." Sam rubs his hands down his pants.

"Fine." Lou-Lou rolls her eyes. "I'm assuming there's more?"

"Two." I add a finger to my upheld one. "The things on the list have to be achievable."

Sam raises his eyebrows.

Lou-Lou throws up her hands. "Obviously."

"No, hear me out. If we say something like 'road trip through the States' it's not likely to happen."

Sam nods. "Okay, I can see your point."

I look to Lou-Lou.

She purses her lips. "Yeah, okay, fine. No crazy big aspirations. Does that mean we're stuck here?" At the last part, she slumps in her seat.

Sam turns his attention on me.

Hmm. I sit back and tap my chin. "Let's make that rule number three. Something about accessible distance."

"Like what? Within a couple hours of here?" Sam asks.

Lou-Lou perks up. "Oh, please say yes."

"How about one hour? Since it's not like we can spend the night somewhere if we were to get stuck or something?" I suggest. "If we keep it in the one-hour range, then we're close enough for Kenzie or Dad to pick us up if something were to go wrong."

The two conspirators share a look. "Agreed."

Lou-Lou folds her hands on the table. "Is that all Miss Anderson?"

"I think so, unless anyone else has anything to add?"

"It has to be fun things," Lou-Lou says. "Nothing boring like 'study ahead for when school starts.'"

I swallow a laugh. "Got it."

Sam takes a moment to rub his mouth, but it does nothing to hide the gleam in his eyes.

"As long as that's clear, we may proceed," Lou-Lou says.

"Do you have paper?" I turn to Sam.

"Paper is so old school. We have phones." Lou-Lou peers over the rim of her glasses like I am the worst disappointment she has faced in her lifetime.

Ouch. "Listen kid, there is something magical about putting a list on the fridge with a magnet. If it's in view every day, we're more likely to do the things we put on there."

"Riley, Riley, Riley." She shakes her head.

Sam holds up both hands, one pointed toward each of us. "How about a compromise? We make a paper list, but we keep copies on our phones?"

"Can't hurt." I shrug and eye Lou-Lou.

She dips her chin. "All right."

"Paper and pen?" I look to Sam. I have a good idea of where his mom used to keep a notepad, but it feels weird to rummage through drawers of a house which has sat empty for so long.

Sam pushes away from the table and, ooh, I'm correct. Second drawer on the right of the refrigerator. When he returns to the table, Sam sets a yellowed notepad and three pens in front of me.

I raise my eyebrows.

"In case one of them is out of ink."

"Good thinking." I grab the first one and click the top.

"Good thinking?" Lou-Lou scoffs. "He just doesn't want to get up again."

Sam wrinkles his nose at her. "Don't rat me out."

Lou-Lou snickers.

"So, what's the first thing on our list?" I ask. "Drive-thru?"

"Works for me." Sam nudges his empty plate away.

I write it down. "Second?"

Lou-Lou bounces in her chair. "Let's go to the beach."

"One hour, remember?" I hover the pen above the paper.

Sam crosses his arms and leans back. "What about the lake? It's not the *beach* beach, but it's something."

Lou-Lou claps her hands. "We could pack a picnic."

They both turn eager looks on me. Who am I to dampen their joy? "All right, go to the lake." I put 'picnic' and 'bug spray' in brackets alongside the notation.

"Backyard barbecue," Sam says.

"Veto." Lou-Lou's hand shoots high. "That's lame."

Sam crosses his arms. "Not when you haven't had one in four years."

"Oh, I am so over the 'I got famous' sob story." Lou-Lou opens and closes her hand like a chattering mouth.

Sam makes a face at her.

"Lou-Lou." I nudge her with my toes. "A backyard barbecue would be fun. Dad and Kenzie would like that and it's achievable. It would even give us an excuse to do another grocery run."

"Fine." She props her chin on her hand.

"What do you want to do?" Sam asks her.

"Go to the zoo."

"The zoo?" I pause as I start to write the word. "Why the zoo?"

Sam looks just as confused.

"We used to go all the time."

"You remember that?" She couldn't have been more than five or six the last time we went.

"Why not, Riley?" Sam stretches his legs. "Sounds good to me unless you're still afraid of the stingrays."

"I am not." My spine prickles and I tighten my grip on the pen.

He folds his arms and leans back in his chair. "You so are."

"Am not!"

"All right, then add it to the list. And when we're there, I dare you to touch a stingray."

My heart pounds a little quicker. But no childhood phobia is going to make me cower in front of the smirk he's wearing. I point my pen at him. "We will go, and I *will* pet a stingray. I think you will find that when it comes to bravery, we Anderson girls are unbeatable." I hold my fist out to Lou-Lou and she taps her knuckles against mine.

Sam's lips quirk. "We'll see about that."

Chapter 12

Twenty minutes and two pancakes later, we have our list:

1. *Drive-thru*

2. *Go to the lake [picnic + bug spray]*

3. *Backyard barbecue*

4. *Camp in the backyard [potentially combine with No. 3 + s'mores are a must]*

5. *Go to the zoo. [Pet stingrays. Gulp...]*

6. *Make popsicles*

7. *Go for a bike ride*

8. *Water fight*

9. *Go to the movies*

"Do you think we can get it all done?" Lou-Lou stares at the paper in my hands.

"It's good." I tap the pen against the list. "We've got this."

"It'll be fun." Sam leans over my chair to get a better look. His warm breath tickles my neck, sending goosebumps across my skin. Something warm sparks to life in my middle.

Lou-Lou sighs. "Are you sure it's long enough?"

"Wait, I thought you were worried about getting it all done?" Sam pulls away to fix his attention on her.

It's cold with him gone. I wriggle in my seat, adjusting my position. I cannot get attached. Sam's leaving. Nine items, a few weeks, and then he's going to be gone. I click the pen to distract myself.

Lou-Lou scuffs her foot against the floor. "It's just…"

"Just?" Sam leans down, equalizing their height.

Lou-Lou peers at him, and maybe it's the lighting, but I swear her eyes shimmer. "You're going to leave when the list is done."

I drape my arm over the back of my chair. "Lou-Lou, you know it's only for the summer. Sam can't stay forever."

"I have obligations," Sam says.

She rolls her eyes. "Ugh. Adults." Lou-Lou crosses her arms. "Fine. I still think it's too short."

Sam looks from her to the list. "You're right. It should be even, don't you think?" He whips out his phone and starts typing on his digital copy of the list.

Lou-Lou leans close to see. "Wow." Her eyes pop wide.

"What?" I crane my neck to see over my cousin, but Sam angles the screen away. "Hey! Not fair."

Sam shakes his head and looks anything but remorseful. "It's a secret."

Oh, so not fair. "But we made the list together."

Lou-Lou giggles. "Let it be a surprise, Ri."

I scramble from my chair and make a swipe for the phone. Sam dances out of reach.

"Let me see." I make another advance.

Sam spins away.

"Sam!" I charge.

He trots backward, holding the phone way too high. "Wouldn't you like to know?"

"Yes." I jump, but he laughs and holds the phone farther away. "Not fair." I make a grab, but trip and fall forward. Sam catches me, one hand at my waist, my hands on his chest. Our eyes connect. We're both breathing hard.

Click.

Sam shuts off his phone and holds it out to me. "There you go."

He thinks he's so smart. I take the device and step away, creating distance between us. Of course, its password protected, but we've been friends for almost our whole lives. I type in his birthday. Nope. But of course, that's too easy. Any fangirl could do a quick internet search and then if they got hold of his phone it would all be over. I try his mom's birthday. The day he signed his record deal. The day he got his first goldfish. Doesn't work. But to be honest, I'm not sure of the exact date anyway. I try today's date to be fair.

"All right, don't lock me out." Sam snags the phone and deposits it in his pocket.

"I want you both to know I am not happy about this." I fold my arms and give them both my most scathing look.

"Riley, you couldn't scare a mouse." Lou-Lou giggles.

Whatever. I stomp to the list and scribble down a tenth item.

10. Watch fireworks

"There. Whatever you two picked doesn't count. Unless you care to share?" I raise an eyebrow.

"Nope," they say in unison. They even wear matching smirks.

Good grief. I think I preferred it when they hated each other.

"When do we start?" Lou-Lou rubs her hands together.

Sam rocks back on his heels. "I don't know about you two, but I could go for something to eat."

I eye the table and sink, both cluttered with dirty dishes. "We just ate."

"Nobody said we have to do the list in order," Lou-Lou says.

"Yes, we do." This time it's Sam and me who speak in unison.

"Woah." Lou-Lou steps back. "I can see you have opinions about that. Okay then, we do the list in order."

"Drive-thru?" Sam raises his eyebrows.

The thought of more food makes me want to gag. "Maybe tomorrow would be a better day to—"

Sam's phone rings. Sam glances at the screen. "I better take this." He looks green.

"Okay." I tuck my hair behind my ear. "We'll take care of things here." I wave a hand to indicate the dishes.

"Thanks." He presses the phone to his ear even as he backs toward the hallway. "We should talk."

"Seriously, Riley, *more* chores? Don't we have enough at home?" Lou-Lou shoots a look of disgust around the room.

"Yes, I know what I said." Sam pinches the bridge of his nose.

I nudge Lou-Lou's back, pushing her toward the table. "Nice try missy, but you helped *make* this mess."

"I'm the one being dramatic?" Sam's voice rises from the hallway.

I gather an armful of plates and bring them to the sink. It must be his manager or someone from his legal team. Who else could add so much frustration to my Sam's voice? Wait...*my* Sam? I shake my head to clear the thought away and run a plate under warm water before positioning it in the dishwasher. If I'm going to survive this summer, then I need to wrangle my thoughts into submission.

Please help me guard my heart, God.

Sam paces, listening to whatever's being said. "There's no call for that and we both know it."

And help Sam through whatever's going on.

Lou-Lou steps closer to me. "Do you think he's going to be okay?"

"I hope so." I dunk my hands in the warm soapy water to keep myself from going to him.

"Fine," Sam all but spits the word. "I'll be back in a few weeks. We can talk then." He ends the call.

"Sam?"

His face is red when he steps into the kitchen. Jaw locked tight. One hand balled into a fist, the other clutching his phone in a death grip.

"We'd..." His voice is too tight. He clears his throat and tries again. "We'd better start the list tomorrow." He glances at the dishes. "Sorry. I need to go make a phone call."

Lou-Lou is curled on the couch with an outdated magazine she found lying around, and I'm wiping the last countertop when Sam returns.

"Is everything okay?" I whisper.

Sam shakes his head and reaches for the rinsed mixing bowl. "No."

"But it will be?" I press.

"I hope so." He swipes a towel over the dish even after the last water droplet is dry.

I squeeze Sam's arm. "We're all here for you. No matter what. I hope you know that."

"Thanks, Ri." He stations the bowl in its proper cabinet.

"Have you talked to your parents recently?"

"I called them last night. They know where I am, and there's only so much they can do." He tosses the towel over his shoulder.

They could be here for him. But that's hardly fair. They have their own lives and they can't jump to the rescue on this one. I can only hope they're truly loving Sam as best they can long distance. Still, I wish they would drop everything and come to his aid. Even if it's just to give him a hug. They must underestimate how much they truly mean to him.

"You got quiet." Sam bumps me with his elbow.

I blink and reach for the towel he holds out, drying my hands. "Sorry. Just overthinking I guess."

"And?"

I can't exactly admit I'm second guessing his parent's love and motives, so I go with the second thing on my mind. "Sam, what happens if you go to the press with your side of the story? Tell them you need a break?"

Sam swallows hard. "I don't see how it would do much. How am I supposed to admit the words have run dry? That music isn't magical anymore?"

"But you can't let everyone smear your good name." Scandal rumors have flooded the internet, most of them too gross or absurd to repeat. If Sam survives this, his name may be smeared for the rest of his career.

Sam goes still. "It won't matter if I quit."

"Do you really mean that?" My heart breaks for this broken boy before me.

"I don't know." Anguish fills his eyes.

A small spark lights inside me, filled with hope. Because I can see there's something inside him still wanting to sing. If he didn't, he'd be having a much easier time walking away for good.

Help him find the words again, please Lord. Lead and direct his steps.

"I'm going to complete our list before I go back. It should give me time to clear my mind and decide what I really want."

It's as good a plan as any. After all, he's the one who can truly decide if he's ready to walk away or not. "Pray about it too?"

He flinches and looks away. "Yeah, that's another thing that hasn't been so easy lately."

I still. "What do you mean?"

"I mean, growing up, it was easy. Faith was my family's thing. We went to church, youth group, Bible studies, but once I was on my own..." He shrugs. "I always thought I was saved. Now, I'm not so sure."

Give me the words, Lord. My heart breaks for this hurting boy before me. "You can be, Sam. All you have to do is believe that

Christ died for your sins. John 3:16. Repent and ask Him into your heart. Pray, read your Bible. God promises He'll be found by those who seek Him."

"Yeah, you're probably right." He toes the ground and all I can do is pray God gives him the ears to listen. To have an open heart.

Please, God.

"Hey, I'm here for you if you want to talk. Anytime." I lean close, hand on his arm.

"Always." Sam's gaze locks on my face. "Riley, I—"

"Are we going to the drive-thru or not?" Lou-Lou stomps into the kitchen.

Sam pushes away from the counter. "Not today, minion. I've got to make some more phone calls." His gaze turns to me. "Rain check?"

"Of course."

"Boring." Lou-Lou huffs.

"It's called being a grown-up," I say.

"Like I said, b-o-r-i-n-g."

"How about this, tomorrow, you pick the fast food place." Sam holds out a hand for her to shake on it.

"Bribery. I should be above it." And yet Lou-Lou shakes anyway.

"It's settled then." I take my cousin by the shoulders and steer her toward the front door. "You coming for dinner?" I call over my shoulder.

Sam's already typing away on his phone. "I better not. I get the feeling this might take a while to sort out."

A pinch travels through my chest. It reeks of disappointment, but that can't be the right label. That would be utterly ridiculous. "Well, if you change your mind, our door is always open."

"It is not. They lock it on a regular basis," Lou-Lou calls over her shoulder.

Sam's laugh follows us out the door.

Chapter 13

I wake to a blow horn in the ear. I scramble into a sitting position, one hand going to my chest where my heart beats frantically, the other pushing a matted tangle of hair from my eyes. "What in the world are you doing?" I glower at Lou-Lou who stands a little too pleased with herself next to my side of the bed.

She tosses her hair over her shoulder. "I'm going to a drive-thru."

"You're twelve. You can't drive." Is this some kind of bad dream?

Sarge whines at the end of the bed, pawing at his ear. Yeah, you can say that again, buddy. This is not the proper way to wake someone up. Especially not on the weekend during summer vacation.

Lou-Lou flicks my forehead, sending a sizzling flare of pain through my skull. "Earth to Riley. Are you awake, or do I need to blow this thing again?" She waves the horn dangerously close to my face.

"Don't you dare." I lug my pillow out from behind me and clobber her before she can move.

Lou-Lou squeals and leaps out of reach. That's all right. I got one solid hit in and that's good enough for me.

"What on earth are you girls doing?" Kenzie throws the door open.

Lou-Lou and I exchange a look and dissolve into a fit of giggles.

Kenzie props her shoulder against the doorjamb and crosses her arms. "Look, I don't know if either of you care, but some of us are trying to sleep."

"You're right, we don't care." I hurl my pillow at her, landing a good hit on her leg.

"Hey." Kenzie's eyes narrow. Ooh, the big sister who doesn't like to be defied is coming out.

I scooch back on my bed, hands raised. "Let's talk about this rational—"

The piercing cry of the blow horn sounds and I clap my palms over my ears as Lou-Lou charges at my sister. Kenzie yelps and darts from the room. The slam of her door seconds later suggests she's taking refuge in one of the few places besides the bathroom where she can turn a lock to keep our cousin out.

Sarge crawls to me and drops his soggy jaw on my knee, sighing big and loud, reminding me how rough his life is. After all, his weekend plans have been ruined too.

"I know, sweet muffin cake. Not my favorite way to wake up either." I massage the top of his head until his eyes drift closed.

"You have five minutes to get dressed and downstairs." Lou-Lou stabs a finger at me from the doorway. "Longer than that, and not only will you not get any coffee, but I'll show Kenzie where you hide the good creamer."

"You wouldn't." I sit up so sharply Sarge jerks, immediately on the lookout for home invaders, cats, or some similar threat.

"Watch me." Lou-Lou whips her phone from her pocket. "And...the...timer...is...set."

Eek! I scramble from bed, trip on the blankets wrapped around my leg, and crawl into the closet where I throw on the first t-shirt and shorts I find on the ground. Maybe they're clean. Maybe they're dirty. Doesn't really matter. I throw my hair into the sloppiest bun I can manage, and skedaddle down the stairs as fast as I can without breaking my neck.

Lou-Lou blows the horn as I skid to a stop on the kitchen tile. "Congratulations. You made it. Have some coffee." She waves to the cup she's poured for me and extends the good creamer my way.

"Thanks." I eye her warily, but she doesn't try anything as I slide into a chair and pour the creamer into my cup, transforming the liquid inside from a dark brown to a rich caramel.

She settles in front of me, chin propped on her hand. "Go on, drink up. I'll wait."

"Of course, you will, because you have nothing else to hold over me." I take a nice long drink of my coffee. Oh, yes. Some days it tastes extra good.

"So, you think." Lou-Lou shrugs. "But don't worry, I'm saving *that* ammo for when I really need it."

Every hair on my body prickles and I pull away from my mug. "What ammo?"

She widens her eyes. "Hmm?"

"Lou-Lou." I lean across the table and grab her arm before she can pull away. "What do you have?"

"Like I would tell." She raises her free hand, prepared to slap her way to freedom.

I tense. Yeah, she never learned the 'we don't hit people' rule. "Don't you da—"

"Good morning, girls. What's going on here?" Dad strolls into the room, dressed in his weekend uniform of joggers and one of those ratty shirts Mom made him promise to only wear around the house.

"Nothing, Uncle Gavin." Lou-Lou shakes me off. "Someone woke up on the wrong side of the bed."

"Maybe because there was a blow horn involved?" I lean back, arms crossed.

She splays a hand over her chest. "I've tried gentler approaches. Believe me, I have. But it's not my fault you sleep like a ship at the bottom of the sea. It's actually dangerous if you ask me."

"Liar." I snatch my coffee mug off the table before she can do something evil like dump it down the drain.

Lou-Lou bats her eyelashes. "Me? Lie? Riley, you wound me."

Yeah, right. I rub my eyes beneath the rim of my glasses. "Listen—"

"Girls." Dad slides into a chair and holds his hands between us. "It's a little early for fighting, don't you think?"

"Sorry, Uncle Gavin. You're right. We're being inconsiderate." Lou-Lou folds her hands on the table. Innocent angel that she is *not*.

"Sorry," I mutter before taking a long drink of coffee.

"What are your plans for the day?" Dad asks once he seems sure we're not about to claw out each other's eyeballs.

Lou-Lou bounces in her seat. "Sam's taking us to a drive-thru."

"Oh, where?"

"Don't know yet."

"I'm sorry, I'm confused." Dad pulls off his glasses and folds them on the table, giving Lou-Lou his full attention. "You said it like it was somewhere special."

"It will be special, because we're going with Sam." She looks to me. "Seriously? You didn't tell him about the list?" It's less question and more accusation.

Well, no, because for most of us, it's nothing earth shattering. "The three of us made a list of all the things we want to do before Sam has to"—it hurts to say the next word—"leave."

Dad studies me, the pause in my sentence not missed.

"We should have made more than ten," Lou-Lou grumbles.

"No, because Sam does have to go, or he's going to be..." In a heap of trouble. "Well, he has to go, so we'll enjoy him while we can." And we're all going to be big girls about it, and we—*I*—will not cry when he leaves. Again.

"Like what things? Other than the drive-thru?" Dad steeples his fingers under his chin and leans forward on his elbows.

Lou-Lou's eyes gleam. "Riley, fetch the list." She snaps her fingers.

I laugh as I climb from my chair and retrieve the paper copy from where I've stuck it on the fridge. I slide into my seat and pass it to Dad.

He returns his glasses to their proper position and studies each item. "Mmhm."

"Pretty good, huh?" Lou-Lou asks.

"Very good. And Sam's okay with all of this?" He looks to me. But he's not worried about the things on the list. He's worried about what happens if we do them. If Sam's recognized.

I clear my throat and point to the list. "Well, most of it we can do here. A hat and sunglasses should take care of the drive-thru." Yes, the cliché disguise will probably have to make a comeback. "And the movie theater will be dark, so we'll only need to worry about getting in and out."

"It's going to be awesome." Lou-Lou pumps her fist.

I turn to Dad, waiting for his approval or lack thereof. If he thinks it's going to put Sam in danger, I'll tear up the whole thing right now or find a bodyguard service and see what their hourly rate is. Not like it will help us blend in any better.

"I think you kids will have fun. Just be careful." He hands the list to me.

Be careful. A normal response for him. And the whole thing does require some amount of caution. For Sam's sake anyway. "We will."

"And call me. If you need anything during any of this." Dad jabs a finger at the list. "Or the police. Actually, make it both of us. I've seen videos of some of Sam's fans."

I nod. My dad may look like a nerdy science geek on the outside, but he could take out a pack of rabid fans if needed.

"Okay then." He pushes away from the table and pours himself a cup of coffee. "If that's all settled, I'll be enjoying this out on the porch." He offers his mug in a toast before moseying from the room.

"He's turning into an old man." Lou-Lou heaves a dramatic sigh.

"Uh, yeah. That's kind of what happens as you age."

She shakes her head like this is the most unfortunate turn of events. "I suppose."

I flick her arm. "Are we having breakfast by any chance?" If I can talk her into making her famous blueberry waffles—

"That's why we're going through the drive-thru. I swear you barely qualify as a person in the morning."

"But I thought we agreed yesterday that drive-thrus are more of a lunch thing?"

"That was yesterday."

I roll my eyes and finish off the last dregs of my coffee, sending a forlorn look at the bottom when I finish. There's never enough to go around.

"Stop staring like it broke up with you, or so help me, I will stage an intervention. Being that obsessed can't be good for you."

I straighten. "That won't be necessary." A couple years ago she forced me to try and quit caffeine. I lasted a week, but the headaches were not worth it. Am I a mess? Yes. But a happy, coffee-loving one.

"All right, wash up and then we should hit the road." She shoos me toward the sink.

I rinse my mug. "Does Sam know about this?"

"I sent him a text twenty minutes ago."

"And he responded?"

"I'm not the boy's keeper."

Yeah, he's probably still sleeping. Bless his heart, the boy doesn't have any idea hurricane Lou-Lou is about to touch down. Am I mixing metaphors with tornado's? Maybe. But I'm too tired to care.

"Let's take Sarge for a walk first." Try to buy the guy ten more minutes. Fifteen if any of my neighbors are early risers and got their dogs out and about first. In which case Sarge is going to have to stop and smell every blade of grass any other canine has touched within the last hour.

Lou-Lou looks like she's about to argue, but then her attention slides to Sarge who is waiting with leash in mouth. It's the proudest thing I've ever taught him.

"Oh, all right," she huffs, pushing away from the table.

"Good boy." I give Sarge an extra good rubbing before clipping his leash into place.

"Let's go, let's go, let's go." Lou-Lou raises the blow horn in threat.

"We're coming," I call, hurrying to shove my feet into some sandals. "Remind me to lose that thing as soon as possible," I mutter to Sarge once Lou-Lou is skipping happily along.

He gives me a long look.

"It's not like I can snatch the thing from her hand. Can you imagine the retribution?" I shudder.

He continues to stare in his soulful way.

I massage the back of my neck. "Okay. At the first opportunity, I'll snatch it and trash it. But you have to defend me when she turns into a livid monster, all right?"

He looks away, plants his nose to the ground like a scent hound instead of a retriever, and snuffles onward.

"I'll take that as agreement."

"They say talking to yourself is one of the first signs of insanity."

I jump and spin to find Sam at the end of his driveway, hands shoved into the pockets of his sweatpants, a hat tipped over his forehead, shielding his eyes from the morning sun. So, the boy isn't abed after all.

I cross my arms, ignoring Sarge's tug on the leash as he strains to get another inhale of someone else's pee. "Or genius."

"True." Sam's lips quirk.

I cock my head. "What are you doing up so early? Aren't celebrities supposed to sleep until noon or something?"

"Lou-Lou texted. We've got our first official adventure today."

"Told you," Lou-Lou calls as she bends to pluck a dandelion puff.

Not fair. "Okay, you two really need to start cluing me in."

"I did." Lou-Lou brandishes the blow horn before puffing the dandelion seeds into the air. "Make a wish."

I roll my eyes, but Sam winks.

"Oh, come on, you didn't really wish for something did you?" I seem to remember Sam giving that up when he was like eight or something.

"Maybe." He scuffs his foot like he's embarrassed.

"What did you wish for?" Sarge tugs on the leash, almost sending me stumbling.

Sam bumps his hat back. "I—"

Lou-Lou springs between us. "Nuh-uh. You can't tell or it won't come true. Shame on you, Riley. You should know better than trying to pull those kinds of secrets from the man."

I quirk an eyebrow. Is she five? Goodness, I wonder if she still believes in the tooth fairy. "Yeah, yeah. Come on, Sarge. You need to use the facilities so we can get out of here."

"Why don't you bring him with us?" Sam asks.

"Yeah," Lou-Lou chimes in. "That would be fun."

"What is he going to do at a drive-thru?" Other than bark at the poor soul who opens the window.

"Please?" Lou-Lou plants her hands under her chin and flutters her eyelashes while pouting her lower lip. "Pretty, please? With coffee and creamer on top?"

Oh, brother.

Sam grins at my cousin before turning those little pearly whites on me. Seriously, what high end product does he use to maintain such a gleam? "Come on, I'll buy him an ice cream cone."

Sarge's ears perk like he somehow knows we're talking about him. Lou-Lou's manipulative eyes I can say no to, but these deep recesses of puppy love? "Fine. He can come."

"Yes." Lou-Lou and Sam high-five.

"Come on, guys, I'm seriously starting to feel like the third wheel of this friendship," I mock protest.

"So insecure," Lou-Lou tisks and shakes her head.

"Don't worry, we still love you." Sam slings an arm around my shoulders and guides me over to his car.

"You're driving that?" I eye the sports car sitting in his garage.

"What's wrong with it?" Sam pauses, spinning his keys on one finger.

I swallow. Hard. What teenage boy has this kind of car? "It doesn't exactly blend in. We don't want anyone to think twice about us."

"Right, right. That's not normal." He folds his arms and blows out a breath. "Your car then?"

"Let me get my keys." I pass him Sarge's leash. "Watch out, he has a thing for cats."

"She's joking, right?" He ask Lou-Lou.

"Nope."

Chapter 14

Ten minutes later, we're pulling out of the neighborhood, Sam in the passenger seat, Lou-Lou and Sarge stuffed in the back.

"What are we in the mood for?" I adjust the review mirror. I swear Kenzie moves every single thing in this car when she drives. I've adjusted the seat three times and it still doesn't feel right.

"Chinese," Lou-Lou crows.

"Burger," Sam mumbles at the same time.

I pause at a stop sign and raise my eyebrows. "For breakfast?"

"Anytime of day," Lou-Lou says.

Sam dips his chin in agreement.

I laugh. "Okay, then, Which is it?"

"What are *you* hungry for?" Sam angles in his seat so I can see him out of the corner of my eye as I drive.

"Oh, I'm not hungry. I'll just have a bite of whatever Lou-Lou gets."

"Um, no you won't." Lou-Lou wedges herself between our seats, opening herself up to a slobber fest from Sarge.

"Hey, no distractions." I lean closer to the steering wheel as if it'll somehow keep my attention locked on the road.

"Sorry." She throws herself against the backseat.

"So?" Sam asks.

"So?" I flip on my indicator and change lanes.

"What are you hungry for?"

"No, no, don't worry about me." I wave a hand before slamming on the breaks as a car cuts in front of me. "Hey!"

"Good grief, Riley. Work on your driving," Lou-Lou says.

Oh, she's lucky both of my hands are on the steering wheel. "No backseat driving, please."

"Let's go to the burger place on 5th Street. Get some fries. A milkshake. Sound good to you, minion?" Sam looks over his shoulder at my cousin.

"Fine." Lou-Lou rolls down Sarge's window, allowing him to lean out and greet the sunshine.

Oh, to be a carefree dog. I head to the closest burger place and get in the turn lane. It may be early, but apparently, we've hit the breakfast rush.

"This might be a long wait." I blow out a breath and maneuver into the *long* line.

"How many people get burger's for breakfast?" Lou-Lou asks.

"Apparently everyone in town," Sam says.

"Yep." I slam on the brakes to keep from colliding with the car in front of me as it stops for the car in front of it or one of the million others in line.

Lou-Lou throws her head back and heaves the world's biggest sigh. "We're going to be here forever."

"Patience." I check my rearview mirror. Three more cars have joined the line behind us. "You two better know what you want or these guys are going to have the biggest hold up ever."

"Easy. Milkshake and fries," Lou-Lou says.

"Good. You?" I slide a look toward Sam as we creep forward. An inch.

"Burger. Milkshake. Fries. Something for our furry companion."

"All right, I'll keep all of that in mind." I free a hand to tap my temple.

After several minutes, we creep through the twisting line to place our order.

"What can I do for you today?" A voice rasps through the speaker, distorted and barely audible.

I lean out my window to be sure they catch every word. "Milkshake. *Chocolate*?" I mouth at Lou-Lou.

She nods.

"Chocolate milkshake. Small fries." One down, one to go. "Your..."

Sam holds up three fingers.

"Triple decker burger, strawberry milkshake, and a small fry."

Sarge nudges my shoulder with his wet nose.

"Oh, and a scoop of vanilla ice cream in a cup."

"Is that it?" The voice asks. Maybe? There's so much static it's hard to tell.

"Make that last fry a large, please," Sam calls.

The voice gives out a warble which might be, "Got it."

I take it as a yes and pull myself back inside my window. "Thanks." I scooch forward as the car behind me fires off its horn.

"Hey," Lou-Lou gasps. "That's just rude. You're not the one making the food."

"Forget it." I shake my head and roll forward another tenth of an inch. After listening to Kenzie's horror stories from working fast food as one of her first jobs, I've got nothing but sympathy for the workers trying to keep up with this rush.

It's a girl with a weary smile who opens the window after a ten-minute stretch. "Hey there. Thanks for your patience. We're a little under-staffed today."

"No worries." I wave away her apology.

Sam passes over some cash and I exchange the payment for our bag of food and beverages.

"Have a great rest of your day," I call before rolling up my window and pulling away from the building.

"Gimme, gimme, gimme." Lou-Lou dives between the seats, grabbing for the bag.

"Hey." I dodge an elbow to the face and slam on the brakes. "Not while I'm driving."

"You're such a baby." But she pulls back long enough for me to cross the street and aim for the closest park.

Ha, we'll see how she feels once *she's* driving. It's a whole world of responsibility this girl knows nothing about. I pull into a parking space beside a mini-van with family stickers boasting of five kids, a dog, and a cat.

"Now will you give it to me?" Lou-Lou bounces into view once more.

"Yeah, yeah." I shut off the engine.

"For you." Sam passes Lou-Lou her order and Sarge makes a lunge for it.

Lou-Lou yelps and throws herself against her door. "Riley, call off your mangy mutt."

"I'll have you know he is a certified, bred to perfection, golden retriever. His dad won all kinds of awards." He was the one thing

Mom asked for when she got sick. A distraction for all of us that came with an extra dose of love.

"Like I care." Lou-Lou squeals and flattens herself further against her car door. Any further and she might melt into it.

Perhaps mercy is the best policy. "Leave it, Sarge."

He pulls back, tongue lulling from the side of his mouth. One big drop of drool hits Lou-Lou's thigh.

"Ugh, that is disgusting. You're sleeping on the floor tonight." Lou-Lou takes a long, loud slurp of her milkshake.

"Uh-huh, my bed my rules." I dig through the food until I find Sarge's ice cream scoop. "If anyone is sleeping on the floor tonight, it's you."

"Don't get ahead of yourself, missy. I know how to arrange an accident. I don't even need it to be permanent. I'm thinking a torn ACL. It'll make climbing stairs too much work. Grounded on the main floor...sleeping on the couch...that kind of thing."

I freeze in pulling the lid off Sarge's cup. "Should I be concerned that you've actually thought about this?"

She snaps off a chunk of fry with a ferocious bite. "Maybe."

I glance over to find Sam grinning. "What?"

He shakes his head and turns his attention to unwrapping his burger. "Nothing."

"No, tell me," I press as I angle in my seat to hold the cup for Sarge. "Here, boy."

It's almost terrifying how quickly my sweet fur baby digs in.

"I was enjoying it, that's all." Sam takes a giant bite of his triple decker, taking off a good quarter of the burger.

Man, if I tried the same thing, I'd pop my jaw. "Enjoying what?"

"You two."

Lou-Lou and I share a confused look.

Is he serious? Lou-Lou asks with a silent raise of her eyebrow.

"Care to explain?" I ask.

"Your banter. The way you love each other but pretend you don't. I don't know...I've...I've missed it. Family, I mean." He covers the words with a laugh and takes another bite.

My heart gives a pang and I pick at something crusty on my jean shorts. "Will you visit them before you go back—" Home. I was going to say home, but I'll never be able to think of anything but the yellow house next door as his home. I leave the sentence dangling.

Sam shrugs. "I don't know. They're busy with stuff right now."

"They'd love to see you, I'm sure."

He ducks his head. Shutting down, ending the conversation.

Fine. I'll respect it. For now, at least. "Pass me a fry, Lou-Lou." I pull the empty cup away from Sarge and swipe a napkin along the dripping edge to keep from turning the car into a sticky mess.

"Uh, no. You're not hungry. Didn't want anything if I recall. You can't have it both ways, Ri." Lou-Lou takes an extra-long time eating the fry in her hand.

Oh, no she doesn't. "Excuse me, I drove us here."

"I can't hear you." She closes her eyes and starts swaying.

I unbuckle my seatbelt, prepared to climb back there and steal a fry if I have to. "Olivia Anne Anderson, you'd better—"

"Not to worry." Sam holds up his hands, stilling our feud before it can truly begin. "Luckily for everyone involved, I foresaw this situation."

"You did?" I sit back and stare at him.

Now it's his turn to share a look with Lou-Lou.

"I'm afraid you do this every time, Ri." Sam extends the large container of fries. "Your fries, my lady."

I accept them. "I do not."

"Yes, you do," Lou-Lou protests.

Sam raises an eyebrow. "Riley, I've known you how many years? Every time."

I shut up and shove a handful of fries in my mouth. Yeah, maybe I do. Something warm flares to life in my belly. Because he noticed. I squirm in my seat and shove the thought aside. "Is there any—"

Sam holds out the small container of ketchup.

Our fingers brush.

"Thank you." I maintain eye contact for a long moment. How does he know something about me I never realized? And how has he remembered after all our years apart?

Sam looks away and takes another bite of burger.

We munch on our meals and then swipe our hands on the stash of flimsy napkins provided for us at the bottom of the greasy bag.

"Are we getting out?" Lou-Lou drums her feet against Sam's chair.

"I don't know..." I scan the park.

It's mostly moms with young kids climbing on the small slides and swinging. A few walkers with graying hair stroll along the paved paths.

"Please?" How does she manage to pack one word with so much whine?

I turn to Sam. "Up to you."

He stares out the windshield for a minute. "Ah, it'll be fine. Besides, we've got our very own guard dog if we need him. Right boy?" He leans over to give Sarge a scratch behind the ears.

"All right, but keep your eyes open. You see any suspicious activity or anyone who looks like they're going to tackle hug Sam, we make a run for it. Got it?" I point a finger first at Sam and then at Lou-Lou.

"Yes, mother." Lou-Lou slides out of the car.

"Better to be safe than sorry," I say.

She slams her door shut.

Oh, no she doesn't. I jump out. "You be careful with Betty, or you will pay for the damages." I yank Sarge's door open and invite the ball of golden fluff into the great outdoors. He plants his nose against the pavement and starts snuffling like a hound. Yeah, I need to double check the certificate the breeder gave us.

"She's a piece of junk." Lou-Lou prods one of the tires with her foot.

"But she's a piece of junk that works." I wrap my free arm around her shoulders and steer her away before she can inflict any real damage. Betty may work at the moment, but it's a precarious tightrope I'd rather not play with.

Sam rounds the car, baseball cap pulled low, sunglasses hiding his dark eyes.

"Seriously? I thought we've been over this." Lou-Lou taps her foot and plants her hands on her hips. "That disguise is appalling."

"Sorry, minion, but it's the only one I've got."

At least he's ditched the hoodie.

"*Fine*," she draws the word out. "But just so you know, you're totally embarrassing me."

Sam laughs, flashing his dimple.

Lou-Lou whips out her phone and snaps a picture of him.

"What are you doing?" Sarge tugs me toward a tree as I try to angle my head to get a glimpse of her screen.

"Evidence." She deposits the phone into her pocket once more.

"Of what?" Sam trails after me as I start Sarge on a proper walk.

Lou-Lou skips to my side. "Of your presence here. That way when your disguise sticks out like a sore thumb and you're discovered I can sell it to the paparazzi."

"No, you will not," I say.

Sam laughs. "Hold on, let's get you a better one." He poses against the tree, hands in his pockets, staring forlornly into the distance.

"Ooh, perfect." Lou-Lou takes the photo.

I shake my head. "You two are crazy."

Lou-Lou slips her arm through mine. "And that's why you love us."

We walk the path circling the park. None of the moms or kids give us a second glance, and all the joggers we pass appear to be too focused on remembering how to breathe to notice us.

"I'm glad we did this," Sam says.

"Me too." We share a smile over Lou-Lou's head.

Chapter 15

"When are we going to check the next item off our list?" Lou-Lou asks as we head to the car.

"We can't do it all at once. We've got to stretch it out at least a little bit." I open the door for Sarge and get him settled before closing him in.

"Agreed," Sam says.

I won't mention how much I dread the day he walks away. Again.

"Fine, but can't we do something that isn't on the list?" Lou-Lou leans against the trunk.

"Like what? If you want to go down the slides or something, be my guest, just don't expect me to join you. I refuse to be one of those people who gets stuck and needs the fire department to free them." I lift an eyebrow.

"Puh-lease. I'm not a child, Riley." And yet she sticks out her tongue.

"Hey, Riley," a deep, familiar voice calls.

I turn with a smile. "Chad, hi."

Chad approaches us, dressed in cargo shorts and a button-down t-shirt. "Long time no see."

A dry breeze blows my hair into my face and I catch it and tuck the strands behind my ear. "How are you?"

"Good, good. Enjoying the summer break." He offers a lazy grin.

"Hi, I'm Olivia." Lou-Lou offers her hand to shake.

Chad cocks an eyebrow at me before shaking my cousin's hand, his expression transforming into one clearly saying he's humoring her. "Nice to meet you."

I cringe at his tone. Lou-Lou may be petite, but she is *not* five.

"No, the pleasure is mine," Lou-Lou croons, all sugar and sweetness which lets me know she didn't miss a thing.

It's then Sarge must look out the window, because he starts barking like a lunatic and good ole Betty does little to muffle the sound.

Chad laughs. "Vicious fellow you've got in there, hey Ri-boo?"

The nickname grates on my eardrums like it does every time he says it. He must think it's cute or something, and if I were braver, I'd tell him how much I hate it, but I'm not the conflict-loving type, so I grin and pretend it doesn't make me want to vomit. Chad's nice and all, but social cues are not his strong point. "Oh, Sarge would never hurt you." I hope, though the way he's growling isn't exactly reassuring.

Chad rocks on his heels. "Could've fooled me."

Sam clears his throat.

Oh, yeah. And then there's him...but how exactly do you introduce an undercover celebrity to some guy from school?

Sam solves the problem by stepping around me and offering his hand for a shake of his own. "Hey, I'm Sam."

"Chad." They perform some kind of handshake/challenge lasting a second beyond a-w-k-w-a-r-d.

"Well…" Lou-Lou performs the world's most obvious fake stretch. "We should really be getting back, right Riley?"

"Hmm? Yep. Totally." I jerk a thumb over my shoulder toward the car. "Yeah, we should go."

The boys step apart.

Chad's brow furrows as he sweeps Sam with a scrutinizing gaze. "Hey, you look familiar. Do I know you from somewhere?"

Sam shakes his head. "Nah, man. I've got one of those faces."

"Yeah, I guess. My bad." Chad bobs his chin. "You doing anything fun this summer?" Once more his focus is centered on me.

"Not really. Just hanging out with these guys." I sling an arm around Lou-Lou's shoulders. "How about you?"

"Working." He nods to a smoothie place across the street. "Trying to save for college and all the expenses that go with it. You know how it is." He laughs.

I join in even though I don't know and don't think I want to know. But I keep silent so he won't look at me like I'm purple with two heads.

"Riley." Lou-Lou elbows me in the ribs. Hard. "We were going…"

"Right. It was good seeing you." I smile at Chad.

"Yeah. Good. You still doing those pictures of yours? You draw, right?" His brow puckers like he's afraid he's mixed me up with someone else.

"Oh, yeah, I still…draw." Why did I say it like it was something bad?

"Actually, she's making money off her artwork now," Sam interjects, his arms crossed. "She's really good."

"Oh, yeah? I didn't know that was a thing unless you worked for some big company or something."

I wring my hands because I don't know what else to do with them. "You probably wouldn't know unless you run in the right circles. But it's not tons of money, or anything. Just enough to pay the bills." Like I have many.

Sarge's howling protest drowns out my words.

Chad cups his ear. "What's that?"

"I said—"

Sarge goes berserk.

Oh my goodness. I'm *that* dog owner. The one with the annoyingly loud pooch you have to swear won't actually rip someone's throat out all while you pray the words are true.

"Are you going to go to school and try to get a job at an animation studio or something?" Chad asks once Sarge stops for breath.

"Actually, I was thinking of..." I swallow hard and force it out, "taking a gap year. Working on my art on my own. Traveling." If all goes well, I might even be able to launch my own graphic design business. But what teenager can pull that off?

"Yeah, I thought about doing that myself, but I decided against it."

Lou-Lou tugs on my arm.

"I think it's a great idea," Sam says. "I kind of wish I'd done the same thing."

Chad's gaze flicks to him, studying more closely. "Really?"

"Whatever works for the individual, am I right?" I tuck my hair behind my ear again even though it's fine.

"Totally." Except Chad is staring Sam down. And then he looks at me. "Hey, the smoothie shop is offering fifty percent off on their tropical pineapple special this week. We should grab one."

"She's allergic to pineapple," Sam cuts in.

How does he even remember? "Yeah, I can't. Pineapple does not agree with me." Even saying the word makes my throat itch.

"Pineapple?" He hikes an eyebrow. "Really?"

"Yeah, it is not pretty." As in I swell up like a balloon and break out in hives. Hideous.

"Let's go." Lou-Lou pulls on my arm again.

Yep, time for a graceful exit. "We should get going."

"Right. Don't let me keep you." Chad steps back, attention shifting between me and Sam.

I smile awkwardly. Why do I feel guilty? I'm going to be re-playing this entire conversation a million times over in my head later. Likely every night for the next twenty-five years as I try to fall asleep.

"See ya." Chad raises his hand.

I offer a limp wave.

"Hey, Ri-boo." He turns to walk backward. "We should get together sometime. If you don't have other plans that is." Once more his focus slides toward Sam.

"That would be nice," I say.

He flashes a grin before turning and heading across the street.

Lou-Lou pinches my arm the moment he's out of earshot. "Ri-ley."

I yelp and jump away. "Hey!" I clamp a hand over my stinging bicep.

"You agreed to go on a date with Mr. Nice To Meet You," she mimics his tone perfectly.

I wince even as heat washes across my face. "I did not."

"Yes, you did."

"Did not." I scramble into the driver's seat.

Lou-Lou is seconds behind me, climbing into the back. "You so did. *That would be nice.*"

"I do not sound like that." I wait for Sam to join us before revving the car to life.

"What about our list?" Lou-Lou demands as I back out of the parking space.

"What about it?" I angle to watch behind me.

"We're not going to have time to do anything if you're dating that guy."

I slam on the brake, almost sending Sam crashing into the dashboard. "Lou-Lou, will you please calm down? I didn't agree to anything. I simply said it would be nice. No numbers were exchanged or dates set."

"But you didn't say no either." She slumps in her seat.

Sulky. I blow out a breath, but why I'm even defending myself is beyond me. I put the car into drive and maneuver onto the road.

"Friend from school?" Sam asks as we ease to a stop at a traffic light.

"Acquaintance?" Even I'm aware of the way my voice rises into a question. "We had a couple classes together. I think we maybe ate lunch together a few times." Okay, more than a few, but always with other people, so it doesn't count, right?

"And he doesn't have your number?" Sam keeps his face angled toward the window.

The light turns green and I start forward again. "No, why?" My palms turn sweaty against the steering wheel. "Is that weird? Do you think I should have given it to him?"

"No," Sam and Lou-Lou's voices overlap.

I jump a little and quickly lock my attention on the road.

"Not if you don't want to, I mean." Sam clears his throat.

"Or never," Lou-Lou mumbles. "Besides, Sarge doesn't like him, do you baby boy?"

Please. "An hour ago, you were yelling at him for drooling on you."

"That was before I knew he was a good judge of character."

"Can we please stop talking about Chad?" I throw on my blinker, waiting for an opportunity to turn into our neighborhood.

"Fine." Lou-Lou's seatbelt locks as she tries to angle between our seats. "But not until you set a date for the next item on our list."

That gets Sam's attention and I swear I can feel their eyes drilling into me.

Is it warm in here? I crank up the AC. "Why do I have to choose?"

"Because we need your guaranteed commitment before anyone else can bust in and spoil our plans." Accusation hangs on her words like such a tragedy has already come to pass.

Man, this girl is dramatic. I run my hands along the steering wheel. "Okay, well, what's next on the list?"

Sam pulls it up on his phone. "The lake."

"Well, that sounds kind of like an all-day thing...Friday or Saturday?"

"Friday or Saturday? Riley, that's like a week away." The punk child kicks my seat.

"Lou-Lou, do you want to cause an accident?" I tighten my grip on the steering wheel and check to be sure nothing tragic has happened in the tiny second my attention has been diverted.

"She may be onto something, minion," Sam says. "We don't want to go through the list too quickly."

"Yeah, I guess."

She could sound a little happier about it.

"We have to pick Friday though," Sam says.

"Why Friday?" I slow as a group of children zip by on their bikes.

"Because that's less than a week away."

"Friday?" I look away from the now empty road long enough to raise an eyebrow at Sam.

"Adding it to my calendar as we speak." True to his words, his thumbs tap against his phone screen.

"Promise?" Lou-Lou stretches across the car, waving her pinky in my peripheral vision.

Of all the... "I'm driving."

"Pull over."

"Hold onto your pants, kid, and be patient." I keep going until we reach our driveway and I pull into the garage.

The moment I shut off the engine, Lou-Lou is practically on top of me and I have to dodge to the side to avoid a pinky in my eye. "Promise?"

I lock my pinky with hers and swing our hands for good measure. "Friday. I promise."

Lou-Lou bounces on the edge of my bed, jolting me and sending my stylus streaking across my tablet screen.

I scowl as a long black line mars the finished art piece. "Lou-Lou." A quick tap undoes the damage, thank goodness.

"Let's do something. I'm *so* bored."

"Just because I don't go in to work like Dad or Kenzie doesn't mean I'm not working."

"Ugh. Come on. Let's finish the puzzle in the basement."

Discomfort settles on my shoulders and I go still.

She watches me, eyes narrowed. She knows exactly what she's asking.

"No, thank you." I tap a few buttons, sending off the art piece with a partial refund and an apology for the late turn-around. I need to set better boundaries if I'm going to make a go of this.

"But you never do puzzles anymore. You used to do them all the time. Don't you think—"

"Leave it, Lou-Lou." I clench my jaw so I won't say something I'll regret.

"Fine." With a huff, Lou-Lou pushes off the bed and moves down the hall to pester Kenzie.

I go to my email and scan the details of my next commission, but all the while, I can't erase the image of the unfinished puzzle in the basement. But even after four years, I can't bring myself to push the last few pieces into place. I hug my tablet close to my chest and turn to face the photo of my mom resting on my nightstand. A pinch of grief pulls at my heart. Even after all this time, the pain is blindsiding and unexpected.

Sarge jumps onto the bed and cuddles close, offering what comfort he can.

I rub his ear. "It's all right, boy. I'm all right." Or at least I will be. Somehow the grief is always worse in the shadows of night. Morning sun rays will bring hope.

Chapter 16

"**R**iley, I'm taking the car," Kenzie shouts over her shoulder as she heads for the garage.

I pause in packing lunch for the lake. "What?"

Lou-Lou almost falls out of her chair as she scrambles to block Kenzie's exit. "You can't."

My sister tries to dodge around our cousin, but when Lou-Lou wants something, it would be easier to wrestle a crocodile than get past her. "I have work today. I picked up an extra shift."

"Can't Uncle Gavin drive you?" Lou-Lou plants herself against the garage door, going so far as to turn the lock.

Kenzie crosses her arms. "No, he already left."

"But we called dibs."

"Lou-Lou…" But even my heart sinks a little. Sam has been holed up at his house most of the week talking on the phone with his team, trying to work out the details of his new album. "We'll just have to reschedule."

"But…but that's not fair." Lou-Lou's nose turns red.

Oh, no. She's going to cry.

My sister sighs and her shoulders lose some of their rigidity. "I'm sorry. I forgot about your lake trip when I agreed to take the shift."

To her credit, Lou-Lou swallows hard enough I can see her throat bob, but she steps out of the way. "I see." Her voice is thick. Husky.

Shoot. Now Kenzie's chin trembles and she fusses with the strap of her bag. "I'm sorry. I-I'll make it up to you."

"It's fine." Lou-Lou wraps her arms around her middle. "Have a good day."

Kenzie locks eyes with me, begging me to fix this.

I mouth *it's fine.* I mean it has to be. What's done is done and we'll all have to remember the world doesn't revolve around us. We'll have to keep going and make the best out of it. *Lord, I was really looking forward to spending time with Sam, but help me to take this with maturity.*

"I'm sorry," Kenzie says one more time before yanking the door open and stepping into the garage.

It falls shut behind her with a heavy thud.

I wince and start pulling the picnic things out of the bag. "Well, maybe tomorrow we can—"

Lou-Lou grabs my arm. "No, you don't. Pack all of those things back up right now."

"Lou—"

"Just do it."

I toss one of the bagged sandwiches on top of the chips. "Happy?"

"Not if you crushed my crisps."

"You're not British."

"No, but I lived there once."

"I don't think spending a week in England counts as living there."

She snags a slice of roasted turkey from the package on the counter. "That reply reeks of jealousy."

"Puh-lease." I cross my arms. Except she's right. Kind of. My little cousin has seen more of the world than I probably ever will. *Someday, right God?*

"Mhmm. I believe you. Honestly, Riley, your face doesn't lie." She grabs the picnic bag and slings it over her shoulder as she marches toward the garage.

Umm... "Where are you going?"

"Leash Sarge up. We should have been on the road twenty minutes ago."

For some crazy reason I follow her, switching off lights as I go. Why I'm listening to her, I don't know. Common sense hits me as I snap Sarge's leash into place. "Wait, what are we doing?"

She throws a look over her shoulder that says *duh*.

Maybe I am dense, because I raise my eyebrows letting her know I really have no clue. If she thinks we're all going to *walk* to the lake, she can count me out.

She pauses at the door, plants one hand on her hip, and taps her foot. "Riley, Riley, Riley. Sam has a car."

"Lou-Lou," I hiss, looking around like some rabid fangirl might have overheard, which is ridiculous considering we're standing in a locked house. "We can't use that."

"Why not? It works, doesn't it?"

"What if someone recognizes it?"

She bats a hand. "Sammy Hong always shows up to official events in either a limo or a black van. How many people do you think actually know what kind of car he drives? Let alone know his specific one on sight. Plus let's not forget they would need to live here to see it. Not to mention they'd actually have to be out and about at the same time as us. That's a lot of odds that would have to magically fall into place, don't you think?"

I bite my lip. Run my fingers through my hair.

"Come on, what does it hurt to ask?"

"I don't know...we'll still stick out like a trio of purple-feathered ducks when people see us get out."

Lou-Lou sighs, long and dramatic before she comes over and plants a hand on my shoulder. "It's time you learned an important truth. Most people are too self-absorbed to notice anything about you."

Everything inside me squirms at the idea, but the last thing I want is to be a party-pooper and be stuck with a moping Lou-Lou all day. If I could shift the decision... "We'll have to ask Sam. It's his car, his call. If he's not comfortable with the situation, you will not push him." I thrust my finger at her nose to get the point across.

She salutes. "Aye, aye, captain."

"I mean it."

"Honestly, Ri-boo, I'm not two."

"Do not call me that." I swat her hip as we step into the garage.

"I didn't hear you tell Chad that."

"I'm not going to correct a stranger about my name." We step onto the driveway and I close the garage door behind us. Why, I don't know, because I'm sure we're going to be coming right back, but I still watch the heavy door rumble closed.

"You sure didn't act like you were a pair of strangers."

"Fine, acquaintances. We've already talked about this. He's just some guy from school, okay?"

"He wants to be more than that if you ask me."

"Nobody did." I storm down the sidewalk and hammer my fist against Sam's door.

He jerks it open after one knock.

Too bad. I could have given the solid panel another good whack.

"I was about to head over to your place." He checks the time on his phone. "Everything okay? You're running late."

I sigh, trying to leave the conversation about Chad behind me. "Change of plans—"

"We're taking your car." Lou-Lou shoves past me and steps into the house. She waves her hands in a cheerful set of jazz-hands.

I shoot her a warning look before focusing on Sam. "But only if you're okay with that. Totally your call. Kenzie surprised us with an extra shift at work, so I can't drive. We could always reschedule, but I know you've been really busy and—"

Sam touches my shoulder, cutting off my rambling explanation. "It's fine."

"Really?" My shoulders sag and for the first time I realize how much I've truly been looking forward to today.

He grins, wide and genuine, making the dimple on his right cheek pop. "Really."

Still...I twist my fingers together. "But if someone recognizes your car..."

"I already told you the likelihood of that." Lou-Lou crosses her arms and stares me down, daring me to ruin her plan.

"Not many people our age have cars like that and—" Wait, am I trying to discourage him from going? Because I don't want to. But if he's discovered and it's because of some ridiculous plan like this that ruins the rest of our summer, I'm not sure I'll ever forgive myself.

"Riley." Sam slides his hand off my shoulder and entwines his fingers with mine. Squeezes. "It's going to be fine. If I remember correctly, the lake isn't that big of a destination for people."

I hold my breath. Stare into his dark eyes. They are safe. Warm and unafraid. "Only if you're sure. No pressure or anything."

"Break it up already." Lou-Lou bursts between us, breaking our hands apart as she skips outside. "Let's go."

I hesitate at the threshold. "You still have time to change your mind."

"Nah, we'll be fine." He steps out of the house and I join him on the porch, waiting as he locks up before heading for the car.

"Let me take that." Sam takes the picnic bag from Lou-Lou and situates it in the trunk.

"Are you sure it's okay for Sarge to come?" I stare at the car, tallying the damage if so much as one of Sarge's toenails scratches the seats. Goodness, even his fur. It's going to be all over the place by the time we come home.

"You look pale." Sam laughs. Somehow, he knows exactly where my mind has gone. He slides Sarge's leash from my loose grip and guides him into the backseat where Lou-Lou has her sneakers positioned against the back of the passenger seat.

I give her a death glare and she drops her feet to the ground.

"Watch yourself, missy," I mutter, moving my lips carefully to be sure she'll know exactly what I'm saying.

She raises her phone, ignoring me by diving into the world of her virtual connections.

Sam plants a hand on my lower back. "Come on. Relax. Everything's going to be fine. Lou-Lou's right. The likelihood of someone recognizing my car is low. I've never publicly appeared with it before."

I can't quite make myself move. "Don't you have a body guard or something? I'd feel better if you gave him a call."

Sam nudges me toward the passenger side. "And ruin my vacation? No thanks."

I yank the door open and ease onto the leather seat like it's made of gold. "Your vacation will be ruined if you get kidnapped. I don't know how much you think I make on commissions, but I'm not going to be able to pay any ransom notices." I yank the door closed, slamming it on instinct like I have to do on our old clunker.

"Riley," Lou-Lou squeaks.

I catch Sam cringing as he circles to the driver's side.

Oops.

"Sorry," I say as he slides into his seat.

"Don't even worry about it." He swivels and stares at me right in the eye. "But seriously, please do not do that again."

My face burns hot. "I won't."

He gives me another long look.

I throw my hands in the air. "A little trust please?"

He laughs and backs out of the driveway and we're soon on our way. Sam flicks the radio on and his own voice comes crooning through the speakers. He startles and reaches to change the station, but I block his hand.

"No, don't. This is one of my favorites." I turn to my window, raising my face to the sunshine, tapping my foot to the tune. It's one of his early releases. Before they hired someone to write for him.

Remember that time

I said you looked pretty

Laughed it off like something silly

Everyone always said we'd be perfect together

Yeah, I think I can see it now

And baby, oh my

I wish you could see it too

Cause it hurts every time I see you with someone new

And now I'mma spend the whole night wish'n I was dancing with
you

And baby, oh my

You look pretty 'n blue

My heart stops

When I'm looking at you

Laughing, smiling,

Oh

Vibrance and sunshine

Everything that makes you, you

Yes, everything I love

Only hope you see me too.

Until time stops, I'll be waiting for you

And baby, oh my

Just tell me you can see me too

Recorded Sam pours out his heart to a girl who doesn't even know he exists. It's the kind of song that had the whole world debating who he wrote it for. After about a month, fans settled on the theory he wrote it for his first Hollywood girlfriend after they broke up. Sam's never set the record straight one way or the other.

"You have a favorite? Of my songs?" Sam's gaze flicks to me.

That's what he's thinking? "Sam, there's like a million girls who have a favorite song of yours."

He shifts in his seat. "Yeah, but…I don't know. For some reason I never pictured you listening to them."

"She couldn't avoid them even if she wanted to," Lou-Lou pipes up from the backseat. "The stores around here are very proud of their local celebrity."

"And this one's your favorite?" Sam slides a look my way.

I laugh because this whole conversation is absurd. "Why not this one?"

He shrugs. "I don't know."

"Which one's your favorite?"

"My favorite?" His brow furrows.

"Oh come on, you have to have a favorite."

"Isn't that like asking him to choose between his kids or something?" Lou-Lou leans between our seats.

I watch Sam. "Is it?"

He shrugs again. "I don't know. I haven't thought about it before."

"But if you had to choose?" Lou-Lou presses.

"This one." Sam drums his thumbs against the steering wheel.

"Oh, come on." I poke his shoulder. "That's a copout. I already said it."

"No, no. There's a reason, I promise."

Lou-Lou and I exchange a look.

"It had better be a good one," Lou-Lou says.

"Mmhm," I agree.

"Let's hear it," Lou-Lou demands.

He flicks on his indicator. "It's my favorite because it has the most meaning."

"Ooh," Lou-Lou hums her approval.

"Really? Who'd you write it for?" He's been dodging the question in interviewers for years. Maybe we'll get him to confess.

Sam runs his hands down the steering wheel. "It was a love confession."

"Um, we already know that," Lou-Lou says.

"A message. Or question, really. It's an invitation. Telling the girl that if she feels the same, I'll always be waiting." His cheeks turn deep red. "I don't know. It's dumb."

"Did she? Ever reply, I mean?" I ask.

Sam meets my eyes for a moment. "No. If she felt the same, I think she would have told me."

"Or maybe she didn't understand the message," I offer.

Sam shakes his head. "She should have figured it out by now."

Chapter 17

The song transitions to an upbeat tune. Sam drums his thumbs against the steering wheel, bobbing his head to the beat.

I slip my phone from my pocket and hold it up. "Smile."

He slides a look my way. "What, you want to blackmail me too?" Except he obliges and flashes a smile. A real one showing his dimple.

I snap the picture before his evasive dimple can disappear. "Nope. This one is just for me."

Sam's eyebrows raise, inviting me to elaborate.

But I don't. Instead, I tuck my phone into my pocket and reach for my tablet and get to work on my new project. An art print for another author. We're still working out the details and this will be a basic line art to get the feel for the character and make sure the author is happy before I pour hours of work into rendering.

"What are you working on?" Sam asks.

I fill him in through broken sentences as I split my attention between him and my sketch.

"He looks like Sam." Lou-Lou cranes her neck around my seat.

"He does not..." Except he does. There's the sharp jawline that has girls around the world swooning. And I even added his annoyingly adorable dimple. I tap around on the screen, morphing the character back into his own face. Heat blisters my cheeks and I angle the air conditioner toward my face.

Lou-Lou snickers in the backseat.

Sam sneaks a glance at my tablet. "Minion, I think you need to get your prescription checked. That looks nothing like me."

"Not anymore," she mutters.

Oh, I hope he didn't hear.

"Unless you're trying to make it look like me? In which case you're the most talented artist in the universe and I can totally see the resemblance. The nose, right?"

I slap his arm playfully. "You are such a liar." Especially since the nose is one of the few details I managed to change before he saw. The noble slope of Sam's nose has been changed into a hooked one.

Sam's lips twitch as he keeps his eyes focused on the road. "Hey, I'm trying to be supportive."

"Whatever." I crank up the volume on the radio and we all dance in our seats like hooligans until the lake comes into view and Sam finds a parking space. Then we pile out of the car.

A cool breeze plays with my hair and I pull my hairband free from my wrist, securing my strands in a loose ponytail.

"Last one to the water is a rotten egg," Lou-Lou shouts, sprinting for the water.

"Not fair," Sam hollers as he reaches for the trunk.

"Sore loser." Lou-Lou cackles as she splashes into the water, clothes and all.

"Foul play," Sam continues to protest.

"She's right. Sore loser." I shove his shoulder before taking off at a run, kicking my shoes off before my feet hit the water. Droplets splash up my legs and drench the back of my cut-off shorts. So cold! Goosebumps climb across my flesh, egged on when Lou-Lou splashes me.

"Hey." I raise one hand to shield my glasses. With my other, I splash blindly in her direction, hoping to at least get her half as wet as she's getting me.

"You two are a pair of cheats," Sam says, somehow carrying the picnic supplies while keeping Sarge from lunging into the water to join us. "It must run in the family."

"It's not our fault you're slower than a sick snail," Lou-Lou taunts.

"I resent that. Give me a fair race and we'll see how the results change." He plunks down the picnic basket.

The instant the food is out of danger, I share a look with Lou-Lou and we both attack, swinging our arms in wide arcs, drenching Sam. Sarge pulls free, springing into the water to join us. I unclip his leash as he passes me, and toss it onto the shore.

"Now I know you're both cheats. Theory confirmed." Sam takes off his baseball cap, combs his fingers through his wet hair, and replaces the hat, backward.

"Aw, don't be such a baby. You're not melting, are you?" I tease.

A dangerous glimmer enters his eyes, and he wades toward me. I squeal, backtracking, but with one lunge, he has me by the waist, and then he's hefting me up until I'm dangling over his shoulder like a sack of potatoes.

"Wait, wait, put me down. Truce." I tap my palm against his back, my legs flailing.

Sam tightens his grip. "I don't want a truce, I want an apology."

"Ooh." Lou-Lou pauses, a stick for Sarge ready to throw. She starts waving it like a flag. "Dunk her, dunk her."

I half laugh, half shriek. "Hey, who's side are you on?"

"My own." She tosses the stick and Sarge springs into the water after it. Some guard dog he is. "Dunk her, Sam."

"Now that is a fabulous idea." Sam trudges deeper until the water laps at his waist and tickles my toes.

I cling to his shirt, my heart pounding against his shoulder. "What about Lou-Lou? She started all of this."

Lou-Lou snickers. "Riley, I am simply an innocent child leaning into my own immaturity. You should have known better. Besides, my short stature and young age allows me the excuse of a head-start."

"Yeah," Sam agrees.

Lou-Lou clasps her hands behind her back. "Cheats should be punished, shouldn't they, Sam?"

Oh, the little punk.

"Right you are, minion."

"Don't you dare." Except I'm laughing and my words have no real threat behind them.

Sam shifts and I sense his muscles tensing, preparing to give me the dunk the pair have determined I deserve.

"Wait, no. My glasses." I tighten my hold on his shirt for real this time. There is no way I'm going to go diving for lost eyewear.

Sam stops. Starts to set me down.

"Allow me." Lou-Lou struts forward and snatches my glasses right off my nose.

"Olivia Anne," my scream is cut short as Sam tosses me into the water. Cold liquid surrounds me on all sides. Stings my nose. I push off the bottom, allow my head to break free, and gulp in a breath.

Sam snags my arm and helps steady me on the uneven ground. "There, I'd say we're even now."

"Whatever." I splash his face with a snicker.

He chuckles, swiping the water away.

"Well deserved." Lou-Lou extends my glasses on the tip of her finger.

I snatch them and slip them into place. Oh, the smirk on her face... "You know Sam, I don't think I'm the only one who cheated."

A spark catches in his eyes again and he snaps his fingers. "That's right."

"Oh, no you don't." Lou-Lou screeches and turns, making a run for the shore.

She is not getting away. I charge after her. She's no match for both of us. Though she fights and wriggles like she's slicked her skin with oil, I still manage to confiscate her glasses and Sam tosses her into the deeper water. She disappears with a screech.

"Good job." I give him a thumbs up.

"All in a day's work." He dusts off his hands.

Lou-Lou pops up, spluttering and wiping at her face. "You'll pay for that."

"Only if you can catch us." Sam grabs my hand and we hightail it to our picnic basket. I lift a towel from the top and wrap it around my shoulders while Sam fishes out the blanket and spreads it over the ground.

We're sitting and sipping on bottles of water by the time Lou-Lou makes it to us, Sarge at her heels, stick in his mouth even though he's already stopped her five times to get her to throw it for him. My cousin's hair drips around her shoulders and she doesn't appear too far off from a drowned rat.

Sam and I share a look and I can't help but snicker.

Lou-Lou wags her finger at us. "Oh, you're laughing now. But I will get the two of you back when you least expect it. Do you hear me? I will get my revenge."

"Sure thing, minion." Sam salutes her with his water bottle.

My cousin narrows her eyes at him.

"Come here." I pat the blanket beside me and allow her to sit next to me, towel draped over both our shoulders.

"Please tell me you packed something good for lunch," she says.

"Wouldn't you like to know."

"Yeah, I literally just said that."

Oh, she is full of sass today. "Pass me the basket," I say to Sam.

He nudges it my way.

I find Lou-Lou her turkey and cheese sandwich and a bag of pickle flavored chips to go with it. "You're the best," she says around a large bite.

All right, give the girl some food, and we're good to go. I hand Sam his sandwich and he also digs in.

I lean back, lifting my face to the sun. *Thank you, Lord, for this day. It's exactly what we needed.*

"You do that a lot," Sam murmurs.

I squint at him. "What?"

He mimics my posture.

I close my eyes and keep my head lifted. "Because sometimes I'm just happy to be alive. Thrilled to feel the sun on my face."

"She's a weirdo. She also does that anytime there's a breeze too," Lou-Lou says around a mouthful of sandwich.

"Hey." I shove her knee.

Sam's attention stays fixed on me. "It's not weird, its..." But his thought hangs unfinished.

Just then, Sarge trots to us, shaking off his wet coat. With a cry, we all scramble to save our food from the beast.

Chapter 18

Sam and I watch Lou-Lou skipping rocks at the edge of the lake, Sarge scampering alongside her, his tail curling against his back, signaling his pleasure with the day.

"What do you want? In the future I mean?" Sam leans back on his hands, crossing one ankle over the other.

I squint at him and shove my glasses higher up my nose. "What?"

"You know. Where do you see yourself ten years from now?"

Ugh. I hate questions like these, so I shrug. "I don't know."

"Aw, come on, don't give me that. You must've thought about it."

I squirm, discomfort settling over my shoulders. Because if I don't say the right thing, don't give the perfect answer, then I won't measure up to whatever invisible rod of judgment the asker holds.

Sam nudges my leg with his foot. "Come on, Ri. Tell me."

I sigh. Roll my eyes. And give in. Because this is Sam and I need to practice answering this kind of question anyway. Except I don't give him the polished answer I practice all the time in my head. No, he gets the raw, bearing-my-heart version. "It's dumb." I pick at the hem of my shorts, fraying the edge even further. "I know I'm young and I should be focused on picking a career or building work experience. But all I've ever wanted…" an unexpected rasp of emotion chokes my voice and I have to swallow before continuing, "all I've ever wanted is to be like my mom. Get married. Have kids of my own. And until that happens, and maybe even after, I want to draw. Travel the world."

Sam is silent for a long moment.

Great. I've embarrassed him. I'm seventeen. Marriage and babies should be the farthest thing from my mind. They probably have never crossed his. I should have given the placating, expected answer instead. 'Make a living off my art,' type of thing. I hold my breath, waiting for an Aunt Auggie style rejection.

But Sam isn't her.

"It's not dumb, Riley." He picks at flecks of sand on the blanket. "So, you want the whole white picket fence thing then?"

I laugh, releasing some of the tension settled between us. "I don't know about that. I think I'd be happy in a tiny house if it meant I could have a simple life."

Sam nods, attention focused on a point far beyond the lake, maybe even the future. "You deserve it."

"What about you?"

"Me? I'm already living my dream, remember?" He flashes a smile. But his dimple doesn't show.

"But you have to get lonely, right?" I deflate as I take him in, out here all alone with a pair of girls he grew up with. No true friends to call his own. This can't be it for him. Sneaking off to secluded beaches. Avoiding rabid fan girls. Doesn't he get more? Some kind of happily ever after to call his own? *Lord, please.*

Sam swallows. Looks away. "Doesn't everyone?"

My heart throbs once more. I wish his parents could see him now. Past the screaming fangirls, tour dates, and the starry-eyed boy who chose it all, to the here. The now. To this hurting young man who must be wondering if it's all been worth it. I know I am.

Sam traces our initials into the earth piled on the edge of the pier. Probably leftover from a kid who thought he could build a sand castle. R+S. A throwback to our childhood when we had to mark everything as ours. When he looks away, I trace a heart around the letters like always. Because it's cuter that way. No other reason. Right.

Lou-Lou drags herself away from the water and flops onto the blanket. "I'm. So. Tired."

Sarge plops himself down beside her, tongue lolling from the side of his mouth, panting heavily in agreement.

"Should we get going?" Sam looks to me.

I turn once more to the water, holding onto the peace of this lake at least for a moment longer.

Lou-Lou tugs weakly on my ankle. "Come on, let's go."

Drama queen. "All right, all right."

I gather our towels and shake them clean as Sam cajoles Lou-Lou into helping him fold the picnic blanket. She stuffs the cloth into the basket and Sam reaches for the towels in my arms. "Here, let me."

I extend the pile and our fingertips brush as he takes them. A light tingle sweeps up my arms, speeding my heartbeat. I wait until he gets a firm grip on the towels before stuffing my hands into the back pockets of my shorts where they won't get me in trouble.

Before long, we're all packed up and settled into the car. It only takes a few minutes before Sarge and Lou-Lou's mingled snoring drifts from the backseat.

"Thank you for today," I say, stretching my legs. "It was fun."

Sam's attention flicks to me. "Anytime. I had a blast."

Is it me, or is there weird tension hanging between us now? But it's only weird if I let it be, right? "How are things with your label?" I shoot a look over my seat to be sure Lou-Lou is really out of it.

Sam's quiet.

I watch his profile. The emotions racing across his face as he chooses his words. "We're figuring things out."

Monotone. Not good. I lick my lips and shoot a quick glance out the window. "And your manager?" I knot my hands into fists and then stuff them under my legs, flattening them out.

"Not happy."

"Have you decided what you're going to do?"

"I'm just...done."

Done. So final. A shiver sweeps my spine.

"Like done forever?" I fidget, reaching into my bag and pulling out my stylus, spinning it through my fingers to give them something to do.

"I don't know, Ri. I really don't know." A muscle jumps in his jaw.

"Have you prayed about it?" I ask, gentle, prodding.

He goes still for a long moment before he sighs. "You're right. That should've been my first reaction. I—"

Thump.

The car jolts.

"What was that?" My throat goes dry.

"Don't know." Sam pulls over. "Let me check it out." He pops his door open and I grab Sarge's collar to keep him from climbing around the seats and following him.

Lou-Lou moans. "What's going on?"

"Something's wrong with the car. Sam's checking it out."

"Ugh." She slings an arm over her face.

Sam slides into the driver's seat and slams his door shut.

Uh-oh. "Everything okay?"

He groans and rubs his hands down his face. "We have a flat tire."

"Oh."

We stare at each other.

"You know how to change one, right?" I ask.

He drapes an arm over the steering wheel and drops his forehead to the cushioned surface. "No, Riley. I don't know how to change a tire."

"Don't *you*?" Lou-Lou leans between the seats. "I thought that was one of Uncle Gavin's requirements for getting a license."

I massage my temple. "He showed Kenzie, and he's been meaning to teach me, but I guess he forgot."

"You mean we're stranded?" Lou-Lou's shriek pierces my ears and Sarge flinches away from her.

"No, we're not stranded. Calm down." I flap my hand in a shushing gesture.

"I'll call a tow-truck." Sam fishes his phone from the cupholder.

"Like that's a good idea. What happens if the driver kidnaps you and holds you for ransom?" Lou-Lou demands.

A smile flicks over Sam's lips. "I think that's a bit far-fetched, don't you?"

"No."

Sam and I stare at each other as if we're both hoping one of us will magically learn the steps to fix this mess.

"Can't we watch a tutorial?" Lou-Lou pokes my shoulder.

I perk up. Between the three of us, I'm sure we can figure it out.

Sam drums his fingers against the steering wheel as he waits for the results from his search to load. "Doubtful. Reception isn't great out here."

Fabulous. I droop against my headrest.

"Let's call Uncle Gavin." Lou-Lou prods the back of my seat with her foot.

Sam and I exchange a glance.

"You think the signal will be strong enough?" I ask.

"Worth a shot."

I mean it can't hurt. I dial my Dad.

"Hey, honey...how...going?"

I close my left ear with my fingers. "Dad?"

Static crackles on the other end of the line as he tries to reply.

"Dad, we need your help. We've got a flat tire."

"What? You're...up."

"Flat. Tire." I pronounce each word, slow and steady, hoping he'll catch them.

"Where...you?"

I give my best guess, based off of the land marks around us, but really, we're in the middle of nowhere. That being said, if he heads toward the lake, he should stumble upon us eventually.

"I...be...soon," he says.

A weight slips off my shoulders and I exhale. "Thanks, Dad."

"Hurry, Uncle Gavin," Lou-Lou yells.

"What's that?" Dad's voice crackles on the other end.

"Nothing. Thank you."

"Honey...can't...you."

"Bye." I end the call and text him with our plea for assistance and a rough estimate of our location on the off chance it gets through. A small circle hovers beside the message as it struggles to send.

"Well, this could take a while." Lou-Lou sags in the backseat. "Do you have any more sandwiches? I'm starving."

I set my phone on the dashboard, hoping it'll somehow encourage the text to send. "You just ate."

"No, that was forever ago. Besides, I need *something* to do."

"How about you get out and see if you can figure out how to change the tire?" I'd love to see her try.

"Oh, you're hilarious. Besides, I'm a child." She splays a hand over her chest. "I shouldn't be going anywhere near the road. What would my parents say?"

I shoot her a look in the rearview mirror. "Right, because the road is *so* busy." Especially since there hasn't been a single car in the past ten minutes we've been sitting here.

She sticks out her tongue.

Yep, there's the maturity coming out.

Sarge whines, shifting on the back seat, ready to get rolling again.

"Sorry, buddy." I rub his neck.

"Eww, he's drooling on my leg. And he smells like a wet dog." Lou-Lou swipes at her thigh. "Sam, can you please crack a window? I'm going to be sick if I have to sit here and smell this monstrosity for much longer."

"Sure thing, minion." Sam reaches for the button that will release her window, but we all freeze when a white pickup truck comes into view.

"What do you think? Help or an axe murderer?" I lean forward, trying to get a glimpse of the driver through their tinted windshield.

"One way to find out?" Sam reaches for his door handle.

"Wait." Lou-Lou snags his sleeve. "You can't go out there. You're Sammy Hong, remember? It's going to take one wrong person and you'll be exposed."

"Come on, minion, I'm not exactly going to send Riley out there."

I twirl a strand of hair. "Maybe she's right. Dad's on his way. If we sit tight, we'll—"

The pickup glides to a stop, joining us on the side of the road.

"Eeek," Lou-Lou screams. "Lock the doors."

Sarge stiffens, barking like he's prepared to chew the stranger's face off. Lick them to death more likely, but we like to let Sarge think he's intimidating.

The car's door opens and it's...Chad.

He strolls toward us, hands in his pockets.

Sam and Lou-Lou both groan.

"Guys, come on," I say, popping my door open.

Sarge lunges, barking like a lunatic, and I quickly shut the door to keep him contained.

"Hey," I push my hair behind my ears.

Chad grins. "Fancy seeing you here. Sweet ride."

"We were at the lake." I gesture behind us even though the lake is far from view by now. "And well, we got a flat." I shield my eyes, squinting against the sun to watch his face.

He nods. "I can help with that. You got a spare?"

"Maybe?" A clear question mark hangs on the end of the word. I mean if Sam has never changed a flat before, then he's never used his spare, and all cars have a spare, right?

Chad laughs. "Let's check it out."

He aims for the rear of the car.

Sam intercepts him, slipping out of the car and shutting the door before Sarge can join him. "Chad, right?"

"Yeah." Chad's brow furrows as he takes Sam in. "Got yourself into some trouble, huh?" He motions to the flat tire.

Sam crosses his arms. "Nothing we can't handle."

Oh, right. Because we've done so well thus far. "Chad knows what he's doing. We should let him take a look."

Sam looks between me, Chad, and the car.

Hmm, he's not one of those guys who doesn't want anyone else touching his car, is he? I shoot him a look. Telling him we need this.

Sam adjusts his baseball cap. But he doesn't protest further.

"Let's get the spare tire." Chad places a guiding hand on the small of my back and directs me toward the trunk.

"Hold Sarge," I call to Lou-Lou as I pull the trunk open.

Sarge barks like a maniac when Chad comes into view.

Chad makes quick work of pulling away the cover from the trunk and I make a grab for the spare tire, but the thing is *heavy*.

"Here, let me," Chad and Sam say the words at the same time.

"Oh." I pause. Look between them.

The hesitation is enough for Chad to swoop in and pull the tire out like it's nothing. I grab the jack and Sam steps out of our way.

"We'll get this baby fixed in no time." Chad winks at me.

"What is taking so long?" Lou-Lou slips out of the car, Sarge on her heels. Thankfully, she had enough common sense to get my golden beasty on a leash. I snag said leash and intercept the pooch before he can let our knight in shining armor know what he thinks about him touching the car. I leave the jack on the ground and back my dog to a safe distance.

Sarge tugs on the leash but soon relaxes as I massage the space behind his ears. "Easy. They'll get this fixed in no time and we'll be on the road again."

He huffs a sigh and flops onto his belly to watch the action unfold.

Chad extends the wrench toward Sam. "Can you loosen the lug nuts? Or is that too much for you, pretty boy?" He laughs like it's a joke, but a note of discomfort settles on my shoulders all the same. Doesn't he know how rude and tasteless the joke comes across?

Sam tenses, but he accepts the tool. "Yeah, I think I can manage."

Chad claps him on the shoulder. "Counterclockwise okay, buddy?"

"*Buddy*?" Lou-Lou crosses her arms and scowls at Chad's back.

"Shh." I ram her with my elbow. "Do not start something. Let's get our tire changed, and then we can all be on our way."

"Whatever."

Funny, she still looks like she's prepared to take Chad down.

"Oh." Chad's call stills Sam as he kneels in front of the tire. "Try not to let them roll away, all right? I don't feel like hunting for lug nuts today."

Okay, enough. "I think he's got it."

"Right, right." Chad throws his hands up and backs off, chuckling.

What is with boys and the need to rib each other?

Sam loosens the nuts in a few quick twists and Chad sets the jack into position. And then the fun begins as he rotates the lug wrench, raising the jack one painful notch at a time. Sweat drips down his flushed cheeks by the time he gets the thing to the proper height.

Chad swipes his arm across his forehead. "All right, lug nuts off."

I wince. Too bad we don't have any leftover drinks to offer him from our picnic supplies.

"Yep." Sam doesn't even glance at Chad as he finishes loosening the nuts.

From there it's a quick change from the busted tire to the spare. Then it's tightening bolts and lowering the jack until both boys are sweaty and red in the face.

"Thank you, you're a life saver." I touch Chad's arm as he dusts off his hands after stowing the tire in the trunk.

"All in a day's work."

"Really, thank you," I say.

"Don't mention it."

Sam joins us, arms crossed. "Yeah, thanks." His tone is short. Clipped.

Chad snorts. "You really should learn how to change a tire, man."

"Oh, believe me, I intend to watch every tutorial that's out there when I get home," Sam mutters under his breath.

I tuck my hair behind my ear and readjust my grip on Sarge. "To be honest, I'm embarrassed I didn't know what to do."

"No reason to be." Chad stuffs his hands in his pockets. "Hey, we should—"

Lou-Lou slides between us, forcing us to step apart to avoid her swinging arms. "Well, we should go. Thanks for your help, *buddy*." She slaps Chad on the back. "We really do appreciate it. Really. Riley, don't you think we should find some reception so you can call your dad and let him know we've lived through the tragedy?"

Oh, right. My dad. "She's right. We should go." I back toward the car. "Thanks again."

"Anytime, Ri-boo."

Gag me. But I smile anyway. Forget a cringy nickname. The guy helped us out of a tight spot.

I guide Sarge into the backseat and we all pile into our respective vehicles.

Chad lifts two fingers off his steering wheel in a wave as he peels onto the road.

Sam gets going, face set in a stone line.

I swipe my hands down my legs. "I'm glad that didn't take too long. Thank goodness for Chad stopping when he did."

A curt nod.

Lou-Lou huffs a sigh.

"I should call my dad." Except when I lift my phone an icon shows reception still isn't good.

Another heaved breath from Lou-Lou.

I release a sigh of my own. "If you want to say something, say it."

"Fine." Her voice is thick with sass.

Here we go. I brace myself.

"Chad is a jerk."

"You shouldn't name call." I reach for my tablet, swipe away the line art I was working on earlier, and pull up an almost finished art piece, angling my head as I try to find a clever way to avoid drawing hands. They are the bane of my existence. Maybe crossed arms...

"I'm not two, Ri-boo."

"Ugh. Please don't call me that." I shake my head and sweep my stylus down the screen. "Look, Chad means well. He's just missing a little...tact."

"Or a lot."

Once we pull onto the main road, I try my cell again.

"Riley?" Dad answers on the first ring. "You guys okay?"

"Yeah, we're actually on our way home. A friend from school stopped and helped us out. I didn't have service, or I would have called you sooner. Sorry."

"Don't even worry about it, honey. I had some errands to run anyway. You kids be safe, okay?"

"Will do."

"All right. Love you."

We hang up and I turn my attention to my screen, adding the arms, and then shading in the details to truly make everything pop.

"What's next on our list?" Lou-Lou kicks my chair.

"Don't ask me what's next. You're the one who insisted on keeping the list digital."

"Ugh, fine." Her nails tap against her screen. "Ooh, backyard cookout. We need to invite Aunt V."

I drop my head against my seat and stifle a groan. Not this again. "You're still convinced she and my dad will magically hit it off someday, aren't you?" Vanessa is the younger sister of Lou-Lou's mom and my cousin has been trying to match make her with my dad for the last two years.

"I told you, I saw sparks."

"You mean when she almost blew up our microwave?" I snort and add some detailing to the brass buttons I'm sketching. There. The author's main character stands stern, severe, and, dare I admit it? Handsome.

"It was a tiny piece of foil stuck to the bottom of the butter. It was an honest mistake. It could have happened to anyone."

Yeah, a mistake that almost cost us our house, but whatever. "Lou-Lou, isn't she like ten years younger than my dad?"

"No, more like four or five years tops. She just *looks* younger."

"Right." I *believe* her.

"It's a genetic family secret. Come on, Riley. Say yes. Plus, if they get married, we'll be doubly related." She bounces on her seat, sending a tremor through the back of mine.

I shift in my chair and tap my stylus against the side of my tablet.

Sam slides a glance my way.

I clear my throat and pretend I'm busy. Except I'm only leaving a looping scribble mark in the corner of my art piece. *I really don't want to do this, God.*

"Please, Riley?" Lou-Lou begs.

So much whine. And hope.

A still, small voice pricks my conscious.

"Fine. But they're both adults. Leave it up to them whether there's *sparks* or not. Okay?"

"Fine." I can picture her eye roll.

"Excuse me." I extend my hand behind my chair, pinky out, and keep it there until she wraps her own finger around mine.

"All right. I promise." She doesn't sound too happy about it, but Lou-Lou's not one to go back on her word. "But remember,

Aunt V isn't like those awful stepmothers in fairytales. This is real life."

"Got it." But even the picture of someone taking the place of my mom in my dad's life sends a tightness through my chest. Except it's cliché, not to mention selfish. *Help me, Lord. If he ever really does start—gulp—dating…help me to love her.* I don't name the *her.* Don't even try to imagine. Even the action of praying for a *her* leaves my palms clammy.

"You okay, Ri?" Sam's voice startles me.

I pull my attention away from the tablet screen I've been staring at blankly for who knows how long. "Yeah, fine. Why?"

He squints. "You're looking a little green."

"I'm fine." I tuck my hair behind my ear, knocking my glasses askew as I do so. Heat stings my cheeks and I quickly send off the finished art piece before my clumsiness and fluctuating emotions can ruin anything. One hundred dollars closer to Europe. I rest my hand on the middle console and stare out the window, watching trees sweep by in a blur of green.

Sam's warm hand covers mine.

Chapter 19

"I'm off." Lou-Lou shoulders her backpack and flicks two fingers from her eyes to mine. "Don't do anything remotely fun without me."

The call came from Vanessa last night, asking if Lou-Lou could spend the weekend with her. While my cousin might be dragging her feet at the moment, she couldn't pack her bags fast enough last night to spend time with her favorite aunt.

"Yes, ma'am." I salute and usher her out the door.

Vanessa's car idles beside the sidewalk. She leans out the passenger window and waves. "Hey, there, Riley. How are you?"

"I'm good, how are you?" Why does she have to be so nice?

"Any day I get to hang out with Lou-Lou is a good one." She winks as my cousin climbs into the car.

"Have fun." I wave them off.

The house is quiet when I step inside. Sarge naps on his dog bed near the couch, Dad's out with a work colleague, and Kenzie is running errands. Just me. I clap my hands against my thighs and blow out a breath.

This is what I wanted, the house to myself to work on my art, but now that I've got my wish, I can't help but miss the hubbub. But, it will return soon enough, so I might as well make the most

of it. I curl up with my tablet, and instead of checking my email to
see if I have any new commissions, I draw for the fun of it, crafting
a girl in a purple kimono, splashes of cherry blossoms all around
her.

When my hand begins to cramp, I check the time. Goodness, it's
almost time for dinner. My phone buzzes with a text from Kenzie
saying she'll be home late and not to wait to eat.

"Well, looks like it's you and me, Sarge."

He barely glances up from his dog bed. Good to know somebody is enjoying the day off.

I grab his bowl and go to the pantry where we keep the kibble,
but the bag is nearly empty. There's enough for dinner, but there
won't be any for breakfast. "Looks like I have errands of my own
to run." I pat Sarge on the head, and place his dinner within easy
access for when his highness decides to finish his nap.

"Oh, wait. I don't have a car." I massage the back of my neck. I
could text Kenzie, but her to-do list was already a mile long, she
doesn't need another thing on top of it, and Dad's dinner won't
be finished for a good while yet.

I pull my phone from the couch cushions and text Sam.

Are you busy?

No. Why?

*Fancy a pet store run? Sarge and I would both be eternally grate-
ful.*

How can I say no to that? I'll be right there.

Thank you. I slip my phone into my back pocket. "Well, boy, you
won't go hungry."

His soft snoring is his answer.

"See you later," I whisper as I tiptoe to the door and step into my sandals.

A moment later, Sam is walking up my driveway and I sneak outside before he can knock and awaken my sleeping, golden beauty. "Thanks for doing this," I say.

"Honestly, it's not a problem."

We climb into his car and he aims for the closest pet store.

"Have you had a good day?" Sam asks.

"Honestly? It's been weirdly quiet." I snort. "Who would have thought I'd miss Lou-Lou and all her drama?"

He smirks. "I get it. My house has practically felt like a graveyard."

I purse my lips and study the cars zipping past us. Should I ask? "Your parents?" I watch out of the corner of my eye for his response.

"We've talked some." He swallows hard. "It's mostly my fault. I should be reaching out more than I have."

"It's never too late."

He nods, but doesn't offer a further response.

The radio hums in the silence, a soft instrumental playlist soothing the tension.

"Have you drawn anything recently?"

I let Sam change the subject. "No. Well, yes, but just for myself. I'm between commissions at the moment."

"Do you enjoy the breaks?" Sam flicks on his indicator and turns into the pet store parking lot.

"I mean it's nice. My wallet might complain a little, but next thing I know, I'll be drowning in work, so I'd better breathe while I can."

Sam walks close beside me, hands shoved into his pockets until we reach the door. Like the gentleman his parents trained him to be, he pulls the door open and ushers me inside.

The pet store smells like dog shampoo from their self-serve dog wash combined with kibble. Ferrets sleep huddled together in their glass exhibit while a rabbit munches on some greenery. Birds squawk their welcome, and the fish and lizards judge us from their wall of terrariums.

"Hi there, what brings you in today?" A guy with blond hair hanging low over his forehead asks from behind the checkout counter. Avery, his name tag says.

"We're just looking, thanks." I wander into the aisles. We're here for pet food, but it never hurts to check on the toys and see if there's anything new or any great deals going on.

I snag an on-sale bone before heading toward the rows of kibble. Bags in bright colors with dogs groomed to perfection shine from the shelves and I wander, trailing my fingers across the bags until I find the kibble Sarge likes. Here comes the hard part. The one problem with being a dog mom is the muscle power it takes to bring food home to your beloved fluffy companion. I sigh and shake out my hands. Here goes nothing...

"Here, let me." Sam hefts the bag for me like it's nothing and we check out. Soon we're in Sam's car once again.

"Can I take you somewhere?" Sam asks.

"Sure." I study his profile, searching for a hint, but his face gives nothing away. Just another skill learned from a life in the limelight.

He remains quiet as he maneuvers us toward the closest park. We get out and Sam leads the way down the winding walking path. It's mostly empty today with only a few others strolling along.

"Are you okay?" I ask.

"I'm fine."

"Why did you bring me here? I mean it's peaceful..." I trail off, inviting him to elaborate.

"I was hoping we could talk."

"About what?"

"You."

"Me?"

"Yes, you." He bumps me with his elbow. "I feel like all we've talked about since I got here is me."

Great. The one thing I hate. Talking about myself. "What do you want to know?" I wrap my arms around my middle and kick a piece of mulch, sending it skittering ahead on the path.

"How are you?" He shoves his hands into his pockets. "I know a lot has changed for you since I left."

Mom. I breathe out a deep sigh. Somehow, she's the easiest and the hardest thing to talk about. Because how can you not talk about someone you love? And yet there's a gloomy darkness there too, lurking around the corner with everyone and their careful words tiptoeing around, ever afraid of overstepping or offending. What do you do when a loved one becomes a taboo subject? "It was hard when Mom died. It would have been hard all on its own, but..." I shrug.

"But?" Sam prompts.

He doesn't know. Of course, he doesn't. He was at the height of his career, swept along from one tour to the next. "When Mom was sick, and after she died, the neighbors and our church group were amazing. They brought meals over, helped to get me and Kenzie to school. Everything they could have possibly done, they did. We even had help paying off the hospital bills."

He watches me carefully, waiting for the next but.

"It was great. But then a local news station got involved. The story went viral as friends of friends shared the news clips, and before we knew it, half the country knew the details and were more than happy to get involved and show their support. Suddenly, strangers knew my name and thought they had the right to know exactly what I was feeling. What should have been private became the feel-good story of the year. I couldn't mourn my mom without finding a camera in my face."

He winces. "I'm sorry, Riley."

Of all people, I know he gets it. Because he can't even walk down the street most places without someone snapping a picture. "I hated it, Sam. Every minute of it." The best moment of my life was when our story was replaced with the next "big thing." The world moved on and forgot all about the tragic end of Molly Anderson and the heartbroken family she left behind.

Sam wraps an arm around my shoulders and pulls me close. "I'm sorry you had to go through that."

I lean my head on his bicep. "I don't know how you do it."

"I guess the big difference is I asked for it." His words ring hollow and I know there's underlying feelings he doesn't want to go into just now.

"All right, this is depressing. Let's do something fun." I shake myself like that can somehow banish the gray cloud of sorrow hanging over us.

"You're right. How about I make you dinner? I remember Lou-Lou saying something about every girl wanting a man who knows how to cook. Let's see how I do."

I let him turn me back toward the car. "But you don't know how to cook."

"Yet. I don't know how to cook yet. But I'm pretty sure I know how to read, so I should be able to follow a recipe. How hard can it be?"

"I think it depends on the recipe."

He pulls away as we reach the car and a coldness settles on my shoulders in the vacancy left by his arm. "Hey, you'll be there to back me up if I need it."

I snort and drop into the passenger seat. "I think you're overestimating my skills. Kenzie's the cook in the family, not me."

"Well, two heads are better than one. We'll figure this out."

Chapter 20

Sam flips through the thick recipe book Kenzie keeps stashed in a cabinet. "What do you think about a frittata?"

"Sounds fussy and maybe a little outside of our league. Next?"

"Pizza?"

"I know enough about that to know we should have made the dough hours ago."

He narrows his eyes. "You're not making this easy, you know."

I slide the cookbook closer to me and flip through the recipes. Certain pages are stained, corners folded down, others are pristine and show little wear. Does that mean we should stick with something reliable?

Sam leans over my shoulder. "Lasagna?"

I frown at the clock. "The cook time is too long. By the time we get everything prepped, we'll be starving."

We flip a few more pages.

"This one?" Sam taps the title of a recipe.

"Green bean casserole?"

"It's perfect. We barely have to do anything."

I roll my eyes and elbow him, but nod anyway. "Fine. Get the cans from the pantry. I'll find the rest."

"Yes, ma'am." He salutes and turns toward the pantry.

"That's 'yes, chef' to you." I skim a finger down the ingredients list before raiding the cabinets and fridge.

"I thought I was the chef. *I'm* making *you* dinner."

"Whatever." I set the oven up and snag the casserole dish from a pullout drawer.

Sam and I meet back up at the kitchen island. I nudge the casserole dish toward him. "Drain the green beans and put them in here." I open a can of soup and we mix the two together until the green beans are slathered in the creamy concoction.

"Next?" Sam dusts off his hands.

I snag the cookbook. "Onion powder."

"Right." He grabs a measuring spoon and scoops a heaping tablespoon from the jar.

"No." I catch his hand before he can dump the onion powder in with everything else. "Teaspoon and level it, please. Cooking is a science." I sound like Kenzie, but the girl can make a mean meal, so she must know what she's talking about.

"I thought that was baking?" But Sam switches out his tablespoon for a teaspoon and dutifully levels the scoop.

I throw my hands up. "I don't know. Does it matter?"

He smirks, dimple popping. "Maybe?"

"You just want to be right." I nudge him aside with my hip and sprinkle a generous helping of cheese over the mixture.

"I'm always right." Sam extends the mixing spoon to me.

"You wish." Our fingers brush as I take it and a jolt of awareness sweeps through me. When did we get this close? I clear my throat and pour my attention into mixing the casserole. I'm making up the awareness between us. And there are *no* butterflies in my stomach. I'm hungry, nothing more.

"Riley..." He trails my name.

A shiver sweeps my spine and I turn.

He back steps, planting himself against the sink, putting distance between us. "I wanted to thank you. For everything. I...I needed this. To come home."

"Well, I wasn't going to let you get yourself caught, now was I?" I tap a finger against the casserole dish. "Oven duty. And don't forget to set a timer. We don't need a visit from the fire department."

He swaggers over and lifts the dish. "Don't think I don't know what you're doing. You're changing the subject."

I open the oven for him. "You don't need to thank me, Sam. Friends take care of each other."

"I'm still grateful."

I chuck the cans in the trash, brain scrambling for a way to change the evening's tone. Because if I don't...well, things are going to get complicated and they're more than complicated enough already. "I wanted to ask your advice on something."

"Shoot." Sam leans against the counter.

"I wanted to help Kenzie with the whole Alex situation. Do you think it would be okay to invite him to the cookout?" I rinse the prep dishes and begin loading them into the dishwasher as Sam contemplates my question.

"I'm not the biggest fan of meddling in other people's lives."

I point a dripping spoon at him. "It's not meddling when it's family. I want Kenzie to be happy. She needs to stop overthinking things and spend time with the guy outside of work, or she'll never get to know him."

Sam laughs and moves to take over the rinsing of the dishes while I load. "I can't argue with you there." He shrugs. "It can't hurt.

A family barbecue is low stakes and they're friends anyway, so no pressure if things don't work out."

"I'll ask him then."

We work in tandem as we wait for the timer to go off, cleaning dishes and wiping down counters. It's an easy, soothing rhythm. One my heart pangs at the thought of losing. Because as much as I wish he could, Sam can't stay forever.

Help me to savor each moment that I do have.

When the casserole is done, Sam and I pull our stools up to the kitchen island and clank our forks together. "Cheers."

Heat engulfs my tongue with the first bite and I cup a hand over my mouth, breathing out.

"It's good," Sam pants arounds his mouthful. "I think."

It's way too hot to tell and I believe I may have scalded every taste bud I possess.

Eventually, heat gives way to flavor and I bob my head. "Not bad, Hong."

Sam grins at me. "Not bad yourself, Anderson."

Chapter 21

Smoke tinges the air with its familiar, trademark scent as Dad stands over the grill. Kenzie hands him a spatula as the wind plays with the hem of her sundress.

"It's perfect." Lou-Lou skips to my side and clasps her hands over her heart. "The sun is shining, not a cloud in the sky, and—" The doorbell rings interrupting her next words. "Who could that be? I told Aunt V to come around back when she gets here."

"It's a surprise." I waggle my eyebrows at her.

She surveys me from head-to-toe. "What are you up to?"

I offer a mischievous smile before I step around her and work my way back through the house where Sarge is on duty, yelping at whoever is on the other side of the door. "Thank you, sheriff." I massage behind his ears and he sits, trusting me to take over guard duty from here.

I peek through the window.

A guy with dark hair stands on the other side, hands shoved in his pockets. He shifts his weight from one foot to the other before rubbing the back of his neck like he's not quite comfortable. Aw, he's nervous.

Lou-Lou pokes my back. "What are you waiting for? Open it."

"All right, already." I twist the lock and yank the door open.

The guy startles. "Hi? I hope I have the right house." Pink stains his cheeks. "I'm looking for Mackenzie?" He peers around me, like he's expecting her to materialize. "I'm Alex."

Lou-Lou's lips pucker in an O as she glances between me and him.

"I'm glad you could make it. I'm Riley by the way." I step aside so he can make his entrance.

"Mackenzie's sister, the artist, right? Nice to meet you."

I nod and push my glasses higher up. He's got a good memory, pays attention to what my sister tells him. Bonus points.

Alex lets Sarge smell his hand and Sarge wags his tail, giving his stamp of approval. Good to know. If Sarge likes him, then he can't be too much of a creep. Another point in Alex's favor.

Lou-Lou props her elbow on my shoulder. "Hey, Alex, I'm Lou-Lou. Kenzie's out back with Uncle Gavin. Just head through the kitchen and you'll find her."

"Great, thanks."

"This way." Lou-Lou ushers Alex onward, leading him through the house to where my sister waits unexpectedly.

I follow the duo outside, Sarge on my heels.

"Hey, Kenz." Alex strides toward the grill where my sister is stationed while Dad attempts to set up an umbrella over our deck table.

Kenzie fumbles the tongs at the sound of his voice, managing to catch them a moment before they hit the ground. "Alex?" Her voice pitches high in a question mark even as her attention flits between me and Lou-Lou.

It was her, Lou-Lou mouths, pointing a finger at me.

"Hey." I pinch her.

Kenzie blushes dark red, but to her credit, she offers Alex a wobbly smile. "How are you?"

"Good. You?" He rocks on his heels, looking every bit as nervous as she does.

Lou-Lou snags my arm and drags me off to the side. "How did you manage that?"

"I have my ways." I toss my hair.

"You broke into her phone, didn't you?"

"It's not my fault her password is easy. Besides, look at her. She's not even upset."

"Oh, look. Sam's here." Lou-Lou bounces beside me.

I turn and watch as Sam swings the gate open and strolls in. He's wearing his baseball cap backward and has on one of the most casual outfits I've seen him in yet. Basketball shorts and a sleeveless top. My stomach does a funny little twist. He's ...my Sam. The one I knew growing up. The only thing missing is some grass stains and dirt on his knees. Well, and he's much taller now.

"Hey, Ri." He strolls forward with a casual swagger.

Sarge bounces into his path, tongue lolling as he falls all over Sam in a desperate bid for attention. Sam obliges, crouching to give him a good scratch behind his ears. Why does my heart melt?

Sweat slides down the back of my neck. No, no, no. This can't be happening. I back up a step as if it'll somehow reseal the crumbling walls around my heart as I watch the pop star kneeling in my yard like he could be any other boy in the universe. Except he's not any other boy. He's Sammy Hong. And I will not be another girl who falls at his feet.

"Riley? Are you okay? You look kind of pale." Lou-Lou squints at me.

"Fine." My voice squeaks. I clear my throat and try again. "I'm fine." I swipe my clammy palms down my shorts. "I'm going to go grab a drink." I flail a hand in Sam's general direction to avoid being rude before I duck inside the air-conditioned sanctuary of the house. I scramble toward the sink and guzzle a glass of water and then another until the pounding beat of my heart ebbs.

Deep breaths.

No need to panic.

I'm being thrown off by the lazy summer vibes. Sam will leave soon, and until he does, and maybe even after, he needs a friend. Just a friend.

"Honey, are you all right?" Dad pauses on his way out the door, a stack of hamburger patties on a Styrofoam plate balanced in one hand.

I startle, sloshing my drink over the side of the cup. "Fine. I'll be out in a minute."

He watches me for a long moment. "You sure?"

"Yep. Fine. Totally fine." I dab the back of my hand against my chin, catching stray droplets.

"Okay." The look he gives me says he doesn't believe me but understands this isn't a great time to ask about it.

I smile weakly even though it's pathetic and won't erase his suspicions at all.

He gives me one last quizzical glance before readjusting his hold on the patties and heading out the door. "Oh, hey, Sam, how are you?"

Sam? I spit out my next drink of water mid-sip.

Not now.

I need time to prepare. If Sam comes in, he'll know something's wrong. I swipe at my mouth in a desperate attempt to conceal my failed drinking attempt.

"Good. Thanks for having me over." Sam's voice drifts closer.

Cheese and crackers! He's coming. I pull my hair forward. But it might appear like I'm *trying* to hide my emotions. Behind my ears it is. No, one ear. That's more natural.

"Anytime, son." If anyone else said it, they might sound old, or even condescending, but affection tinges my dad's tone. Like he really does love Sam like part of the family.

I grip the edge of the sink. Part of the family. Sam's the brother I never had.

"Riley?" Sam's voice sounds behind me.

I swivel to face him, but my foot catches on a pesky puddle created from my less than graceful drinking. For one terrible moment, my gaze connects with Sam's, then a pit opens in my stomach and I'm falling.

Except I don't hit the ground.

Sam's warm hands cup my arms and his heartbeat races beneath my palms. Our eyes lock. My mouth runs dry. Yeah, okay. He's nothing like a brother. Something winged and jittery sparks to life in my stomach.

Sam's eyes search mine. "Ri—"

"Forgot the salt."

Sam and I spring apart at the sound of my dad's words and I almost fall again, but he catches my elbow.

Dad snags the salt and shakes the jar in triumph. If Sam and I look as guilty as I feel, Dad has the grace to let us off the hook.

"Great." I pray he doesn't notice the heat burning my face.

"Good." Sam's voice breaks and he has to clear his throat.

"Come on, kids, let's get cooking." Dad slings an arm around my shoulders and steers me to the backyard. Sam follows behind.

"Hey there," Vanessa's cheery greeting sounds from where Lou-Lou is tugging her through the gate. I can't help but feel a bit vindicated when Sarge shoves his nose up her sundress. Which is terrible. Rude even.

"Sarge, come here," I call, my humanness and sympathy kicking in while Vanessa's cheeks turn pink as she smooths her skirt.

Sarge trots over to me, prancing as if he doesn't have a care in the world. I bend down and rub his head. "You shouldn't do that." But a snicker escapes me all the same. Yes, I am a horrible person and guilt stabs at me a second later.

Forgive me, Lord. Help me love her well and help her feel welcome. Maybe get to know her better? Love your enemies and all that, right?

Lou-Lou kicks my shin. "Teach that dog some manners."

I scramble out of reach. "Him? You're the one who needs manners."

"Riley, how are you?" Vanessa touches my arm, interceding before Lou-Lou can retaliate in any way shape or form.

"Good." I swallow the grimace attempting to take over my mouth. She's so...nice. It would be much easier not to like her if she was a troll. But she's pretty much the exact opposite. Which makes me even more of a horrible person. "And you? How have you been?"

She waves a hand. "Busy. Honestly, this is exactly what I need." She throws her head back, letting the sun warm her face. "Sometimes you just need a dose of sunshine."

I can't disagree. As much as I would like to. Instead, I find myself tipping my own face to the glorious rays.

"Vanessa." My dad joins us. "I'm glad you could make it."

Vanessa beams and I have to admit she does have a pretty smile. "Thanks for having me."

Is it me or has their attention snagged on each other a little too long? I shift my weight from one foot to the other, my palms growing slick. Maybe Lou-Lou's fantasy isn't far off from reality after all.

"Riley, Riley, Riley." Sam wraps an arm around my shoulders and guides me away.

"Hey," I protest, but only verbally.

"Leave them be."

"But—" I should be running interference. Creating a theory proving Lou-Lou's insane. Grown-ups, especially ones with a niece in common act friendly toward each other all the time. No biggie.

"Look." He turns me when we're a safe distance away, forcing me to view the scene with a fresh perspective. The way Vanessa leans in and touches my dad's arm, *gag*, the way my dad's eyes light up. Wait...what?

"You think he actually likes her?" The words are a hoarse whisper.

"Would that be so bad?"

It shouldn't be. It really shouldn't. More than anything my dad deserves to be happy, especially after everything he went through after Mom...but couldn't he wait? Until I'm like in my forties or something?

"You look sick."

"I don't think I can do this, Sam." My stomach churns and moisture pricks at my eyes.

"If you want my advice, and before you say it, no you didn't ask, but I think you should try. Besides, there might be absolutely nothing that comes from it."

"And if something does happen?" I wrap my arms around my middle. Why does change have to be so dark and ominous, looming like a shadow?

Sam taps me with his elbow. "Then you'll deal with it when it does. One day at a time, Ri."

Lou-Lou jogs over to us. "What are you two standing around for? Let's get this party started!"

As if on cue, Kenzie's phone syncs with the speakers, sending a pulsing beat through our backyard.

Sam snags my hand and tugs me to the deck where the others are gathered. The awkwardness between Kenzie and Alex has melted and they're laughing as Alex tells some story from work. Dad flips burgers, grinning along. Vanessa catches her blonde locks which are attempting to tangle with her lip gloss as she listens.

Lou-Lou slings her arms around my waist and squeezes so tight it's a miracle my ribs don't crack. "Thank you."

"For?" I hug her while trying to remember how to breathe.

"For this." Lou-Lou beams at me. "It's fun, right?"

I want to deny it, but then Dad tells one of his dad jokes and everyone is cracking up and I'm laughing too. Yeah, this is fun.

Chapter 22

As the sun sets, Dad and Kenzie wave goodbye to Alex and Vanessa as they make their way to their respective cars. Lou-Lou attempts to close the sliding door with her foot as she steps out onto the deck, arms loaded with everything we could possibly need for s'mores.

"Um, whatcha doing?" I work my way behind her to shut the door before she tumbles over in her attempts.

"Backyard campout. The next item on the list. You're the one who said we could combine it with the barbecue." She readjusts her grip on the multitude of packages precariously stacked together.

"I'll dig the tent out from the basement." Dad rounds the house, hands tucked into his pockets.

"Ooh, will you be joining us, Uncle Gavin?" Lou-Lou waggles her eyebrows.

"Not on your life, kiddo. While you get eaten by mosquitos and wake to a crick in your back, I will be enjoying my luxurious king-sized bed, thank you." He bows and steps inside.

Lou-Lou wrinkles her nose at his back before rounding on my sister. "Kenzie," her voice is all sugar and sweetness.

Kenzie stiffens. "Nope. Don't even ask. I'm an adult and have full vetoing power when it comes to camping."

"Aw, adults are so boring." Lou-Lou huffs and deposits the s'more things near the fire pit. "Let me guess, Sam, you're going to bale on us too?"

Sam drops into a lawn chair and crosses one foot over his knee. "You kidding? Wouldn't miss it for the world."

"Riley?" She looks to me, stink-eye in full effect, promising pain and torture if I think for one second, I'm going to get out of this.

Not that I want to. Camping out here is the perfect way to end this glorious evening. "Simmer down. I wouldn't quit the list, now would I?" I perch on another of the lawn chairs.

Lou-Lou squeals and dives onto my lap. "Best day ever."

A moment later, Dad returns with a tent bag in hand. "Here you guys go. I hope this old thing still has all the poles and stuff." He deposits the bag at my feet and turns to head inside.

"Woah, woah, woah," Lou-Lou protests. "You're not going to help us set it up?"

"Nah, it's time you kids learned the full joys of camping." He waves a hand over his head. "Have fun."

"What did you do to make him mad, Riley?" Lou-Lou looks from the closing sliding door to me.

I pinch her side. "Nothing. It's called learning life skills."

"Ugh. Remind me to get filthy rich when I'm older so I can have a butler to do this kind of thing for me."

I nudge her off my lap. "Come on. Let's try to get this thing put together before it gets dark."

"Yeah, yeah." But she helps me pull everything out of the sack and organize it on the grass. "You going to help, Mr. Celebrity?"

Sam unfolds himself and joins our duo. Between the three of us, we soon get the tent up and ready for use.

"I'll get the fire going," Sam says. "Any chance you guys have some sleeping bags?"

"We should. I'll go check." I jog into the house and dig through a spare linen closet before I come up with the well-worn sleeping bags my family always uses on camping trips.

When I make my way to the backyard, Sam has a fire going and Lou-Lou has taken over my chair and has a pair of marshmallows positioned over the glowing flames.

"Scooch." I nudge her sideways with my hip and reach for my own pole and bits of cushiony white goodness.

Sam watches me, something mischievous passing through his features.

I narrow my eyes. "What?"

"Are ghost stories still banned?"

I blow a raspberry and try to wave away his words. Like ghost stories? What's a ghost story?

Lou-Lou narrows her eyes at me before leaning toward Sam. "Oh, ghost stories are completely banned. I told one last summer and I don't think Riley slept for a week."

Sam's eyebrows shoot up. "Really?"

I curl my toes into the grass. "Okay, I don't think we need to—"

"Yep, she's still a complete chicken." Lou-Lou drops her chin onto her hand. "You'd think she'd have outgrown such things by now, but our dear Riley is still a complete wimp."

"Hey." I nudge her with my elbow. "Aren't you supportive."

Sam laughs and reaches for his own s'more supplies. "So, ghost stories are out. What are we supposed to do to entertain ourselves?"

"You could sing." I enjoy the way his cheeks pinken in the firelight.

His gaze catches on mine, flames reflected in his pupils. My heart skips a beat and my throat goes dry. I swallow hard.

"Yeah, sing." Lou-Lou bounces beside me.

"Just remember, you asked for this." He throws his head back and belts out a tune in a horrendously off-pitch voice that would have any dog pawing at its ears. Well, any dog but mine. Sarge sleeps uninterrupted on the deck. Some guard dog he is. It sounds like we're getting torn apart by a pack of rabid raccoons.

Lou-Lou claps her hands to her ears. "Okay, okay."

I give Sam my best impression of one of Lou-Lou's stink-eyes. "That's not what I meant."

He stifles a laugh and clasps a hand to his chest. "Ouch. Luckily, I'm used to critics or I'd be wounded right now."

I pull my marshmallow away from the flames. Perfectly golden, a stark contrast to the charcoal lumps dangling from Lou-Lou's roasting stick. A chunk of chocolate and a pair of graham crackers later, and my mini-tower of yumminess is complete.

Lou-Lou frowns at my creation. "So undercooked."

"At least it won't taste burnt."

"Crisped. Not burnt. Crisped to perfection." As if to prove her point, she pries one black lump off her stick and pops it in her mouth. I wince on behalf of every taste-bud she's probably just scalded.

"You do it your way and I'll stick to mine, thanks." I take a bite of my s'more, moaning at the perfect mix of sticky marshmallow, gooey chocolate, and the crunch of the crackers. Perfection.

Sam rounds the fire to collect my empty roaster. He pauses, looking down at me.

I still. "What?" The word comes out mangled around the unladylike amount of s'more I'm attempting to chew.

"You've got something..." He taps the corner of his mouth.

Oh. I swipe at my lips and look to him, eyebrows raised.

He shakes his head. "Here, let me." He bends and swipes the pad of his thumb over my bottom lip.

Sparks tingle beneath my skin where his thumb lingers. My breath catches as a dozen dangerous thoughts dance through my mind. And for once I struggle to push them back. To remind myself of all the reasons these sparks are forbidden.

"Riley, you should really learn to use a napkin." Lou-Lou breaks the spell.

Sam clears his throat and steps back.

I duck my head, swiping at my mouth as if it'll erase the moment.

Lou-Lou launches into a story of a disaster of a camping trip she once took with her parents, neither of which are outdoorsy, but they tried their hardest for her sake. Of course, it wasn't their fault it rained, or that the tent flooded, or a bear got into their food supplies. Let's just say the trip was memorable even for those of us who only know about it secondhand.

Sam settles into his chair across the fire, laughing in all the right places, like nothing happened between us.

Because nothing did. This summer and the laziness of the evening are getting to me. I readjust my position, rebuild my walls, and drop a mental cinder block on my head so I can knock some sense into myself.

Chapter 23

A yawn pulls at me, but I swallow it and push one finger under the rim of my glasses to rub at my eye. But the stars are too pretty to miss. We've moved to the deck for the best view.

Sam sighs beside me.

"What's wrong?" I ask.

"I'll miss this."

"Stargazing?" I gently stroke Lou-Lou's hair as her soft snores blow against my leg. The girl has worn herself out and is now using my thigh as a pillow. Sarge returns the favor with his chin propped on her leg.

"More than that. Just sitting here. No schedule or flight to catch. Just...being."

It's not the first time he's voiced the sentiment. "Sam?"

He looks to me, the depths of night reflecting in his eyes.

"Have you thought about staying?" I pause, not breathing, waiting for his reply. Something warm and bright sparks to life in my middle. Hope?

He blinks. Looks away. "Staying?"

"I mean I know you have to sort things out with your label and everything. But after that...what if you stayed?" My heart beats too quickly as I wait for his answer.

"Give it all up?" Sam purses his lips and turns his face toward the sky.

Would it be so bad? I want to ask. But I don't. "Only if that's what you want."

"I won't pretend it doesn't sound appealing. But I don't know. I've been praying about it a lot...Ri, do you ever get the feeling that you're not done? That there's still a purpose for you where you're at?"

A part of my heart leaps to know he's been praying, but something cold slithers through my stomach at his reply, replacing the light, airy feeling. Because this is the wrong answer. He's supposed to walk away from the pop star persona. It would fix, well, everything. But I shouldn't be surprised. I always knew he was just here for the summer. I shouldn't have gotten my hopes up. "I mean I guess. But seasons change, Sam."

He shakes his head. "I just don't think it's time."

"You want to worry about being trampled by a mob of rabid fangirls every time you walk through an airport?" Fury marks my voice. Why am I angry? I shouldn't be.

He flinches. "You know I've never been in it for the fans."

No, he hasn't. For him it's always been about his love for music. Except now it's like he's choosing them over me. Again. "Yeah, I know," I snap.

Why would you let him leave again, God? Why can't he stay?

"You're angry." He picks at something on his shorts.

"No, I'm not." But I can feel the heat vibrating through my body. If I'm not careful, I may say something I'll regret.

"You are." He leans close, eyes intense in the glowing beam of light from inside the house. "Why are you angry, Riley?"

My lips part, but I have nothing to say. I shouldn't be angry. I have no claim on him or his choices. His gaze flickers to my mouth and alarm bells go off in my head. I all but shove Lou-Lou off my lap, jolting both her and Sarge awake.

Sarge takes off, running the length of the fence, barking like a maniac in an effort to deter whatever intruder disturbed the peace.

"Huh?" Lou-Lou blinks groggy eyes.

"It's late." I poke her back. "Bedtime." I scramble to my feet.

Sam is a beat behind. "Ri—"

"It's late." I step backward, putting distance between us, and shove my hands into the back pockets of my shorts. "We should go to bed. Get some beauty sleep." I clamp my teeth together to cut off any further rambling.

Hurt flashes across his face, but Sam nods. "Yeah. Okay."

What a rotten human I am.

"Sweet dreams." I could gag on the amount of sugar I've used to sweeten my tone. It comes across as fake and hollow. I turn and bolt into the cover of my sleeping bag. The shuffle of fabric and the press of a warm, small body against mine suggests Lou-Lou has followed my example. Sarge flops down at my feet.

It's a long time before the zipping of the tent signals Sam's entrance.

"Riley?" Lou-Lou rolls close, smooshing herself against my side.

"Hmm?" I stare at my bedroom ceiling. Like I have been ever since we crawled into bed at two in the morning because Lou-Lou couldn't fall asleep in the tent and I jumped at the excuse to distance myself from Sam. I should sleep. I want to sleep. But my mind won't let go of my conversation with Sam. It plays on repeat. Over and over and over again.

"Are you mad at Sam?"

I wriggle, or try to, but Sarge is sprawled across my feet. Yep, big baby that he is, he had to join us inside the house too. "No. I'm mad at myself."

"Are you going to tell him that?" Lou-Lou props her chin on my shoulder.

"No." I tense to still the urge of shrugging her off.

"I don't think that's fair."

I swallow hard. "Go to sleep."

"Are you going to tell me why you're mad?"

I cross my arms. "No."

"But—"

"I don't even know why I'm mad, all right?" My voice rises, making Sarge twitch, and I hurry to correct my tone, "It's silly."

"But it's about Sam?"

"No." Yes.

"Have you convinced yourself yet?"

I huff. "Go to sleep."

Chapter 24

The next morning, I slink through my morning routine with all the curtains around the house pulled tight so Sam won't know I'm awake. My glasses sit low on my nose and my bun lists to one side. Do I look like a hot mess? Probably. Goodness knows I feel like one.

I work my stylus over my screen in quick strokes as I attempt to create the chiseled jaw of a girl's boyfriend she's commissioning in a comic book style for his birthday, except the only face that appears is Sam's.

"Of all the—" I slap my stylus to the table and take a long gulp of coffee.

"You okay?" Kenzie grabs the milk carton from the fridge and eyes me as she pours it into her cereal.

"Fine." But I still haven't figured out how to face Sam today. Maybe he'll be caught up with lawyers and what-not. That would be almost worse though. The longer I avoid him, the greater the chasm and hurt between us will grow.

"You don't seem it." My sister drops into the chair across from me and stirs her spoon through her cereal speckled milk. "Where's Dad?"

I don't feel it. "He left already. You and Alex seemed like you had fun last night." I waggle my eyebrows.

"We did." Pink colors Kenzie's face. "In fact…"

I lean forward, a squeal already building in my chest.

"We're going out tomorrow night." She shrieks and bounces in her chair.

"Yes." I pump a fist and release a whoop of my own.

Kenzie laughs. "Okay, okay, settle down."

I nudge her leg underneath the table. "Seriously, I'm happy for you."

"Yeah, well, we've liked each other for a long time. I know I should be furious with you for stealing my phone, but it turns out it was exactly what we needed. To *communicate*."

Suddenly, her stare is too intense. I squirm in my chair. "That's great. I'm glad things worked out." I take another gulp of coffee and snatch my stylus. Maybe if I look like I'm busy, she won't—

"It's okay if you like him, you know."

I spit the coffee across the table.

"Ew, Riley." Kenzie flinches away.

"Sorry." I grab my tablet off the table before the liquid can reach it. With my other hand, I grab a handful of napkins and fling them overtop the mess.

"That's disgusting." My sister glares at me.

True, but at least it provided a distraction.

"Seriously, though. It's okay if you like Sam."

Or not. I push the soggy napkins to the edge of the table. "What makes you think I like him?"

"I'm not blind, Ri. None of us are."

I lean back and cross my arms. "It's not okay."

Kenzie's mouth drops open. "Why on earth not?"

"Because I swore I never would."

"Well that was silly."

I can't argue. It does sound ridiculous now that I've said it aloud. Still, the point remains. "I won't be like those fangirls. They don't even know him. They build up these wild fantasies in their head, all the while Sam is a human being." A boy who grew up next door. Who shoved worms down the back of my shirt. Who spilled a milkshake on himself every other time we had them. I've seen the guy throw-up. He's as human as any of them. Heat burns my face and my heart rate picks up. I snatch the soiled napkins and march them to the trash.

"And?" Kenzie shakes her head. "You see the real him. There's nothing wrong with that."

She doesn't understand. I stalk to my chair and sit so hard my bottom stings. "I don't want that lifestyle. I want to go to the grocery store and walk around the neighborhood in my pajamas without worrying if some paparazzi person is hiding in the bushes ready to snap a picture. Besides, every girl he's ever dated has received death threats."

"None of them have died," Kenzie offers.

I give her a long look.

"Yeah, not funny. I can see where you're coming from." She purses her lips. "The celebrity thing does complicate stuff, I'll admit."

"I won't do it." Tears burn my eyes. I clench my jaw and shake my head. "I won't do it, Kenzie."

"Aw, Riley." Kenzie reaches across the table and takes my hand. "Don't cry."

I blink, forcing the tears away.

She squeezes my fingers. "It's okay. No one says you have to fall head over heels for him. But Ri…" Her voice dips.

Uh-oh. Here comes some kind of truth bomb. I brace myself.

"I know you care about him. Make sure you take time to think this through. Do you really want to let him go?"

I look away.

"Promise me you'll pray about it? Be sure before you give a final answer to anything."

I roll my eyes, except that makes a hot tear slide down my cheek. "He hasn't asked me anything."

"Not yet."

I slash away the tear, pull free from her touch, and spring away from the table. "You know what, I don't think this is helping." I turn on the sink water nice and hot until the steam warms my face. Hopefully it disguises the continued tears.

"Ri—"

I ignore her, slamming my cup into the dishwasher. "Have a good day at work." I make a dash for the stairs and lock myself in the bathroom.

"Riley Alyne, you get out here right now." Lou-Lou pounds on the door.

I swipe a bit more mascara onto my lashes. "Go away."

The door quivers beneath her fist. That or she's resorted to kicking the door. If she starts huffing and puffing…

"You cannot mope in your feelings all day."

Watch me.

"Unlock this door."

"Why don't you try huffing and puffing?" I pull my hair from its towel and shake it out around my shoulders.

"Seriously, which one of us is acting like a toddler?"

I ignore the comment and dab on some tinted lip balm.

"Open up or I'm going to get a butter knife."

Cheese and crackers! I never should have shown her how to do that. "I'll be out in a minute." I sit on the counter, snag my phone, and start scrolling through social media.

"You're impossible." She stomps away.

Ha, I win.

Except less than a minute later, her footsteps are thundering up the stairs. She's not going to…

Click.

I guess she is.

"I hope you're decent, because I'm coming in."

I don't even have time to slide off the counter before my cousin bursts into the bathroom.

The humidity trapped in here attacks her hair and fogs her glasses, but that doesn't keep Lou-Lou from directing her butter knife my way. "Get your booty off of there right now."

I cross my legs and keep scrolling.

"You are acting like such a brat."

"Me?" I splay a hand across my chest and blink, widening my eyes in innocence.

"Riley Alyne, I have had enough of your dramatics." She stows her knife in the waistband of her sequined skirt and crosses her arms. "Out with it."

"Out with what?" It's my turn to pocket my phone and fold my arms over my chest.

"Whatever it is that made you go all drama queen." She taps her foot.

"It doesn't matter." All of a sudden, it's too hard to meet her eyes. I stare at my lap and link my fingers together. Twisting, twisting, twisting. Too bad I can't wring out all the hurt from my heart too.

Lou-Lou sighs. Places a hand on my knee. "Look, you don't have to tell me, but please can you come downstairs?" She pouts. "I'm lonely."

"Fine." I slide off the counter.

Lou-Lou tucks her arm through mine. "You're the best."

"No, you are, kiddo." I pull my arm free and sling it around her shoulders instead.

"Remember that, okay, Ri?" She looks up at me.

My eyebrows creep up. Does she have to look so serious? "Sure."

Lou-Lou stops at the top of the stairs and extends her pinky. "You have to promise."

Now who is being the drama queen? But I link my finger with hers anyway. "I promise."

"Good." She grabs my hand and scampers down the stairs.

"Slow down. I don't want to break my neck today." I stumble after her, taking every ounce of coordination my body possesses to not trip and fall.

"You overthink everything." Lou-Lou gives a sharp tug and I have to jump from the last two stairs to keep up with her.

I do not. "What's the emergency?" I pant.

She yanks me to the kitchen, then in some ninja move, she's behind me and shoving me forward. "Remember, you will thank me for this someday."

"What—" I crane my neck, trying to catch her gaze.

"Hey, Riley."

I freeze.

Sam Hong stands in my kitchen.

Chapter 25

I'm not emotionally ready for this.

My knees tremble and it takes every ounce of willpower I possess not to turn and run.

Lou-Lou pokes my spine. "Be mature," she hisses.

Mature. Not something I excel at. Still, in a few months I'll be an official adult, so better to start practicing now. I pull in a shaky breath and square my shoulders.

Sam watches me, his torn-up heart reflected in the intensity of his gaze.

Great, now I feel like trash.

Sam clears his throat. "Can we talk, Riley?"

Riley? We're on a full name basis? My stomach sinks and now a sheen of hot liquid washes across my vision. What have I done? *Help me to fix this, please, Lord.*

Lou-Lou tiptoes away.

"Sam..." Oh, how to start? I'm such an idiot, letting my insecurities about nothing he's actually said or claimed, ruin everything. I wrap my arms around my middle, because maybe, someway, it'll keep my heart from breaking.

Sam steps closer. "Look, I don't know what exactly I did, but Riley..." His gaze holds mine. Powerful and full of so many emotions I have to swallow hard. "I'm sorry."

That snaps me and I'm rushing forward. Shaking my head. "No. No, Sam. It's my fault. I was being utterly ridiculous about something and—"

Sam's finger lands on my lips, shushing me.

When did I get so close? Maybe he moved forward too.

"Let's decide we both said some things we probably shouldn't have. That we're both sorry. Friends?" Sam holds out his hand.

I shake. "Duh."

"Yes." Lou-Lou whoops from the living room, sending Sarge flying toward the door, barking like some intruder has somehow burst into our house and made my cousin shout while he wasn't looking.

"It's okay." I laugh and go to the window to prove there's nothing out there. After a tense moment of being on duty against invisible threats, Sarge flops to the ground with a long sigh like babysitting all of us is too much for his old soul.

Lou-Lou skips to my side and hugs my arm. "Soooo..."

Uh-oh. Nothing that drawn out can be good. I brace myself.

"Does that mean the list is back on?" She blinks at me, pouring the thimble-full of her remaining innocence into her eyes.

Sam and I share a look.

"You bet." I tickle her ribs, making her spring away with a laugh.

"Yes." She pumps her fist and does a little victory dance. "We're going to the zoo."

I clamp a hand on her head and nudge her down to earth. "Not today, minion. We need a little more notice than that."

"Aw." She deflates.

"Not to worry. We'll rearrange things. There's got to be something we can do today." I cross to the fridge, snag the list and a pen, and flatten it out on the table.

    1. *Drive-thru*

    2. *Go to the lake [picnic + bug spray]*

    3. *Backyard barbecue*

    4. *Camp in the backyard [potentially combine with No. 3 + s'mores are a must]*

    5. *Go to the zoo. [Pet stingrays. Gulp...]*

    6. *Make popsicles*

    7. *Go for a bike ride*

    8. *Water fight*

    9. *Go to the movies*

    10. *Watch fireworks*

Well, the first thing to do is eliminate what we've already done. I cross them out with big, bold strokes.

    1. ~~*Drive-thru*~~

    2. ~~*Go to the lake [picnic + bug spray]*~~

    3. ~~*Backyard barbecue*~~

4. ~~Camp in the backyard [potentially combine with No. 3 +~~
   ~~s'mores are a must]~~

Obviously, going to the zoo is out for the day, we're not going to the movies without having checked the schedule to see what's showing, and we can't conjure fireworks on a whim. Good, that narrows down our options.

"We can either make popsicles, go for a bike ride, or have a water fight today." I tap the pen against my chin as I study our remaining options.

Lou-Lou sidles up beside me. "Ooh, popsicles."

I turn to Sam. "What do you want to do?"

He shakes his head. "You know I can't turn down a good water fight."

Lou-Lou crosses her arms. "Popsicles. I'm the youngest, so you have to do what I want."

"And who made up that rule?" Sam asks.

She points to herself.

I hold out my hands. "Hey, now. I have a solution."

Their attention turns to me.

Lou-Lou props her hip against the table. "I'm all ears."

Sam raises his eyebrows.

They're either going to love me or murder me for this. "Let's do both." I pump my voice with as much cheer as any cheerleader could possibly dream of.

Sam's eyes widen. Good, I've caught him by surprise, but not unpleasantly so. I shift my focus to Lou-Lou. Her eyes narrow into slits. Ooh, not good.

"I thought we were supposed to do one thing on the list at a time. Stretch it out." Her voice is low. Possibly dangerous. Should I run now or try to talk her off the cliff?

"Hey, you're not trying to get rid of me sooner, are you?" Sam asks.

Heat streaks my cheeks and I imagine they must be lobster red. I wave my hands through the air like it might somehow help me take the words back. "Oh, no. No, I didn't mean that. I—"

"I'm kidding, Ri." He laughs.

"Oh." I still, but then shrug. At least we're back to nicknames.

Lou-Lou eyes the list. "I don't know...this feels a little bit like breaking the rules."

"Please." I bat her words away.

Sam studies me. "I thought you were a ruler follower."

"Not when we *made* the rules. Besides, guys, it's hot and the balloon fight will give us something to do while the popsicles set."

Sam looks to Lou-Lou and they share some kind of silent communication.

"Well?" I demand.

Sam nods to her. "Your call, minion."

Lou-Lou purses her lips. "Fine. On one condition."

Her and her conditions. It's my turn to cross my arms and offer a stare down.

"I get a five-minute head start when it comes to the water balloon fight." She raises her chin, daring me to argue.

In what world is that fair? "No way."

"R-i-l-e-y," she groans my name.

Sam laughs. "Don't you think that's a bit much, minion?"

She shimmies her eyebrows with every ounce of sass she possesses. "Do you want to do them both or not?"

Ugh, she is impossible, but I guess her parents have taught her how to drive a hard bargain. But my dad is in business too. He taught me how to negotiate. "One minute."

"Four." Somehow, she manages to raise her chin higher.

I straighten. "Two."

"Three." She leans forward and I find myself drawing back. Victory lights her eyes. "Take it or leave it."

I've lost.

"Fine." I offer my palm.

We shake.

Chapter 26

Ten minutes later, I massage my temple and am seriously considering dropping my head on the counter for a quick nap as Sam and Lou-Lou argue over what flavor the popsicles should be.

"Peach," Lou-Lou says, popping up on her tip-toes to make herself look taller.

Sam shifts, blocking her way to the freezer and the frozen fruit locked inside. "Strawberry. Everyone knows that's the best."

"Everybody who?" Lou-Lou plants her hands on her hips.

"Everybody important."

"*Guys.*" I draw the word out. Wait for them to notice me. But they're too tied up in their argument.

Lou-Lou angles her chin higher. "Peach. It's summery. Light. Refreshing. *Yellow.*" She says the last point like it's the most important of them all.

"Strawberry is universal. It goes with everything," Sam says.

"That's code for boring."

Sam's eyes narrow. "I'm not sure I can trust someone who doesn't like strawberry."

Lou-Lou bristles. "Like I care."

They're toe-to-toe now.

"Guys." I work my way between them. "I propose a solution."

Lou-Lou rocks on her heels. "Better make it good, Ri."

No pressure or anything. I push my glasses higher on my nose and glance between them. "We'll make strawberry peach popsicles."

Sam slants a look my way. "Not bad, Anderson."

Lou-Lou sweeps me with her gaze. "I'd rather hoped you'd take my side, seeing as we're family and all, but I see I was too optimistic."

"Lou-Lou." If she keeps this up, I'm going to have to—

"Fine. We'll do it your way." Lou-Lou offers a flippant shrug.

"All right." I jerk my chin at Sam before she can take back her approval.

Sam makes quick work of shuffling through the freezer until he comes up with a bag of each fruit. Lou-Lou snatches them and dumps half of each into the blender. A scoop of flax seeds followed by a spoonful of chia seeds goes in next.

Lou-Lou groans. "Aw, now you've gone and ruined them."

"Not another word, or I'll throw in some kale. I'm sure Kenzie has some in the fridge."

Lou-Lou's lips part, but Sam stops ladling yogurt into the mixture and clamps a hand over my cousin's mouth. "Don't say another word."

She glares over his hand, but holds her peace.

I lean against the counter and eye Sam. "You're not scared of a little green, are you?"

"Of course not." He shakes his head, eyes wide with false innocence.

Lou-Lou peels his hand away. "Nobody wants healthy popsicles, Riley."

"I do."

"That's because you're a freak."

I wrinkle my nose at her.

"Yeah, Ri. A real freak." Sam ducks his head and grins as he goes back to ladling the yogurt into the blender.

"Oh, real nice." I grab a towel and toss it against his chest.

His head snaps up.

Uh-oh. I hold up my hands. Back away. "Wait a minute—"

He lunges.

I shriek, but he's too quick and he's got one arm wrapped around my waist as he swipes a streak of yogurt down my nose.

"Sam! Let me go or I'm going to throw every green thing in the fridge inside those popsicles." But I'm laughing and my threat carries no real weight.

Sam holds me tighter. "You'll have to get there first."

A throat clears.

We both pause, attention jumping to Lou-Lou.

"Children," she arches one haughty eyebrow, "if we could please focus on the task at hand."

We step apart.

Sam's dimple doesn't fade as he swipes his thumb down the length of my nose. "Here, let me get that for you."

As if he didn't put it there.

Something light and fluttery sparks inside my stomach as his skin brushes mine. His dimple deepens and suddenly all I want in the world is to keep that dimple from vanishing. I reach a finger to touch it. But I stop myself mid reach. Because if I take that step, there's no going back. No erase button like with my tablet.

So, I step away before I can step forward. "Right, let's get this treat blended." I sound too sweet. Too bubbly. Fake. False.

Twenty minutes later, I'm standing on the deck, a water balloon in each hand, wearing a bathing suit and shorts. Sam stands in his swim trunks at one end of the yard, a bucket of balloons at his own feet. Lou-Lou faces off opposite him, the hose and her own arsenal awaiting use.

We all wait. Tense. Watching each other for any sign of a flinch, something to giveaway an on-coming attack.

"Three minutes starts now," I shout to Lou-Lou, squinting without my glasses in order to make her out.

Fierce determination paints her face as she sprints forward. I brace myself, waiting to see which way she'll weave. Me or Sam.

Part of me thinks she'll attack him. The other part braces for impact.

She grins wickedly as she hurls a balloon at me. I skip out of the way, but still take an indirect hit to my leg even as Sam shouts. I glance over. She's soaked him.

Two more minutes.

With a wicked cackle, Lou-Lou turns and dashes for her weapons.

I exchange a look with Sam.

He gives a nod.

Lou-Lou snatches a pair of water balloons and resumes her charge.

One minute.

This time her aim is off and the water balloon sails over my shoulder and crashes against the house. The one she throws at Sam hits the grass inches from his feet.

Game time.

With a war cry that would make any ancient warrior proud, I leap from the deck and hurl one of my balloons, hitting my cousin square in the back even as Sam's hits her in the legs.

"No fair," she squeaks as she scampers away.

But I still have an intact grenade, so I give chase. Even as she bends to arm herself, I send my second missile splattering against her hip.

"Oh, you're on." She ditches her balloons and goes for the big guns.

I shriek and backtrack, but she's quicker and an icy dose of hose water drenches me, sending goosebumps prickling over my skin. It's then a projectile slams into my side.

"Traitor," I yell at Sam even as I dash for my bucket of weaponry.

He laughs before gasping as Lou-Lou soaks him with a blast of the hose. "That is cold."

"Ha." My cousin crows.

I point a finger at Sam even as I gather a fresh balloon with my free hand. "You deserve that."

"Game on." He strides to his own bucket like he has all the time in the world.

"You're going down." I heft the balloon in my hand, judging the weight. Nice and full.

He arms himself and flashes the dimple I love so much.

No, wait.

The dimple I *like* so much.

Smack.

A missile from Lou-Lou crashes into my shoulder.

"Get your head in the game, Riley," she taunts.

I shake my head to clear it of all conflicting thoughts and emotions surrounding Sam and instead swivel my attention between the two as they approach from each side. Sam fires first. I jump to the side, dodging the blow even as I hurl a balloon at Lou-Lou, making her retreat.

Sam nails me in the shoulder and a spray of icy water soaks my swimsuit. I gasp as goosebumps flash across my skin once more.

"Yes." Lou-Lou and Sam high-five.

And they're distracted. I launch a bombardment, grabbing balloon after balloon as they scramble to get out of range. Both are dripping by the time they get to a safe distance.

"Take that." I pitch one last balloon at Sam's back. It hits the ground a disappointing few inches away from him, but I stick out my tongue anyway.

Sam jabs a finger my way and combs a hand through his wet hair. "You'll pay for that."

Lou-Lou stares me down, hands propped on her hips, her own damp hair drooping into her eyes. "Did you notice something, Sam?" She cocks her head to the side, studying me.

I stand there, gloating with a smirk, waiting for them to either go after each other or try to come at me again. Let them try.

Sam mops water off his face. "What's that, minion?"

"She's out of balloons." A wicked gleam lights my cousin's eyes.

Out of...cheese and crackers! I back up, hands outstretched. "Hey, now...we can talk about this."

Lou-Lou stalks forward. "Where you going, Riley? There's nowhere to run."

Where am I going? She's right. I'm trapped.

Sam and Lou-Lou advance, circling from both sides.

There's nothing to do but make a break for it. I dash down the deck steps, dodge a swipe of Sam's arm and swerve past Lou-Lou. I ditch my home base and instead cut through the grass, aiming for Lou-Lou's abandoned bucket and the balloons bobbing in the water.

"No fair," Lou-Lou's protest is distant, but I'm sure she's giving chase. I scoop up a balloon—

Ice water douses me from head to toe and my shoulders bunch tight as the liquid drips down my body. Blood rushes in my ears as my mind struggles to connect the freezing cold water with what's happening around me. And then the static gives way to roaring laughter and I become aware of Sam stepping away from me, my empty balloon bucket in hand, now void of water as well. Lou-Lou clasps her stomach as she guffaws a few feet away.

Sam's dimple flashes. "I think it's safe to say we win." He holds out a fist to Lou-Lou and she taps her knuckles against his.

I cross my arms to ward off the chill soaking through my limbs. "I didn't know we had teams."

They share a look.

Lou-Lou pats my shoulder. "That's okay, Riley. You don't have to be the smartest one in our trio."

I poke her ribs. "Rude."

She springs away.

I'm too cold to give chase, so I settle for a glower instead. Sam retrieves a towel from the deck railing and drapes it around my shoulders.

I burrow into the fuzzy warmth. "Thanks."

He extends my glasses next and I towel off my face before slipping them into position.

"Popsicle time," Lou-Lou calls.

How is she not cold? Oh, to be young again. I wrap my towel tighter around myself. "How about we get dry first?"

"Weakling." She lays on her own towel in the sunshine, letting the rays bake her dry.

"I'll be right back." I slip inside the house and change into dry clothes, throw my hair in a bun to keep it from soaking the back of my t-shirt, and fish the popsicles out of the freezer along with a container of puppy ice cream. The sliding door squeaks as I join the others. "Come on, Sarge. You deserve a treat too."

He follows me, pausing to frolic in a particularly deep puddle before he settles on a dry patch of grass and I leave him to lick out the miniature ice cream carton in peace.

"Oh, give me, give me, give me." Lou-Lou wiggles her fingers in command and I pass her a popsicle before joining Sam on the deck steps.

"Cheers." I clack my popsicle against his.

For a moment we're six-years-old again, without a care in the world.

Sam grins at me, his dimple deepening and something warm and bright bursts to life in my stomach. Yeah, the boy next door has grown up. I find myself scooching ever so slightly closer.

Chapter 27

I stand in the kitchen, staring at the newly revised list.

1. ~~Drive-thru~~

2. ~~Go to the lake [picnic + bug spray]~~

3. ~~Backyard barbecue~~

4. ~~Camp in the backyard [potentially combine with No. 3 + s'mores are a must]~~

5. Go to the zoo. [Pet stingrays. Gulp...]

6. ~~Make popsicles~~

7. Go for a bike ride

8. ~~Water fight~~

9. Go to the movies

10. Watch fireworks

Number five is circled in bright pink marker Lou-Lou must have added last night. She even stuck a glittery star sticker next to it. I have got to get them to choose something else. Sam is supposed to be here in ten minutes and I need to come up with a plan before I break out in hives. I shoot a look out the window. It's cloudy. It could rain. Who wants to walk around the zoo in the rain? We should go see a movie instead.

Upstairs, Lou-Lou wails one of Sam's songs as she gets ready. Turns out a zoo outing requires a whole planned outfit and accessories combined with a cute hair-do.

I pace the kitchen, trying to form a persuasive argument in my head. But I can't confront them without facts. A plan. I pull up my weather app on my phone. Today we have a grand ten percent chance of rain. Ten percent. But it's still a chance. I tuck my hair behind my ear. Right. I can do this. Game on.

The doorbell rings.

"I still need five minutes," Lou-Lou screeches.

"Take your time," I call as I nudge Sarge out of the way so I can let Sam in.

"Hey, you ready?" He's got sunglasses on, but other than that, he's dressed like any other teenage boy.

I widen the door, inviting him inside. "Actually, there's something I wanted to—"

"R-i-l-e-y." Lou-Lou thunders down the stairs. "You've got to help me." She holds up one sloppy braid half the size of her other. "I look horrible."

"Lopsided, but not horrible. Turn around." I take her by the shoulders and rotate until her back is to me. I unravel both braids and part her hair down the middle. "I think we should postpone the zoo." Indefinitely or at least until all stingrays are banned.

Sam raises an eyebrow. "Postpone?"

"No." Lou-Lou wriggles, but my grip on her hair stops her from full on throwing a fit.

"It could rain." I'm halfway done with her braid.

"Rain?" Sam swipes his phone from his pocket. Scrolls. "Riley, there's a ten percent chance."

"But it could. Lou-Lou, you're wearing white. You don't want to get wet, do you?" I give her a shake to get the point across.

"Don't you think you're overreacting?" Her voice vibrates as I give her another shake for good measure.

"Wait a minute." Sam crosses his arms and smirks. "You're scared."

Cheese and crackers, he knows. "Me? Scared? Ha!" My voice rings too loud. "I think we should wait for nicer weather and it's a Tuesday. Everyone and their grandmother are going to be at the zoo on a Tuesday and we can't risk exposing your identity."

"My identity. Right." Sam smirks. "That's what you're worried about."

"And the weather. Don't forget the weather."

A burst of fresh sun rays stream through the windows.

Lou-Lou snickers. "I think your ten percent chance of rain blew over."

Sweat prickles the back of my neck. My palms. "What about sunburn? Lou-Lou, you know you'll burn to a crisp."

"I practically showered in sunscreen. I'll be fine."

I tie off her second braid. "I tried to warn you, I did." My mouth is too dry.

She spins around and grabs my arm. "Will you stop being a baby already? Let's go." She yanks the front door open and pulls me over the threshold.

Sam snags me from my cousin's grip and guides me to the car with a gentle hand on my lower back. "Don't worry, I won't let any stingrays eat you."

"That's what you said last time."

Lou-Lou shoves the car keys into my clammy hand.

"For the thousandth time, that stingray did not bite you, you scraped your hand on the exhibit wall." He opens the door for me.

"Says you." I lock my knees.

Lou-Lou scowls as she rips open the door to the backseat. "Get in Riley, or I swear I'm going to throw you in."

Like she could pick me up.

"All right." Sam takes the keys from my limp fingers. "Let's try this instead." He maneuvers me to the passenger side.

"Maybe today's a better day for a movie?" It's a squeaky, weak protest. I've lost and we all know it.

Sam gives me a gentle nudge. "Get in."

I can think of a million things I'd rather do, but somehow my limbs obey even as my brain scrambles for one last protest. Sam shuts me inside before I can grasp one. And then he's climbing behind the wheel and I'm watching the garage door roll down.

"You know, Sarge doesn't like being home alone. Why don't you two go to the zoo and I'll stay here?" I try one last time as Sam flicks on his indicator to turn out of the neighborhood.

"He's spoiled rotten. He can take a few hours alone, besides, Kenzie will be home soon enough," Lou-Lou says.

Like that makes me feel better. I gnaw on my thumbnail. I should have grabbed my tablet before leaving the house.

Sam catches my hand, pulls it away from my mouth, and wraps his fingers through mine. "Sarge will be fine, I promise. And so will you, Ri."

Somehow, with my hand in his, I believe it.

"Riley?"

"Hmm?" I glance up from watching a bear meander through his enclosure.

Sam looks away. "Never mind."

I turn my attention to the bear, but soon the hairs on the back of my neck prickle with the feeling of being watched. I turn to find Sam's reflective sunglasses-covered stare locked on me.

"What?" I laugh.

"Nothing." He looks back to the bear.

I eye Lou-Lou as she becomes the bear's personal stalker, snapping what must be a million pictures to send to her mom. After a second, that prickling sensation returns. I turn and tap a finger against Sam's chest. "All right, out with it. What's up?"

He shifts. Crosses his arms. Feigns interest in the bear who has plopped down in the grass. "It's just...I've noticed you don't do puzzles anymore."

"Oh." I don't know what I expected, but not that. I pull the zoo map from my pocket and roll it between my hands, searching for words to reply.

Sam watches me.

I clear my throat and force the words out of the cavern of my heart where I've buried and left them. "It was always kind of my thing with my mom. And with her gone..." I shrug. "I don't know, it didn't seem fun anymore."

"Even word search puzzles?"

I shift my weight. "I didn't mean to give them up exactly. Life changed rapidly, and we all were adjusting, and now my art keeps me busy. And you know, school...I don't have a lot of extra time for hobbies."

He goes so still a shiver runs through my middle.

"Sam?"

"When was the last time you did a puzzle, Ri? Any kind of puzzle?"

"I guess it would have been right before my mom died. We were working on this aquatic puzzle together. We were going to frame it when we were done." My voice grows husky and I have to swallow hard before continuing, "We never finished."

"I'm sorry," he whispers.

I reach out. Shove his shoulder to break the mood. "Come on. Lou-Lou, I think your mom will be able to see the bear from every angle."

"I'm coming, I'm coming." She stashes her phone in her back pocket. "Where to next?"

I unroll the map. "Elephants?"

Lou-Lou glances at Sam. "Is it true you got to ride an elephant on one of your Asia tours?"

He rubs the back of his neck and looks around like he's afraid someone might overhear. "Maybe."

She bounces. "What was it like?" The girl is practically vibrating.

I take quick inventory of our backpack. Three sodas are missing. Great, the girl is completely hyped up on caffeine.

"Let's just say I'll never forget it," Sam says.

We visit the elephants, watch a woman training a seal, and then the dreaded building comes into view and a sign says: *Come pet our stingrays! Stingray food $3.*

My mouth goes dry and my feet fuse to the pavement.

Sam's hand splays across my back. Warm. Could be described as comforting if not for the fact he's propelling me forward. Lou-Lou snags my hand and yanks me through the doors into the exhibit where a large pool sits in the middle of the building where parents, grandparents, and a cluster of children happily feed the beasts.

"Wash your hands up to your elbows and gently pet with two fingers," the on-duty attendant says though I can barely hear over the blood rushing in my ears and the pounding of my heart.

I think Sam murmurs some sort of acknowledgment even as Lou-Lou shoves three dollars into the woman's hand in exchange for a cup of stingray food reeking of sea life.

My companions shove me forward and somehow, I find myself at a sink, washing my hands. Am I really going along with this? And then my hands are clean and there's no room left for procrastination.

Sam entwines his fingers with mine and leads me over to the pool set low in the floor. The wall sits at knee level and the stingrays bob around, circling toward people in a desperate frenzy, no doubt looking for food. My fingers for example.

My knees shake as Sam guides me to a stop. "You know, stingrays have killed people before."

"I don't think this kind have."

"Exactly you *think*. You don't *know*." I sidestep a puddle of water which has splashed from the pool.

"Aw, Riley, don't be such a baby." Lou-Lou settles in beside me and selects a pinch of food from her cup.

"Wait, don't—"

But before I can fully get out the protest, she's sprinkled the food into the water, bringing a dozen stingrays in our direction.

Sam leans over the wall, stroking two fingers over one of the stingrays. "Come on, Ri. I promise they're not going to hurt you."

Like that's a promise he can keep, but I don't see these two letting me leave this building before I acquiesce, so I extend two shaking fingers and...

I can't do it.

Heat washes my face. Part of me truly wants to, but the fear is stronger.

In the next instant, Sam's hand covers mine, helping me lower my arm until my fingers slip into the cool water and brush against a stingray. I hold my breath, savoring the moment as I stroke the sea creature, Sam's chest warm against my back, his presence making me brave. When I pull away, all of my flesh is still intact.

Okay, maybe that wasn't *so* bad.

Sam grins and for one moment, I wish he'd pull off those sunglasses so I can see his eyes, but it's way too crowded in here, and we can't risk him being recognized. It's a long race to the parking lot if some of the teenage girls decide to swarm him.

Instead of begging him to toss the sunglasses in the trash, I extend my hand once more, stroking the closest stingray.

Lou-Lou smirks.

"Not a word," I say.

"Fine, fine. My lips are sealed." She mimes zipping her lips. "I will, however, readily admit that I am enjoying this."

"Just give me some food." I extend my hand and try not to cringe at the smell as she passes me a pinch.

"David, no running," a frazzled mom shouts from somewhere in the building.

I wince on her behalf. Here's to hoping her kid doesn't slip on the wet floor. I bend over the tank, aiming the food toward a baby stingray. Yeah, I admit, he's a cutie—

Wham.

Something collides with my back.

My balance wavers.

I stumble sideways and I think I'm safe, but then my shoe hits that bothersome puddle.

My stomach drops.

And then my feet are no longer in contact with the floor. For one desperate second, I flail my arms in a frantic attempt to gain my balance, but it's too late.

Crash.

I hit the water, sending the stingrays scattering.

Chapter 28

Water drips from my hair and a chunk of stingray food rolls off my shoulder, hitting the water with a plop. For one dreadful second, everything is silent and then everyone is talking at once.

Cheese and crackers.

I try to stand, to run away from the sea of staring strangers, but my shoes find no traction and I fall onto my bottom with a second mighty crash, sending water splashing out of the pool.

Lou-Lou stares at me, mouth gaping wide.

Beside her, Sam is ripping off his shoes, preparing to come get me.

People have their phones out, no doubt getting ready to make me go viral as the girl who fell into a stingray pool.

I'm in a stingray pool.

My breaths come sharp and gasping.

A stingray brushes against my leg and I yelp. Hot liquid burns across my eyes and I lose it, thrashing, unable to catch my balance long enough to stand.

Water splashes behind me, and then someone has their hands under my armpits and hefts me up. A protective arm wraps around my shoulders and guides me past the pack of stingrays hoping for a bite of my flesh, and then I'm out of the pool and those hands are wrapping a warm towel over my shoulders.

"You okay, Ri-boo?"

Ri-boo? I blink the sheen away from my vision and force my rescuer to come into view.

Chad stands beside me, concern furrowing his brow.

Am I okay? No, no I'm not. I'm shaking. "What are you doing here?" Those ridiculous tears form again.

"I volunteer here during the summer. Looks good on paper, you know." He shoves his hands in his pockets and rocks on his heels. "You all right?"

"Fine." I swipe the towel over my face, hoping he can't tell the difference between my tears and the water drenching me from head-to-toe.

"Hey, probably not the best timing, but I was hoping to run across you again. I'd like to take you out sometime."

He's right this is *so* not the time. "I—"

A woman approaches. Touches my arm. "Are you okay, sweetie?"

"Fine." Heat burns my cheeks. Maybe I should dive back in the pool and hope the bottom falls out and sucks me into a different universe.

A crowd has congregated around me, everyone checking to see if I'm alive.

"I'm fine," I assure each newcomer even as water drips off of me and pools around my feet.

Sam and Lou-Lou are stuck behind a patch of curious onlookers.

"I'm fine. Just fine." I try to step out of the gathering, but they're closing in. Looking as hungry as the stingrays.

Chad puts a protective arm around me. "She's fine, folks. Please go back to enjoying your day." He snags a hoodie off a rack of ones for sale and passes it to me. "Here, it's on me."

"Thanks." I crane my neck, looking for the door. I have got to get out of here. Now.

A woman steps into my path, a little boy's hand clutched in her grasp. He wriggles against her hold, avoiding looking at me. "I'm so, so sorry. Tell her you're sorry, David."

He ducks his head into his mother's side.

"David." She gives him a shake.

I hold out a hand, skirt around them. "It's okay, really."

"Are you okay?" Another mother stops me, her children gathered like a flock behind her, gaping at me like I'm the best source of entertainment they've ever seen. In fact, they'll probably remember this moment for the rest of their lives.

Great.

Fabulous.

"I'm good." There's the door. I start speed walking.

"About that date..." Chad's hand stays at my back as he keeps up with me.

"Yeah, sure." Almost there, almost there.

A man steps into our path.

"I'm fine," I say before he can ask and dodge around him. Just a few more feet.

"Cool. Friday at seven?"

"Sounds great." I push against the door and step into the blessedly warm sunshine where the world and the other zoo goers have no idea of what's transpired. I whip the towel off my shoulders and start squishing my hair. Ugh, I smell like fish.

Chad stops beside me and digs a pen and paper out of his pocket and scribbles something out. "Here. Text me your address."

I blink at him. "My address?" What, so the zoo can mail me some kind of apology or something? Great. The last thing I need is some memento. I'm already going to replay this moment in my head for the next fifty years.

He pushes the paper into my hand. I accept it because it'll help me get out of here quicker. He jerks his thumb over his shoulder. "I better get back in there and help with the clean-up."

Right. I've probably traumatized everyone in the building, not to mention the stingrays. "Yeah, yeah, go. I'm good." I spin and march toward the parking lot, leaving Lou-Lou and Sam to catch up at their own pace.

"See you Friday."

Wait, what? I turn, but he's already entered the building.

Chapter 29

"You sure you're okay?" Sam pulls his gaze away from the road long enough to shoot a look my way.

I swipe the sleeve of my new hoodie under my nose. "I said I'm fine. Let's just forget it, okay?"

"Sure." Yet his tone remains heavy with worry.

Lou-Lou coughs. "Can someone please crack a window? Riley, you reek."

I'd like to argue, but I really have no grounds, so I roll down my window, letting fresh air waft through the car.

"Riley, I'm sorry," Sam murmurs.

A watery sheen attacks my eyes again and I turn my face to the side and watch trees sweep past in a blur.

It's a quiet drive back to the house.

I scramble for freedom the moment Sam puts the car into park.

"Riley, wait."

Can't he let this whole miserable day go? I march toward the front door.

"I've got your keys."

Oh. I spin. "Right. Thank you."

He approaches, eyes searching mine like there's a thousand things he wants to say.

I look away.

"I had a great time today. Before the stingrays anyway." He places the keys in my hand. His fingers linger.

I meet his gaze. "Yeah, me too." And then my lips twitch and I laugh. "I don't think you're ever going to talk me into going to the zoo again."

He steps back, shoving his hands into his pockets. "We'll see about that, Riley Anderson. You'll have a good experience someday. I promise."

Somehow, I believe him. But I'm going to have to wait a solid decade before I give him the chance to prove it.

Lou-Lou bounces over to my side and pinches her nose shut. "What's next on the list?"

Sam winces. "I have to make some calls tomorrow. Maybe we can do something Friday?"

Friday. Oh no. A prickling sensation shoots up my spine even as my stomach drops.

"You okay?" Sam squints at me. "You look kind of pale."

"It's that smell." Lou-Lou waves her hand in an attempt to clear the air.

"Guys, I think I agreed to go on a date with Chad on Friday."

"What?" Sam blinks.

"Chad?" Lou-Lou gasps.

I fumble for the piece of paper he gave me. And there in bold, blocky writing is his number. Gulp.

"Well, maybe Saturday we can go for a bike ride or catch a movie," Sam says.

"Yeah, sounds good." I tuck my limp hair behind my ear, because what else is there to do? Who even accidentally agrees to go on a date with someone in the first place?

"See ya." Sam offers a wave before cutting through the grass to get to his own house.

"See you," I whisper to his back. But why does it hurt to watch him go? Why is there a part of me longing to call him back?

"How could you agree to go out with *Chad*?" Lou-Lou jabs a finger at my nose.

I hold up my hands. "I didn't mean to."

"Sure. Whatever you say, *buddy*."

I plant my hands on my hips. "Look, Chad's not so bad. Maybe we'll even have fun." This could be for the best. Except my attention flicks to the yellow house next door in hopes of seeing one last glimpse of the boy who has disappeared inside. I shake myself and focus on Lou-Lou. "Maybe this is fate."

"Fate my toenail."

Now it's my turn to bop her on the nose with a finger. "Have an open mind."

She growls. "But what am I supposed to do while you're gone?"

"Hangout with Dad and Kenzie. You have more family members, you know."

"Whatever." She snatches the keys from my hand and unlocks the door. "I can't believe you're abandoning me."

"I am not abandoning you."

She kicks off her shoes and heads for the stairs. "I don't want to talk to you again until you've taken a shower and rethought your life choices."

I stick my tongue out at her back even as I kick the door shut.

Sarge springs up from his dog bed and greets me like it's been ten years instead of a few hours since we've seen each other. It's sugar and sweetness until he starts rapidly licking every inch of my exposed skin. I'm not sure if he's trying to eat me or help me clean up.

"Yeah, I guess a shower is a must." I dodge a swipe of his tongue and scamper up the stairs.

Maybe if I'm lucky, I'll stops smelling like fish before Chad picks me up on Friday.

Chapter 30

This Friday cannot get any worse.

I'll be there in 10.

I stare at Chad's text hoping it will somehow rearrange to say he has to cancel last minute. But it stays the same.

My own little dot bubble hovers on the screen. What do I say? I can't exactly tell him I've got a thundering headache I believe may be linked to stress. Not only did I have to plan an outfit that gives off the impression I'm ready for a fun night (but don't know if I want to make this a regular thing), but Kenzie picked up an extra shift at work last minute to cover for a coworker. I secretly suspect it's because Alex is working tonight. Throw in a last-minute business dinner Dad got himself into, and I'm stuck with Sarge who's whining in the bathroom where I've shut him so Chad can get in the door without being barked at, and a pouting Lou-Lou who sits on the edge of the bed.

Can't wait!

I regret it the moment I hit send. Sounds way too peppy. Like I've been counting down the minutes or something. Should have gone with *see you soon* and left off the exclamation mark.

"I cannot believe I have to go on this lame date with you and Chad. Even Aunt V totally flaked on me."

I don't think getting a cavity filled can be described as flaking, but I don't have time to argue the point. Besides, if Lou-Lou hadn't accidentally started a small fire on the stove the last time she was home alone, completely freaking her parents out, we wouldn't be in this mess. I whip on some mascara, go back and forth on a streak of lip gloss. Nah, that would make this feel too much like a *date*, date.

"Will you relax? It's going to be fun," I say it to convince myself as much as her.

"You're not the one stuck as a third wheel."

"Three can be fun. You don't complain when it's you, me, and Sam."

"That's different. That's *Sam*."

The doorbell rings and Sarge goes berserk even though there's no way he can actually get to the door. Well, unless he somehow figures out how to turn a doorknob or knock down said door.

I swivel to face Lou-Lou. "Keep an open mind. It's just for a few hours. You'll survive. And maybe you'll even start to like him."

"Fat chance of that."

"Open. Mind." I tap my temple.

She rolls her eyes. "Fine."

The doorbell rings again.

"Come on." I scamper down the stairs and pull the door open.

Chad stands there in khaki shorts and a button-down shirt, hair slicked back with mousse. "Hey."

"Hi." Am I too underdressed? I glance down at my t-shirt and denim shorts. But I put in earrings, curled my hair, and even did some makeup, so I can't be too bad, right?

"Chad." Lou-Lou approaches, arms crossed.

"Olive, right?" Chad nods in greeting.

Lou-Lou's expression totally asks if he's an idiot. "*Olivia*." She drags out each syllable.

"Right. Right." His focus zeros in on me. "You ready to go?"

"Uh, there's actually something I need to talk to you about." I shoot a look between him and Lou-Lou. "So, my dad and sister had some things come up last minute. Would you be cool if we brought Lou-Lou with us?"

"With us?" He motions between him and me like he hasn't heard right.

"I'll pay for her of course," I hurry to assure him.

He sweeps her with a scrutinizing gaze. "Sorry, but aren't you like ten? Can't you stay home by yourself?"

She narrows her eyes. "Twelve. And no, my parents aren't comfortable with that. Rules are rules." A wicked gleam lights her eyes like she's won some great victory.

I step in front of her. "Look, I'm really sorry about this. Everything was last minute and by the time I found out, you were already on your way. If it's a problem, we can reschedule."

"No. No, it's not a problem." Is his smile a tad too tight?

Lou-Lou slips her arm through mine. "Great. Let's get this party started."

Chapter 31

Chad drives us to a classy pizzeria and I have to admit, for a first date, he's got good taste. A hostess seats us at a round table near a window and an overhead chandelier adds a glowing ambiance.

I ease back in my chair and blow out a breath.

Not bad.

Like I told Lou-Lou, I just need to have an open mind.

A waitress comes over. "What can I get you to drink?"

"Sorry, could you speak up?" Chad waves a hand near his ear. "I can't really hear you."

The girl's cheeks turn pink. "What can I get you to drink?"

Chad and I each order a soda.

Lou-Lou folds her hands over the table and opens her mouth to speak, but Chad cuts in before she can, "She'll have an apple juice or something from the kid's menu, right?" He laughs and winks.

Lou-Lou pushes her glasses higher up her nose. "*Actually*, I'd prefer a glass of sweet tea."

"Gotcha." The waitress jots down her order. "I'll give you some time to look over the menu and I'll be right back with your drinks."

"Thank you," I say before excusing myself to use the bathroom.

When I return, Lou-Lou is tapping her fingernails against the table while Chad scrolls through his phone. He tucks the device away when I approach. "I hope you don't mind, but I went ahead and ordered."

"Oh." I slide into my chair. "That's fine." I guess...I rub my hands down my legs and shift to unstick my thighs from the chair. *Help me to have an open mind, Lord.*

"Riley," Lou-Lou hisses out the side of her mouth.

"What?"

"He—"

"Here we go." The waitress arrives with a wide circular pan balanced on her arm. She slides the pizza into the middle of the table and my stomach tightens. "Enjoy."

Chad rubs his hands together. "I hope you like Hawaiian. It's my favorite."

I stare at the yellow chunks of fruit sprinkled over the cheesy pizza. I should say something. My gaze flicks to Chad. He's grinning as he lifts one of the slices and slides it onto my plate. He's so excited. I can't crush that. One slice. And then I can crawl off to die in the bathroom or something so I don't have to go through the embarrassment of him calling an ambulance.

"Riley," Lou-Lou grinds out my name.

"Dig in." Chad takes a generous bite of his piece.

Sweat dampens my palms and I swear I'm going to break out in hives just thinking about putting one of those in my mouth.

"Um, actually, Chad..." my voice warbles and I have to clear my throat. "I'm allergic to pineapple."

He blinks. Lowers his pizza. "You're allergic. To pineapple."

"She told you that at the park, remember?" Lou-Lou splays a hand across her chest. "*I* tried to tell you."

Chad's brow furrows. "I guess I thought you meant like a personal preference or something."

Because that's the definition of allergic. *Help me, Lord. Grace and mercy.* "Yeah, no. I break out in hives and my throat swells up."

"You know, *allergic.*" Lou-Lou smiles, all false sweetness and sugar.

"Bummer. I'm sorry about that, Ri-boo. My bad. You can pick it off, right?" Chad's already back to munching on his own pizza.

I lick my lips. How I wish I could say yes and smooth things over. Instead, I squirm in my seat. "Well, the juice has already soaked into—"

"She needs a new pizza." Lou-Lou glares at him. "If you had listened to me—"

"Consider it done." Chad snaps his fingers at the waitress. "Hey, could we get some help over here?"

She comes over, smile tight. "How can I help?"

"Could we get a personal sized cheese pizza? And we need a new plate."

"Please," I add. "If it's not too much trouble." I bite back my request for a veggie pizza instead, noting the girl's patience is already wearing thin.

"Sure thing."

Chad chomps down on a second piece of pizza.

"Thank you," I attempt to push as much kindness into the words as possible.

She nods and heads off.

"It's a shame, Ri-boo. This is really good pizza." Chad swipes a napkin over his lips.

Lou-Lou snags her own slice and takes a bite. "Yeah, it's not ba—"

"So, about that guy you're always hanging out with, who is he anyway?"

"Sam?" I take a sip of my soda.

The waitress returns and slides a fresh plate and cheese pizza in front of me. "Here we—"

"Yeah, that guy." Chad crumples his napkin. "There's something familiar about him, I just can't put my finger on what."

"Thank you so much," I say to the waitress.

She nods and hurries to check on her other tables.

"Sam's a friend." I bite into the pizza and let the cheesy goodness saturate my taste buds.

"A *good* friend," Lou-Lou adds.

"From childhood." Why on earth do I feel the need to explain?

"Right, right. Gotcha. Hey, did I tell you about that time Lukas and I—"

Lou-Lou slurps the dregs of her tea nice and loud as if to inform us her plate of pizza is long devoured and she's ready to go. Except Chad is currently diving into a story from his last football game and it would be rude to interrupt. Even if this is the tenth time he's taken us through one of his glorious victories.

I shift on my own chair, booty aching from too long in the seat. I nibble on a piece of crust more to give myself something to do than out of any real hunger. With my free hand, I doodle on my napkin with a crayon some kid lost under the table. Under careful strokes, the waitress's face begins to form. Not bad, although I'm remembering why I like my tablet best. Going old-school requires more attention to detail and a steady hand because there's no erase button within reach.

"And so, I had to bring him down, right? I don't think I've ever run so hard in my entire life." Chad animates the story with big hand motions.

"Mhmm." Probably not a good time to admit I know next to nothing about football.

Lou-Lou kicks me under the table.

I yelp and jump, slamming my knee into the wood, making the entire thing tremble. Glassware shakes.

Chad breaks off mid-story. "You okay, Ri-boo?"

"Fine." I rub my knee and glare at Lou-Lou. Classy, cuz.

"Anyway, there I was—"

Lou-Lou fakes a yawn and gives a big stretch. "Whoa, this has been *so* much fun, but I am wiped out. Must be close to my bedtime."

Chad checks his phone. "It's only eight-thirty."

Only?

Lou-Lou and I share a look.

I clamp my teeth together, stifling the groan threatening to emerge.

"You know my parents are real sticklers for bedtime. They are strict." Lou-Lou leans across the table.

If you can count being in bed by midnight strict. Now I kick her under the table.

"Don't worry, I won't tell if you don't." Chad winks at her.

Her hand balls into a fist on her lap.

"We probably should get going, they'll be closing soon." My attention flicks to the corner where our waitress wipes down the last table with an eye aimed at us.

"Ah, don't worry about it. The customer is always right, am I right?" Chad winks again.

I press my lips tight.

"As I was saying—" The buzz of his own phone cuts him off this time. Chad swipes it from his pocket. "Sweet. Jonathan and Lukas are throwing a party. We should go."

"Um, hello?" Lou-Lou waves.

"Chad, I don't think that would be appropriate for a twelve-year-old." I shift my weight on the seat. "And I'm not exactly a party-goer myself."

Chad points his phone at Lou-Lou. "Easy. We'll drop her off at your house and we'll be good to go."

"Drop her off?" Are my ears full of cotton or what am I missing?

"Excuse me?" Lou-Lou scoffs.

"You don't expect us to babysit all night, do you? Besides if she climbs into bed like a good girl, no one will even know. If she's sleeping she can't get hurt, so she doesn't need a babysitter."

I inhale deeply. "Chad—"

"No, no, I have it all planned out. Everything will be fine, and besides, I'm sure your dad will be home soon. I mean old people go to bed at nine, right?"

Did he call my dad old? My ears burn hot and my heart pounds too fast in my chest. "Actually, Chad. I think I'm ready to go home."

He gestures to his phone. "But the party—"

"Please, Chad," I grind out the words and try to smile through them. Hopefully, it doesn't come off as a grimace. My cheeks ache from the effort of faking it.

"Aw come on, you can't actually expect me to go alone? All the other guys will have their girls there."

Their girls? One corner of my mouth twitches and I strain to keep my smile in place. "Thanks for a lovely evening, but—"

He huffs, throwing up his hands. "I can't believe you're doing this to me."

Lou-Lou slaps her hand against the table. "Listen *buddy*, Riley says she wants to go home. So, let's get going."

Chad snaps his fingers in front of her face, shutting her down. "You know, I've had about enough of you."

"Don't talk to her like that," I say.

He turns on me. "Don't you think someone should have taught her some manners?"

"Check please," I say the words way too forcefully, but the waitress trots over anyway.

"Here you are." Her gaze searches mine like she's trying to figure out if I'm all right.

"Fine." Chad's face goes hard and he reaches for his wallet. "Home we go." And then he searches one pocket. Then the other. "Aw, man. I hate to do this, Ri-boo, but I forgot my wallet." His cheeks turn pink.

"Of course, you did." Lou-Lou rolls her eyes and crosses her arms.

"Yeah, it's fine." I pull my own small purse from my pocket and lay out enough bills to cover our meal plus a generous tip. I lay the doodled napkin on top of it all with a 'thank you' written across the top.

"I am sorry, Ri-boo—"

"Don't call me that." I snap the check holder closed and shove my purse into my pocket. "I should have said something to you long ago. I'm sorry I didn't, but I hate that nickname. My name is Riley. R-i-l-e-y."

"Wow." Chad blinks at me.

I pinch the bridge of my nose. "Like I said, I should have said something sooner."

His jaw goes tight. "Yeah, you should have. Listen, we should get going or we're going to be late." He places a hand at the small of my back.

I wriggle away from his touch. "Late for what?"

"For the party. We still have to drop off the squirt and—"

"Lou-Lou. Her name is Lou-Lou. And there's no we, Chad. I'm not going to a party." Tears burn my eyes and I blink quickly. I will *not* cry in front of him.

"Oh, for crying out loud, Riley." He looms closer. "Can we please not do this here? So, I got a few names wrong, big deal."

I shrink in on myself.

"Let's go." He makes a grab for my am.

"Don't." I jerk away and his fingers graze my skin.

"You're being overdramatic. Let's go."

"No." I step back and almost collide with Lou-Lou. "Go ahead. Don't let us stop you."

He huffs. "I don't have time for this."

"Then go." I wave a hand toward the exit.

His nostrils flare. "Fine. If that's what you want." He storms out.

I stand there, shaking as heat surges through my body and those ridiculous tears burn hotter.

"Um, Riley?" Lou-Lou tugs on my arm. "As ecstatic as I am about what you just did, you do realize we're stranded here without a ride and they're about to close?"

Oh. Right. Those tears leak down my cheeks. "Come on." I pull her outside in time to watch Chad speed out of the parking lot. Fine. I didn't come out here to beg him for a ride anyway. I'd rather walk all the way home. Instead, I pull my phone from my pocket and dial one of the few numbers I know by heart.

"Riley?"

"Sam." I dab the back of my hand against my nose. "Can you come get me?"

Chapter 32

After fifteen minutes, Sam's sports car rolls into the parking lot. I lower my phone even as I watch Sam hang up his through the windshield. By now, he's more or less got the gist of the evening if he understood me at all through my tears.

"Sam." Lou-Lou springs up from her cross-legged position on the sidewalk.

He stops the car and steps out. Before I know it, his arms are around me, squeezing hard. I wrap my arms around him and lay my head on his chest.

"Did he hurt you, Ri?"

"No. I'm fine. It was just an awful evening."

His arms tighten. "Let's get you home."

I step away and swipe at my tears. "Thank you for coming."

He reaches out and catches a tear with his thumb. "Anytime, Riley."

There's so much safety in knowing he means it.

Thank you, Lord, for Sam.

"You girls okay?" The waitress steps out, keys in hand. I have a feeling she's been delaying locking up for our sake.

"Yeah, our ride is here."

She waves and heads to her car. "Have a good night."

"You too." I sniffle and dab at my nose again.

Sam wraps an arm around my shoulders and then tucks Lou-Lou under his other arm and ushers us toward the car. "Let's get you girls home."

We pile into his car and soon we're pulling into the sanctuary of our driveway. A light is on in the kitchen, signaling either Kenzie or Dad has come home.

I unbuckle and turn in my seat to face Sam. "Thank you. Really."

He reaches across the console and takes my hand. "I mean it. Anytime. I'm just sorry your night was so bad." His thumb brushes across my knuckles.

A shiver sweeps through me and for the first time I wonder what it would be like to not pull away. To instead lean across the console and brush my lips against his. To give him a kiss goodnight and call him 'my Sam' out loud.

And then Lou-Lou's foot bumps against my seat as she makes her exit.

I slip my fingers free from Sam's but something makes me linger. "Are you free tomorrow?"

He drapes a lazy arm over the steering wheel. "I could be." His lips twitch and his eyes dance in the light cast from the motion sensor light which goes off as Lou-Lou trudges to the front door.

"How about that bike ride?" My heart races as I wait for his answer. It shouldn't matter. It's just another item on our list. Except I don't want him to be busy.

"All right." His dimple makes an appearance. "What time?"

"Ten? Before it gets too hot?"

"I'll be there."

"Riley, let's go," Lou-Lou hollers from the front step.

"See you tomorrow." I slide out of the car, push the door closed, and then walk backward toward the front porch.

Sam backs out and seconds later pulls into his own garage.

"Hello, earth to Riley." Lou-Lou waves her hand in front of my face. "Man, I think you have hearts popping out of your eyes."

Heat burns my ears and cheeks. I cross my arms and scoff. "No."

She cocks an eyebrow.

"What would you know?"

"I may be young, but I am far from oblivious."

The last thing I need right now is to lecture her about all the reasons why Sam and I are an impossible illusion, but I can't risk her even teasing him about the idea. "Look, Lou-Lou—"

The door swings open. "Hey, girls, I thought I heard you pull in." Dad stands there in slacks and a dress shirt, tie slung haphazardly over one shoulder. He must have just arrived or he'd be in sweats by now. He squints at the driveway. "Did Chad leave? I was hoping to meet him."

I step inside and wrap my arms around my middle. "No worries. Chad, um...won't be coming again."

Dad's eyebrows arch. "Is everything okay?"

"Yeah, fine."

He squints. "You look like you've been crying."

"It's just—"

"Chad is the biggest jerk in the world of jerks. Like, he's the definition of jerk." Lou-Lou slams the door shut and locks it like it'll erase the whole night from our memories. She swivels for the stairs. "Now if you'll excuse me, I find myself much in need of pampering." A few moments later the sound of rattling drawers suggests she's raiding Kenzie's supply of face masks.

Dad's focus stays locked on me, reading with a look how awful the date went. "I'll put some tea water on."

A pang cuts through my middle. With Sam's return home, we haven't had our late-night tea party in pretty much forever. "Yeah, I'd like that," I say. "I'm going to shower really quick."

"Sure thing. Caramel?"

"Always."

I hurry up the stairs and shower, scrubbing like mad in hopes it might wash away my entire date with Chad. Unfortunately, life doesn't work that way, but I still feel cleaner when I slip into my pajamas and wrap my hair in a towel.

Dad waits for me on the couch with two steaming mugs of caramel tea with just the right amount of sugar.

"Tell your old man about it." He mutes the news playing on the tv.

So, I do. Everything from Chad picking me up, to the pineapple pizza, to having to pay.

Dad nods along. "Are you okay?"

"Yeah." I run my finger around the rim of my mug. "I didn't even *like* like Chad anyway. And Sam came, so it all worked out."

"Sam." Another deep nod.

"Dad." I draw out his name, begging him not to continue that train of thought. Because I'm not ready to go there myself. What does life look like if I like Sam Hong? Worse, what will I do if he doesn't feel the same way?

"Okay, we won't talk about Sam." He fixes me with a no-non-sense gaze. "But we can. Anytime you want."

"Thanks. I appreciate that." I'm not ready to pour out my heart when I'm not sure I'm ready to face what I'll find.

"Well, if we're not going to talk about Sam, I think we should talk about Vanessa." Dad adjusts his weight on the couch and starts fiddling with the handle of his mug.

Oh. I'm not sure this is a conversation I want to have either. "Vanessa?" Hopefully my voice doesn't sound as strangled to him as it does to me.

He heaves a sigh. "I never thought I'd be having this conversation with you."

That makes two of us.

"Dad." I don't know how to follow that up, but it's clear he's struggling. I will be strong. I will accept whatever he says next. *Help me, help me, help me.* I dart a glance toward a picture of Mom sitting on the mantel. She'd want him to be happy. For all of us to be happy.

Dad meets my eyes. "For the business dinner, I was invited to bring a plus one. I asked Vanessa to go with me."

He was on a date of his own tonight? "Oh?" I try not to sound hurt or think about how Vanessa lied about getting a cavity filled in. But I wouldn't exactly want to confess to Lou-Lou that I was on the date she's been dreaming of her whole life either. There's no way those beans would go un-spilled.

"I've been praying about it, and it seemed like the right time, but I didn't want to make a big deal about it. That's why I didn't say anything, and you know Lou-Lou..."

True. If she'd gotten wind of a date between her favorite uncle and aunt, she would have the wedding planned before Dad even got out the door. "I get it." I do. I really do.

"Vanessa and I had a lot of fun chatting the other night at the barbecue."

Why did I ever put that on the list? Why did I let Lou-Lou talk me into inviting her? Nope. I'm a big girl. I can handle this. *Please, God. Help me to handle it.* I clench my jaw, ready for him to spit out whatever's coming next.

"And we had a lot of fun tonight."

Ouch. There it is.

His gaze gets even more serious. "I don't need your permission or your blessing, Riley, but I would like it."

"To," *gulp,* "date her?"

He nods.

I force myself to take a deep breath. Dating her isn't the same thing as a marriage proposal. And even if it leads to that, Kenzie and I aren't going to be here forever. Do I want my dad to be alone?

"Talk to me, kiddo."

I take a sip of my tea. A delaying tactic as I struggle to find the right words. "That's great, Dad. Really great."

He expels a deep breath and for the first time I wonder if maybe this conversation is as hard on him as it is on me. "Thank you, Riley. I appreciate it."

I smile to keep from crying. "Mom would be happy."

He grins, slow and weighed with remembrance. "She and Vanessa always did get along."

"That's awesome."

He shifts. "Riley, about Sam..."

No, no, no. I can't take another serious conversation. I open my mouth to ward him off, but Dad beats me to it.

"Will you invite him to dinner tomorrow?"

I blink. Recalibrate. "Tomorrow? Dinner?"

"Seems like it's been a while, and the kid needs to eat."

"Sure. Yeah, I'll do that."

"Good."

My attention snags on the tv and the image of a pink haired Sam splayed across the screen.

"Dad, turn the sound on." By the time I get the words out, he's already unmuted the sound system.

"So, where is Sammy Hong?" The news anchor lays the drama on thick. "It's a question many of us have been pondering for a few weeks, but tonight, we might have our answer. A fan claims to have seen Sammy Hong at a local zoo."

The image on the screen changes to a grainy picture of Sam at the zoo. He's got his sunglasses on and he's looking over his shoulder. He could be anyone if I hadn't seen the outfit he wore that day. Anyone except for that dimple as he grins at me off screen.

"Oh, Sam," I breathe.

The story cuts to the news anchor. "Sammy Hong's manager refuses to confirm whether or not Sammy Hong has returned to his hometown."

They throw up a few recent photos of Sam living the Hollywood life, paparazzi spread thick on either side of the street.

"Meanwhile, Sammy Hong's fans continue to show their support."

Posts with *#webelieveinSammyHong* and *#weloveSammyHong* scroll across a social media feed. A group of girls picket outside Sam's record label with signs proclaiming their undying love for my childhood friend. There are even photos of a pair of girls arrested for breaking a window of his manager's house and sending death threats to her. Apparently, they've found her silence distasteful.

"So, where is Sammy Hong? We hope to know soon." The news anchor delivers it like a grim death sentence.

I snag the remote and switch everything off.

"You okay?" Dad sets his tea aside.

I'm breathing hard and fast. Why is it that just when I start to see Sam as the boy I grew up with, reminders like this come flying in my face. Because this is what a relationship with Sam would mean. Broken windows and death threats. Not an ounce of privacy.

"Talk to me."

Hot liquid burns my eyes. "I think," my voice breaks. "I think I'm in love with Sam."

Chapter 33

Dad wraps an arm around my shoulders. "And that's a bad thing?"

"I don't want that." I fling a hand toward the tv. "Death threats? And this town is going to be crawling with paparazzi by morning. I don't want to have to look over my shoulder for the rest of my life."

He nods. "I don't want that for you either."

"Then what do I do?"

"Think about it. Pray. Give it some time. For now, focus on being Sam's friend, especially as he rides this whole thing out."

"And if I want to be more than his friend?"

He squeezes my shoulders. "It's not an easy life, for you or Sam. But I think it would only be fair to be honest about your feelings. Both with yourself and Sam. If that's what you decide you want."

"I don't know." I drop my head into my hands.

"You don't have to decide right now. Riley, you're seventeen. You've got time. I just don't want you to make a decision you regret."

"You think I'll regret becoming part of that?" I wave my hand at the tv.

"That, or you might regret it if you let Sam walk away."

I wake with the sunrise and tiptoe out onto the deck with my Bible and journal.

Lord, I don't even know how I feel or what to do...

It's all so much.

Lead me. Guide me. Grant me your wisdom.

By the time the sun begins to heat the world, I have peace. Not a decision, but peace, and it's a good place to start.

The sliding door yanks open behind me. "Come on, Riley. Sam's going to be here in an hour."

We fix a couple smoothies and I sneak some kale in when Lou-Lou isn't looking. She slurps hers so fast it's a wonder she doesn't get a brain freeze. With breakfast out of the way, she plants herself at the window while I clean up.

Sarge watches from a puddle of self-pity on the floor. How he knows we're leaving even though we've yet to get our shoes on is beyond me.

I kneel and scratch under his chin. "Trust me, baby, this is not your idea of fun."

He huffs in disagreement.

"Here he comes." Lou-Lou squeals, springing away from the window and tripping as she scrambles to get her shoes on.

I give Sarge one last pat before hurrying over to stuff my feet in my own sneakers.

Lou-Lou yanks the door open. "Riley, let's go."

"Coming." I hurry outside.

Sam waits for us, wearing a lazy smile.

Has he even seen the news? I take a deep breath and remind myself the people in this neighborhood under the age of retirement are few and far between. Plus, it's Friday. And early. Most of the not retired neighbors will be at work. As long as we keep a low profile, everything should be fine.

"Hey."

"Hi." I push my glasses up, jitters awakening in my stomach. Oh, no. I need to play it cool. There's no need to spoil our friendship with a schoolgirl crush unless I'm absolutely sure it's what I want. For now, it's best to be just friends. At least until everything with Sam's disappearance has resolved.

"Well don't stand there, let's get the bikes out." Lou-Lou's voice drips with the biggest implied *duh* ever.

Right. I tear my gaze away from Sam and open the garage door. After a bit of shuffling through junk, we manage to unearth our bikes and three dusty helmets. Soon, we're on our way. Lou-Lou takes off on my old bike which is a tad undersized and still boasts sparkly streamers and a spare seat for a doll.

Sam rides my dad's bike and I take Kenzie's baby blue one. We follow behind Lou-Lou at a more sedate pace. I worry my bottom lip as we work our way through the streets. Should I bring up the news? Like is he going to be in danger now that everyone knows or at least suspects where he is? Cheese and crackers, what if paparazzi line the bushes as we speak?

But he's got his face tilted toward the sun, grinning like a kid, and I can't bring myself to say anything. Not now anyway. I throw my head back as we glide down a hill, letting the breeze play with the ends of my hair beneath my helmet.

Sam pulls up alongside me. "We should have done this sooner." He lets go of the handlebar, showing off as he balances with no hands.

"It really is the simple things in life, isn't it?"

"Yeah." He slows, grabbing the bars once more. "The older I get, the more I appreciate that."

It's not something I've thought much about until he showed up, but experiencing this summer through Sam's eyes truly has shown me how to appreciate the little things. A night under the stars, a homemade popsicle, a bike ride. *I'm sorry for taking it for granted, Lord. Thank you for opening my eyes to the simple things.*

Sam twists his hands around his bike handle. "Riley…"

Uh-oh. There's a weight to his voice. "What?"

"Did you…" he trails off. Looks away.

"Did I what?" I pull to a stop and plant one foot, giving him my full attention.

He stills and fixes me with a weary gaze. "Did you watch the news last night?"

"Yeah." I eye him. "What are you going to do?"

"I got a call this morning." His attention locks on the blacktop. "My lawyer has set up a meeting with my label. My bodyguard is on his way, same with my manager. They're coming to escort me back. Word is they've hired on a writer to help with the album."

"Oh, Sam." I touch his arm, his skin warm from the sun.

"I—" He swallows. "I'd like to go see my family before they get here."

For a moment I'm speechless. But I have to say something. "Wow. That's…that's great."

His shoulders slump.

"It's not great?"

"Ri, there's something I need to tell you."

I catch a flyaway and push it under my helmet. "Shoot."

"They're not the ones who cut things off, Ri. I stopped seeing them."

My breath catches. "But you—" but all this time I thought they were too busy to see their only son.

Sam shakes his head. "I got so busy, so wrapped up in my career, in myself, that I lost sight of what's important. My family. You. After a while, it was easier to stay away and Hannah was just a kid. My sister deserved a childhood. And then there was security to deal with."

I squeeze his arm. "I never blamed you for losing contact." His career maybe. But never him personally.

"But I should have stayed in contact. With you. With them. Now it's too late."

I lean forward, catching his gaze. Our foreheads are mere inches apart. "It's never too late, Sam. Not for family, not for me."

"Will you go with me?" His dark eyes search mine.

"Are you sure you want me there?"

"Please?"

"I'd love to." I don't even hesitate. Because suddenly I get the feeling he could ask me to go anywhere. Do anything. And I would say yes.

"Yeah?" He's beaming.

"Yeah." My attention flicks to his lips. It would be easy to lean forward...

"Come on, slow pokes," Lou-Lou hollers from several yards ahead of us.

Sam laughs and kicks off, speeding after her.

I follow at a more sedate pace, giving my crazy heart time to calm down. And then I catch sight of Sam. He's drawn even with Lou-Lou and he's looking back at me, dimple popping out. My pulse races all over again.

Cheese and crackers.

It's official.

I've fallen for Sammy Hong.

Chapter 34

"I can't believe we have to hide in our own house," Lou-Lou grumbles.

"Trust me, this is much better than having to outrun the paparazzi." Besides, there's no way we can get to a movie theater now. Not with Sam's location disclosed. I stretch on my tiptoes as I balance on an ottoman, hanging a blanket over the window, darkening the room.

Sam enters the living room with a bowl of popcorn. "Improvising is good for you, minion."

Lou-Lou flops onto the couch. "Fine. But know I'm holding you responsible for this." She juts a finger at Sam.

"Sorry, minion. I'll try to be anonymous next time."

I hop down from the ottoman and join them on the couch. Try to smile and pretend like nothing is wrong as I snatch a handful of popcorn. But all I can think of as I settle in beside Sam is there won't be a next time. Not like this anyway. Sure, he might be able to come visit, but he won't be allowed to disappear twice. Next time he'll come as Sammy Hong, not my Sam.

But that's a worry for another day.

Help me to focus on the here and the now and soak in every moment You give us, please Lord.

We may not be able to conjure fireworks, but we can finish this ninth item on the list before Sam goes.

It'll have to be enough.

Sam moans as he shovels in another bite of food. "Oh, Kenzie. I didn't realize how much I missed your honey chili chicken."

"Well, there's plenty more, so eat up." My sister passes the chicken bowl his way.

Sam's knee brushes against mine as he shifts to accept. Sparks shoot through my veins.

"Riley, I love you!" Sam shouts, hearts popping out of his eyes. He snags the flowers from the center piece, gets down on one knee and says, "Riley, will you marry me? Be mine forever. You're the love of my life. Oh, Riley. You are my one and true muse."

I gasp. Place a trembling hand over my mouth.

Lou-Lou bawls. "I've been dreaming of this moment my entire life."

Sam snags my hand. Slips a ring on my finger. "Oh, Riley, baby..."

"Wow, earth to Riley." Kenzie's voice snaps me out of the daydream.

"Huh?" I blink the world into focus and find Sam plus my entire family staring at me. Cheese and crackers! Sheep cheese! Toenail fungus! Heat blasts through my face. "What did you say?"

Dad raises his eyebrows. "I asked if you've gotten any new commissions lately."

Commissions…I gulp a drink of water and nod as a delaying tactic. Come up for air and swipe the back of my hand against my mouth. "Yeah, I was hired to design a logo for this lady who's going to start her own bakery."

"That's great." He smiles graciously.

Lou-Lou squints at me. "Are you okay? You're acting weird."

"Fine. Totally fine." I shove a huge forkful of rice into my mouth and chew like there's no tomorrow so they won't ask anything else.

Sam places his hand on my knee. "Seriously, what were you thinking about?"

Choke. Sputter. Another gulp of water. "That's none of your bison or your biscuits."

"What?"

Oh. Right. I laugh. "Sorry. Lou-Lou and I made it up. It means not your business."

He sits back, pulling his hand away from my knee. "Not your bison or your biscuits? I like it. You know, I think I'm going to use it from now on."

"It's nonsense." I shake my head.

"Hey, watch it missy." Lou-Lou points a finger at me. "Don't disrespect our secret code."

"Sorry, sorry." I hold up my hands.

"When will you guys head out?" Dad asks.

I glance at Sam who filled Dad in on our plans to visit his parents. It's a three hour drive each way since they've stationed themselves in a countryside estate. The gated kind where you have to give notice to visit. I wonder if Sam's told them we're coming.

"Nine?" Sam shoots a questioning glance my way.

"Sounds goo—"

"I can't believe I don't get to go." Lou-Lou slumps in her seat.

Kenzie pokes her. "You and Vanessa are going to have tons of fun. Besides, if you ask me, a spa day is better than six hours in the car."

"I guess." But Lou-Lou's eye roll suggests she's unconvinced.

Now it's my turn to nudge her under the table. "Come on, Lou-Lou. You'll be so busy you won't even notice. You might even have so much fun you won't want to come home."

She crosses her arms. "Keep leaving me out of things and I won't."

Unfair considering she bounced up and down this afternoon when Vanessa called to set the aunt-niece date. But, she's not in the mood to be reasoned with, so I stick out my tongue, letting the action do the talking for me.

She cranes her nose in the air and turns her attention on Kenzie. "You could at least let me come on your date with Alex."

"I'd love to take you, but we're having dinner with his parents."

"Riley let me go on her date with Chad."

"And look how well that turned out." My sister laughs.

Lou-Lou pooches out her bottom lip. "I never get to have any fun."

Dad chuckles. "We'll have a movie night or something. If you behave, I might even let you pick the movie."

"Yes." Lou-Lou pumps a fist and straightens up.

She's lucky we all love her so much.

We finish up and all help clean the table. Dad washes dishes, Lou-Lou loads the dishwasher, and the three of us dry the rest.

I walk Sam to the door once the clean-up is finished.

"I'll see you in the morning." He walks backward down the driveway, hands in his pockets.

My heart stutters. I wrap my arms around my middle and lean against the doorjamb. "See you."

His dimple pops. And he keeps walking backward, gaze locked on me.

My pulse races. Does he somehow sense things have shifted? "Turn around before you trip."

"Yes, ma'am." He salutes and spins on his heel.

I watch him go.

At the end of the driveway, he looks back.

"Goodnight," I call and push the door shut.

"Wake up you lazy sack of potatoes." Lou-Lou whacks me over the head with her pillow.

"Lou-Lou." I groan and push her away with my elbow.

She starts pushing on my legs, rocking me back and forth. "You have to get up. It's eight-thirty."

Eight-thirty? Cheese and crackers! "Why didn't you say so?" I throw off the comforter and scramble out of bed, slapping around on my nightstand until I find my glasses.

"Uh, I tried? I've been trying to wake you up for the past five minutes."

Fabulous. At this rate, I'm going to have to make my coffee to-go. I scramble to my closet and snag a clean t-shirt and shorts. Next, it's a race to the bathroom where I scrub my teeth in a desperate attempt to rid myself of any morning breath. A shower is in order, so I jump in without even waiting for the water to heat.

Fifteen minutes later, I'm dressed, hair blown somewhat dry, and gulping a bowl of cereal. I shoot a text off to my dad who left bright and early for the grocery store, telling him I love him and to have a good day. It's a habit I started after my mom died. Anytime I'm gone longer than a few hours, I want to make sure we've said goodbye.

Lou-Lou watches me with an expression I can only describe as pity.

"What?" I ask around a mouthful of cereal.

She holds up her phone and wiggles it in front of my face. "You know these little pocket devices? Yeah, well most of them come with a handy little alarm that gets you up in the morning. You can even customize that time to fit your schedule."

"Thanks for the tutorial, smarty." I push her hand away. "I'm doing fine, aren't I?"

She extends a napkin. "You might want to wipe the milk off your chin."

I obey, cringing at the flake of cereal I swipe off. Great. Way to make a first impression. Yay, Riley. Except it's the millionth impression. And see? This is why I swore I'd never fall in love with Sam in the first place. I can't take the pressure. I smash the jittery butterflies of attraction in my stomach. Nope. I'm not doing this. Today, I will simply be Sam's friend. Nothing more, nothing less.

"What's wrong?"

I blink. "Nothing."

Lou-Lou cocks her head to the side. "You sure? You kind of got this warrior woman look on your face."

I change to the most dull and placid expression I can muster. "Nothing's wrong. Just thinking."

"Well, stop thinking about whatever you're thinking about, or you'll scare Sam off."

How little she knows... "Thanks for the tip." I lift my bowl and guzzle the last of my cereal.

"Ew, Riley, that's disgusting. Have some manners." My cousin wrinkles her nose.

"Manners have to take a backseat when there's a time crunch."

"That's not what your Aunt Auggie says." Lou-Lou extends her pinky and lifts her nose in the air. "'Manners must never be forgotten under any circumstances.'"

"Well, Aunt Augustine isn't here."

The doorbell rings.

"Nope, but Sam is and you don't want him thinking you're some kind of cavewoman." Lou-Lou scrambles from her chair.

"Too late. He's the one I used to have burping contests with."

"Ew!"

I laugh and nudge Sarge aside so I can answer the door.

Sam squats to greet the drooling welcome committee. "Hey, buddy. How you doing?"

Is there anything more heart melting than watching a guy love on your dog? Wait, nope. Nope, not doing it.

"You ready?" Sam looks up at me.

"Yeah." I glance at Lou-Lou. "You're good, right?"

"Kenzie's upstairs and Aunt V should be here soon. I'm fine."

"All right, have fun with your aunt and try not to let her spoil you too much." I sling an arm around her shoulders and give her a squeeze goodbye.

She sighs and looks to Sam. "Will you please get this clingy girl out of the house?"

He laughs and touches a hand to my lower back. "You heard her, let's go."

"Wait." Lou-Lou shoves my tablet and stylus at me. "You have that bakery logo due on Monday."

Right. I've been so distracted with all things Sam, I forgot. "Who needs a calendar when I have you?"

"If you're feeling so grateful, you might consider making it a paid position."

"In your dreams."

Sam laughs. "See you later, minion."

Chapter 35

S am pulls into the drive-thru of *Ducky's*, a favorite mom-and-pop coffee place among locals.

I glance up from my tablet. "What are we doing here?"

"Grabbing drinks for the ride. Want anything?"

"No, I'm okay." In fact, I'm in the zone. I tap and pinch the drawing on my screen, zooming in and then out as I touch up the details. My best work yet? Maybe. Everything is a blur of brush strokes as Sam maneuvers through the line and places his order.

Sam pulls up to the window and accepts his drink. Only it's two cups he positions in the cup holders. One a vanilla iced coffee, the other a caramel macchiato with extra whipped cream and caramel drizzles. My go-to.

"Sam, you shouldn't have."

"Aw, come on. It's the least I could do. You agreed to come with me after all."

"It's my pleasure. But really, thank you." I reach for the drink and take a long sip. Mmm. Perfection.

Sam turns out of the parking lot and onto the road. I switch on the radio, and tap my foot along to the music as we cruise toward our destination.

My palms turn slick as we turn off the country road and glide up the first quarter of Sam's parents' driveway. The car rolls to a stop when we reach a looming black gate set into a stone blockade.

Okay, maybe not a blockade, but intimidating none-the-less.

Sam rolls down his window and reaches for the intercom.

"Yes?" A voice crackles through the speaker.

"Can you please tell Mr. and Mrs. Hong that their son is here to see them?" His posture goes tight as he waits for a response.

"Right away." With a sharp buzz, the gate slides open.

Sam looks to me.

I stare back. "You ready for this?"

He rolls his shoulders. "I guess."

I lay a hand on his arm. "They're your parents. They'll be happy to see you."

"Let's hope so." He rolls the car forward and the gate sweeps closed behind us.

I clasp my hands between my knees. *Oh, Lord, please let this go well.*

After a half mile of driveway and tall pines lining either side, a sprawling estate comes into view. The car brakes squeak as we come to a stop in front of the tiered steps.

"Wow." I knew Sam was rich. There were plenty of magazines to tell me as much, not to mention the car I'm sitting in. But something about seeing the house he gifted his parents makes the idea settle in my mind.

Sam runs his hands down the steering wheel.

I catch one of his hands and wrap my fingers through his. Squeeze. "It's all going to be fine. Maybe Hannah will even be home."

"Maybe." His exhale is shaky.

Give him peace. "I'll be with you the whole time."

"Thanks for coming with me, Riley."

I swallow under the intensity of his gaze. Smile. "Anytime." I hope he knows how much I mean it.

He runs his hands down his dark jeans. "All right, let's do this." He pushes his car door open and I follow his example after stuffing my tablet in the glove box.

The estate dwarfs us both as we approach the steps.

May they be happy to see him.

The giant front doors swing open and Sam's mom comes flying down the stairs, her hair tied in a messy bun, wisps of gray having joined her blonde locks. She's wearing sweat pants which is a relief. Somehow, I had her pictured in a formal dress or something. She wraps her son in the biggest embrace any mama could give. Sam hugs her tight, leaning down to bury his face in her shoulder. His sniffling gives away his tears.

I hang back, watching as Kun, Sam's Dad, descends the steps, his hair as black and pristine as ever. "Samuel."

Sam pulls away from his mom and focuses on his dad.

I hold my breath, waiting to see how this reunion will go.

Mr. Hong says something in Mandarin and Sam responds. Despite his best efforts to teach me when we were little, it's not a language I've ever picked up. With whatever words of greeting they've exchanged, the pair move forward and meet with a fierce embrace.

"Riley Anderson, is that you?" Mrs. Hong pulls me into a hug and squeezes me like we're not practically strangers after all these years.

I pat her back before pulling away. "It's good to see you."

"Riley." Mr. Hong hugs me, his accent barely identifiable anymore.

I take a moment to watch these people I once knew well. Mr. Hong's face is lined with wrinkles, and Mrs. Hong has laugh lines set deep at the corners of her eyes and mouth. But his wide grin is the same and the smell of fresh baked goods still lingers around her.

Sam looks between them. "Where's Hannah?"

Mrs. Hong winces. "In her room."

"Ah." Sam nods, but not before I catch the hurt flickering through his eyes.

Mr. Hong wraps an arm around his son's shoulders and ushers him toward the house. "Come in, come in."

Mrs. Hong catches my hand and presses my fingers. "Thank you for bringing Samuel home."

"He wanted to come," I assure her.

She turns to watch her husband and son ascend the steps. "It's about time. We've been worried."

I search her eyes. "How much do you know?"

"Enough. Mostly from the news, but he's been calling Kun more often." Her serious gaze turns on me.

"He misses you," I say. "All of you."

She splays a hand over her chest. "Trust me, we've missed him just as much."

We enter the house, and my breath catches at the sheer elegance of everything. I root my sneakers to the tiles to keep from breaking anything.

Mrs. Hong touches my shoulder. "I hope you won't think less of us, dear."

"Less of you?"

"It all must seem frivolous." She waves a hand at the entry way. "Sometimes, I wish we'd stayed in that little yellow house, but I was desperate to escape the paparazzi." She sighs. "If nothing else, we do have privacy out here."

"It's a beautiful home."

"Cora has put together a feast to welcome Sam home," Kun whispers to me, grinning from ear to ear at his wife. Sam's mom has always been an amazing cook and Mr. Hong has never been shy about letting people know it.

My heart gives a little pang. Oh, how I've missed these people. I sniff deeply and my stomach gurgles. "Whatever you're cooking smells delicious."

"Pot roast. Once upon a time it was Samuel's favorite." She winks.

Sam rubs his stomach. "You can never go wrong with pot roast."

Cora shoots me a worried expression. "I wish we'd known you were coming. You don't have any allergies I've forgotten about, do you?"

"Just pineapple."

"Then you are safe here." Kun winks. "I can't abide the fruit."

"Sam, why don't you go upstairs and find your sister. We'll have dinner on the table soon." The Hongs move off toward where I assume the kitchen must be, heads bent close together.

"She's not going to give us directions?" I whisper to Sam.

He laughs. "Come on. She said upstairs, so I suppose we should start by finding a staircase."

"Good thinking." I snicker and let him lead me through the house.

We pass a family room with a massive tv and leather furniture that hardly looks lived in.

"Ah, there we go." Sam points to a sleek staircase around the next corner.

Let's hope they lead exactly where we need to go. I swallow as my sneakers collide with the white carpet lining the steps. Oh, I hope they aren't as dirty as they feel in this moment. I ease out of them, and even then, it seems scandalous to touch my socks to the plush floor. I keep my hands fisted at my sides and lean away from the polished banister. Last thing this place needs is my smudgy fingerprints.

Sam has no such convictions. His hand follows the banister all the way to the top of the stairs.

Great big doors line one side of the hallway with a smattering of oversized windows facing opposite them.

"Hannah?" Sam calls.

No reply.

I arch an eyebrow at him. He shrugs and moves to the closest door. A turn of the handle reveals a linen closet. Nice to know people who live in houses like these still need such basic necessities.

I try the next door and find a sprawling bathroom. It's like the size of my room combined with Kenzie's. A clawfoot tub sits in the middle of the floor.

Nice. "Wow."

"Find her?" Sam pokes his head over my shoulder.

"Nope. Remind me to sweet talk myself into a soak in the tub later."

Sam laughs and we move on. He knocks on the third door.

"I'm busy," a girl calls.

Hannah.

Sam pushes the door open.

A girl with jet black hair lounges on a bed overflowing with what must be fifty pillows, scrolling on her phone.

"Hey." Sam hovers on the threshold.

"Oh, I'm sorry? Who are you?" She looks up from her phone long enough to slow blink at him. Her dark eyes are stunning. I've always thought so, but rimmed in black cat-eyeliner, they're even more so. Little Hannah has grown up.

Sam massages the back of his neck. "Come on, Hannie."

Her attention fixes on her phone. "I out grew that name a long time ago. Which you would know. If you were ever around."

Oof. It's like something slams into my gut. I place a supportive hand on Sam's back.

"Look—"

"Why don't you give me a shout-out on one of your social media platforms? That's what you do when you want to give one of your fans a personal touch, right?"

All right, missy...I try to wriggle around Sam to shake some sense into the punk—I mean angel.

He extends an arm, holding me back. "I'm sorry, Hannah. I should have been around more. That's on me."

She doesn't move to acknowledge his words. How much muscle does it take to remain so still?

Sam blows out a breath. "Look, I can't make you forgive me, or even talk to me, but I do want you to know I'm sorry and I plan to change things."

Her eye roll is impeccable. "Whatever."

Sam's shoulders slump and he turns away.

"Where are you going?" I catch his arm.

"To help Mom." I watch him retreat down the hallway, fist pressed to my chest. The door behind me slams shut, making me jump. Of all the—I swivel on my heel and shove the door open once more. I stalk toward the bed where Hannah has returned to her statuesque posture.

"You know what, you could at least give him a chance."

"Oh, you mean like when he missed my thirteenth birthday? Fourteenth? Fifteenth? We could list Christmases too if you want."

I exhale through my nose. Nice and steady. Unclench my teeth. "He's trying, okay? Give him a chance."

"No." She swings her feet off the bed and faces off with me, one green tipped nail pointed at my face. "It's not 'okay.'"

I lean back to avoid getting the tip of my nose stabbed.

"You might hang on every word he speaks, but I learned my lesson years ago."

"He loves you."

"Yeah, well, he claims to *love* about a million girls he's never met, so." She shrugs.

Heat burns in my cheeks. "He's here now. Doesn't that count for something?"

She examines her nails, but it's not enough to hide the sheen washing over her oh-so-beautiful eyes. "Get out of my room."

"Fine." It takes all of my self-control not to spit the word. "But Sam's right. He can't make you forgive him. He's sorry and he's trying to make things right. The rest is up to you."

I exit to the sound of her slamming the door behind me. I lean against the wall and squeeze my eyes shut against the hot liquid stealing across my own vision. Oh, Sam...

Chapter 36

Sam and his parents laugh and exchange stories while Hannah sulks at one corner of the table. Cora keeps shooting warm glances my way as if she attributes this family dinner single handedly to me. And it is so, so good to see them all together, even if Hannah doesn't appreciate it yet. In fact, I'm not sure when the last time was that Sam smiled so big.

After a dessert of last-minute chocolate chip cookies—Sam's mom makes the *best*—I help load the dishwasher while Hannah dries, and Cora washes. Sam and Kun step out the back door for a tour of the estate grounds.

"Thank you for today," Cora says.

I wish she knew she didn't have to keep thanking me. "It was more Sam than me."

Hannah snorts in the background.

I clench my jaw. Does she not have any grace for her brother?

Cora's phone buzzes and she wipes soap suds off her hands and checks the number. "Excuse me, I have to take this." She swipes to answer and steps out of the room.

I turn toward Hannah. "Sam's trying. Would you please give him a chance?"

Her eyes narrow and she crosses her arms. "Oh, I did. For the first two Christmases he missed. After that, I figured he really was done with us."

My nostrils flare as I take a deep breath. "Look, he's trying—"

She advances. "He abandoned me!"

"He abandoned me too," I yell right back at her, my chest heaving. And for the first time, I realize I felt exactly the same way four years ago.

Hannah's gaze searches mine before going cold. "He's my brother."

"He's the boy I—" *Loved.* Because when he left, I was getting old enough to understand what a crush was. "He's my best friend. He's trying, Hannah. I can't excuse his past. But, I know he regrets it. And he's right. Sam can't make you forgive him."

She flinches and looks away.

"Give him a chance."

"He's had plenty of chances." She picks at a cuticle, but her voice has lost some of its fire.

I touch her shoulder. "At least be honest with yourself, is this how you want your relationship with him to end? No one can undo the past, but you get to choose the future."

She shrugs off my hand. "Whatever."

I let her go, because there's nothing else I can do. She's the only one who can make the choice to forgive. *Lord, open her heart.*

Cora returns as I turn on the dishwasher and lift the last glass to its spot in the cabinet. "Thank you for helping with the clean-up."

"Oh, of course." I wave off her words with a washcloth.

She leans against the counter. "How's your family?"

"Good. Kenzie graduated college this year, and has been working a lot at this cute little store. Do you remember Lou-Lou?"

"Little Olivia?" Cora chuckles. "It would be impossible to forget that girl."

I laugh. "She's been staying with us for the summer."

"And your dad?"

Dad? I swipe at the counter. "He's good. He um, he's started," I choke out the word, "dating again."

"Oh? That's great."

"Yep."

"But you don't seem thrilled."

I forgot how good she is at reading people. "I don't know. It's just...weird."

She steps closer and places a hand on my back. "I know. He loved your mother very much. Their marriage was something special and made me work on mine like never before. But Riley, honey, we weren't meant to be alone."

"I know. I'm trying. I really am."

She squeezes my hand. "That's all you can do. I'll be praying for you."

"Thank you."

"Anytime."

Sam bursts into the room and snags my hand. "You've got to come see this."

"What?"

But he's already pulling me out the door. My bare feet hit stone as he leads me out onto a terrace. Fireflies speckle the night, their small lights flickering on and off as they fly over a great expanse of land uninterrupted by city lights or neighbors. Above us, the light of stars shines oh so bright, joining in the summer beauty.

"It's gorgeous." *What a magnificent world you've spun, Lord.*

"Yeah, it is." Sam squeezes my hand before letting go.

I turn in a slow circle, taking it all in. And for the first time, I think I understand what seduced the Hong's away from their cozy yellow home next to mine.

Sam drops onto a cushioned couch and I slide down next to him. Okay, loveseat is a better description than couch. But there must be water nearby, because a cool breeze keeps me from putting space between us.

Sam yawns and drapes an arm across the back of the loveseat, his arm resting inches from my shoulders. "Thank you for coming with me."

"Sam. It's no big deal, I was happy to." I relax further into the cushions and his arm drops those last few inches to wrap around my shoulders. I lean my head back and find his shoulder a ready cushion.

"You were right. Mom and Dad...they've already forgiven me for neglecting them. Just like that..."

"Isn't that how forgiveness is supposed to work?"

His sigh tickles the top of my head. "Yeah, but I don't know, I feel like I should've had to work for it."

"It's called grace, Sam." I pat his knee.

He's quiet, his steady heartbeat echoing beneath his chest.

When did I angle so far against him? But I don't move. It feels perfectly right, being here like this.

"What do I do about Hannah?"

"Keep trying to reach her. I have a feeling she'll come around eventually." *Oh, Lord, I pray so.*

His thumb strokes my arm, sending a shiver through my middle. "I guess you're right."

I angle to look up at him. "Samuel Hong, I'm *always* right."

His laugh is interrupted by the sliding door squeaking open.

Cora steps onto the terrace, wrapping a cardigan over her shoulders. "Do you want to spend the night? I'd feel better if you two weren't out driving tonight and I'm sure Gavin would feel the same. You can get an early start in the morning."

Sam looks to me. "Is that okay with you?"

"Yeah, sounds good. Let me call my dad, and double check, but I'm sure it'll be fine." I rise and fish my phone out of my pocket.

Cora squeezes my arm as I pass. "I'll get the guest room ready."

"Thank you." I make a quick call to my dad and he agrees with Sam's mom. "We should be back by noon I would think."

"No rush," Dad says. "Just make sure Sam drives safely."

"He always does." I wish he could see my playful eye roll.

"Be safe. Love you, kiddo."

"Love you too."

We hang up and Cora shows me to the guest room.

I slip into a borrowed pair of Hannah's pajamas and slide into the king-sized bed. It's big and cold without Lou-Lou and Sarge to help fill it, but I'm so tired from the flip-flopping emotions of the day it doesn't take long for sleep to claim me.

Chapter 37

I wake to the sound of Hannah and Sam squabbling in the kitchen. Well, and the smell of frying bacon.

Ugh.

But also, yum.

I resist the urge to pull my pillow over my head to block out the siblings' bickering, but my stomach gurgles, lured by the bacon. And if memory serves me correctly, Cora knows how to cook bacon perfectly. I'd never admit it's better than Kenzie's though. Not to my sister's face anyway.

I slip out of bed, freshen up as best I can in the adjoining bathroom, and throw on yesterday's clothes.

I get lost halfway to the kitchen, take a detour through a gorgeous library, and then finally step into the tiled space filled with the tantalizing scent of frying bacon and something more on the yeasty side.

Hannah groans. "Sam, you are so immature. The pancakes do not need to be shaped."

He makes a tisking noise as he pours a batch of batter onto the griddle in the shape of a smiley face. "Focus on the eggs and let me work my magic."

"Whatever." She rolls her eyes but cracks an egg into a skillet all the same.

"Good morning, Riley," Cora calls from her position at the stove.

Hannah grunts and rubs her face like she's not quite awake yet. Sam grins at me. "Morning."

He looks at home here with his mom and sister. He wears a grey t-shirt and plaid pajama pants he must have borrowed from his dad. He hasn't even combed out his bedhead. My heart does a funny little flop.

"Grab a plate, and we'll get you fixed up." Cora points a spatula toward a stack of plates near the sink.

I grab a plate and fork and step into their assembly line. Cora serves a generous amount of bacon, followed by a pair of sunny eggs from Hannah, and I find myself waiting for Sam. "Do I get to choose the shape?"

"Nope. This one's done." He slides a heart shaped pancake onto my plate.

"Boo. Poor service," I say even as my attention fixes on the heart. How silly is it that I suddenly want this to mean more than a cooked pancake?

"You okay?" Sam squints at me.

I blink. Laugh. "Fine."

Cora points to the fridge. "There's orange juice in the fridge or milk...help yourself to anything that sounds good."

"Coffee's over there." Sam nudges me toward the island where a pair of French presses sit beside a jar of homemade creamer. He pushes a mug into my hand.

Bless him.

I take my time putting my drink together, making sure to get the proper ratio of creamer to coffee which won't leave the mixture either too bitter or too sweet. When the blend is perfected, I take my food out to the patio and slide into a chair at a large glass table positioned to take in the land. There's a large pond I missed in the darkness yesterday, but I make a mental note to walk over later and check it out.

The back-door squeaks open and Sam joins me, his own coffee and plate in hand. He sits and releases a deep sigh.

I nudge his leg under the table. "You okay?"

He blows out another breath before lifting his fork and cutting through his first pancake. "Yeah, it's hitting me how much I wish I could stay."

Oh, Sam. "Maybe you could come back for an extended visit soon."

"Yeah, maybe." He picks at one of his eggs, popping the yoke.

"Any word from your bodyguard or manager?"

"They'll be here by Monday at the latest. I've been ordered to lay low until then."

The words are a sledgehammer to the gut. I swallow hard. Nod and smile. I knew this day would come, but foreknowledge doesn't make it any easier.

"I have to man up and face this. And..." He shakes his head.

"And?" I prompt before stuffing a large bite of pancake into my mouth to keep from crying.

"And I don't feel called to leave the industry. I've gotten right with God, and I think He can still use me."

"That's amazing, and He can, Sam." Somehow, I know it in the depths of my soul. God is not done with Samuel Hong. "Have you thought about doing things the way you used to? Before, I mean?"

Before the record deal. Before a marketing team turned him into the next teenage heartthrob.

Sam's brow furrows. "You mean the hymns?"

"The hymns. Sharing your faith publicly. That's what you loved in the beginning."

He nods. "There was meaning back then. I could see the good in it all."

"Maybe it could be that way again." I shrug.

Direct his heart, Lord. Make his path clear.

Sam bobs his head as if listening to a beat beyond my hearing. "You might be onto something, Riley. I'd have to consult my team…"

"It's worth a try. The worst they can do is say no, and then you're no worse off than you are now. God's given you your platform. Use it for His glory."

"Okay." He blows out a breath. "Okay." A slow smile transforms his face.

Please open this door, God. And then give Sam the courage to step through.

Sam stares off in the distance, shoulders still sagged.

"What else?"

His gaze flicks to mine. "I don't think I'm ready to go back to all of it. The lights, cameras. I can't go anywhere without someone asking for an autograph. I'll miss…this." He throws out a hand, gesturing to the peaceful countryside surrounding us. "You." His stare fixes on mine.

I force a wobbly smile. "We'll always be here." I bump my foot against his. "Just don't stay away for so long this time."

His dimple makes a weak appearance. "I won't."

"Good."

After a round of hugs and promises of weekly phone calls, Sam collapses into the driver's seat of his car. I buckle in and reach for my tablet. I have got to get the bakery logo done and sent before Monday.

Sam sits, watching his family as they gather on the front steps, waving goodbye.

"It'll be different this time," I say.

He pushes out a breath before throwing the car into drive. "You're right. It'll be different. And I'll be back for Christmas."

Don't go, my heart cries. "Exactly." I bend my head so he won't see the tears blurring the bakery logo on the screen in my lap.

As Sam pulls out of the gate, bright lights flash, blinding me. "What is going on?" I raise a hand to shield my eyes.

"They've found me." Defeat hangs heavy in his words.

I fan my fingers, squinting to watch paparazzi lining the road, cameras flashing, eyes gleaming as they fight to get the most note-worthy shots.

Something dark creeps through my middle and I hunch down in my seat, raising my tablet to cover my face. No, no, no. This can't be happening. But my pounding heart assures me otherwise.

"Sammy Hong—"

"Who's the girl, Sammy?"

"What have you been doing all this time, Sammy?"

The questions fly as the pack crowds closer to the car.

"Sorry, Riley." Sam groans as he cranes his neck, searching for a way out of this.

"Can you get us out of here?" Or call the cops? I whimper and lower even further into my seat.

"Hang tight." Sam lays on the horn. "Move."

Undecipherable shouts rise up. Whether in glee or in protest, who knows.

Someone hammers on my window and I yelp, turning wide eyes toward Sam.

"Who is your girlfriend, Sammy?"

"Smile for a picture, sweetheart."

Sam mutters something under his breath and reaches into the back seat, retrieving a dark sweatshirt with a hood. "Put this on."

I slip into it as quickly as I can, keeping my head bent low, hoping my hair has fallen forward enough to shield my face. I zip the sweatshirt up to my chin and pull the hood low over my face.

Sam slams the horn again and revs the engine.

The people appear to get the message this time and back off, cameras still flashing. Sam peels off, sending them running for the cars parked along both sides of the road. I massage my temple, already picturing the scandalous story of the star with road rage sure to appear in the headlines sooner rather than later.

"Hold, on, we'll lose them." Sam turns down a back road and then several more. I don't relax until we've gone twenty minutes without seeing another car.

Sam blows out a breath, some of the tension seeping from his shoulders. "I'm sorry, Ri."

"It's okay." It's not. My heart still thunders wildly in my chest. "It comes with the territory." I offer him a wobbly smile.

His eyes call me a liar, but he turns his attention to the road and a heavy silence falls between us.

Chapter 38

The car rumbles up the driveway where my house greets us with lights and warmth, and all the familiarity of home.

Sam puts the car in park. "Thanks again for coming."

"Anytime. I had fun." Other than the little fiasco at the end. I hope he knows how deeply I mean those words. I make sure my smile is cheery and bright as I slide my seatbelt off. Because I will not ruin the last of our time together with hysterics. There will be plenty of time for tears after this.

He pushes his door open and joins me as we head toward the front door.

My stomach twists as we walk side by side and yet so apart. And yet I slow my steps, making this last, because I don't know when we'll get the chance to do this again. *Please, Lord. Don't let this be the end.*

Sam stops me with a touch on my arm. "Riley, there's something I want to talk to you about." His fingers slide down and find my hand.

Days ago, I would have run. Even now, my knees tremble, but I hold my ground. "Okay?" My heart rate quickens. *God, what do I do?*

"Riley, I—" His thumb strokes my knuckles and his eyes search mine. "Riley, I care about you. A lot. You've always been my best friend, and I've always hoped we could be more."

My stomach flips and a thousand fireworks go off in my head, but a shiver running up my spine silences all the good in his declaration. With the flash of a camera, everything has been ruined. I can't look at him as my Sam. No, Sam comes with cameras and shouted questions and fists pounding on windows. Everything I've always dreamed of and never wanted collide with his declaration.

"Riley." Sam shakes my hand lightly. "Say something."

"Sam..." I try to pull my hand free, but he won't let go. "Sam, I can't. The limelight, the paparazzi...the death threats." My palm turns slick.

Hurt flashes through his eyes and his hand falls away.

No, no, no. The last thing I want is to hurt this boy. I touch his face, thumb finding the indentation where his dimple is. "I care about you. A lot." Love. I love you a lot. "But—"

His hand covers mine. "No, buts. Please."

I tug free from his grip. Step away and wrap my arms around my middle. "You'll always be my best friend."

"Wow." He also takes a step backward, jaw going tight. "Friend zoned, huh?"

My heart shatters. "Oh, Sam, no. It's not like that."

"Then what is it like? Help me understand." He runs his fingers through his hair.

"You'll always be someone special to me." So special. And he'll never know how much I care. "But I told you. The limelight. That's not the life for me." Especially not after experiencing it today. *I can't, God. I just can't.*

His dark eyes turn glassy and wet and he retreats. Another step and he'll be off the porch entirely.

My own chin trembles. *Not like this, Lord. Please don't let our friendship end like this.* "Sam..." But I don't know how to follow up. I'm not about to make a promise I can't keep.

Sam hesitates, toeing the ground. "We could keep it secret."

"I want to be more than some dirty secret tucked into the back corner of your life."

His nostrils flare. "That's not what I—"

The front door swings open and Dad steps onto the porch. He pulls the door shut behind him, a deep furrow creasing his brow. "You're home." He shifts his weight from one foot to the other.

"Is everything okay?" I force a laugh. "You're acting weird."

His scrutiny travels over both of us, and he must be able to tell things aren't okay, but the furrow in his brow deepens. "Listen, there's something you need to know—"

The front door swings open and a woman with perfect hair and shadowy makeup steps out, a hulking man in a dark suit behind her. "Sammy!"

Sam's face washes pale. "Annabelle."

Chapter 39

Dad clears his throat. "Maybe it would be best if you all brought this conversation inside." He steps back, widening the door.

Right. I slide in between Dad and Annabelle who's got her hand on Sam's shoulder like she owns him or something. But maybe as his manager, she kind of does.

"Sammy, you could look happier to see me." The woman finally steps away from him.

Sam shoves his hands into his pockets, and positions his back toward the wall like he expects an attack from behind. "What are you doing here, Annabelle?"

Annabelle shoots a look toward the man I assume is Sam's body-guard before turning an irked gaze on my friend. "We're here to bring you home. I told you we were coming."

"On Monday."

"By Monday."

I slink toward the kitchen.

Sam shoots me a pleading look and I stop my retreat. Okay, I'll be his backup then. Forget what happened five minutes ago. Sam is still my best friend and I'll be here for as long as he'll let me. I change directions and station myself next to Sam.

Annabelle doesn't miss the movement and her heavily shadowed eyes narrow on me.

I narrow mine right back. Bring it on.

Dad clears his throat. "We saw Annabelle and Steve waiting outside your house and Lou-Lou recognized her. Thought we'd get her inside before someone put two and two together."

Part of me wishes we could throw her back outside, but it's not worth the risk of compromising Sam's cover. Although, with his bodyguard here…but he's not exactly an ally, is he? He's here to drag Sam back.

"We caught an early flight and our next one leaves in a couple hours." Annabelle checks her watch. "Pack your things and let's get going. Steve's got everything mapped out." She reaches for Sam. "Let's g—"

"You're back." Lou-Lou comes racing into the room on socked feet and skids to a haphazard stop, cutting off Annabelle before she reaches Sam.

Good job, girl. I shoot my cousin a discreet thumbs-up.

Annabelle glances around at each of us and fidgets with the ring on her index finger. Clearly, she understands where she stands with us. Her lips nearly drop into a scowl as she takes in my closeness to Sam once more. Nearly. And then a perfect smile is in place and her attention fixes on my best friend. "Sammy, isn't there somewhere we could talk?"

Don't go. Don't go. Don't go. My brain pounds the words with every beat of my heart, and my fingers twitch to wrap around his, but I force myself to be still. To let Sam take the lead on this.

"Yeah." Sam steps away from me. "Let's go out back." And then, he's ushering her out onto the deck, Steve on their heels.

Nausea twists in my stomach.

"Are you okay?" Lou-Lou squints at me. "You're looking a little green."

"I'm fine." But my voice sounds small to my own ears.

I gnaw my thumbnail as I watch Annabelle pace the deck, her hand gestures wide. Sharp. Sam watches her with crossed arms. Their mouths are moving quickly. Red cheeks and heaving chests. It doesn't seem to be going well.

Kenzie joins me at my bedroom window where they won't see us unless they intentionally crane their necks in our direction. "Not going well?"

I flop into my desk chair. "Kenzie, seconds before Dad opened that door, Sam pretty much confessed that he has feelings for me. Well, not pretty much. He *did* confess his feelings for me. What a mess." I drop my head into my hands. Everything's a muddled ball of confusion. How can I care for Sam so deeply and yet my pulse pounds at the idea of getting caught by another onslaught of paparazzi? Why can't I have the one without the other?

"It's about time." Kenzie cheers and flops onto my bed. "What did you say?"

I gape at her and shake my head. "I told him how much I care about him." I swallow hard. "As a friend."

My sister gasps. "You friend zoned him? Riley, no."

I cross my arms. "A really good friend."

She throws a pillow and it smacks against my shoulder. "Riley!"

"What? Did you not see her?" I jut a finger toward the window. "She's here to drag him back, and then everything will be how it was before."

Kenzie rolls her eyes. "Um, hello? Long distance is a thing. Sam will be back."

"You don't know that." My heart pangs with the memory of all the broken promises from the first time. "Besides, he's told me he's not done with that life." A picture flashes through my mind of Sam at some epic premier, a shiny actress on his arm. A shard of my broken heart cuts through my middle and my throat thickens. "Before long, he'll find a glamorous actress or something. Someone pretty. Used to dodging the paparazzi. They'll get married and have one of those celebrity marriages that actually lasts. Three kids and two ridiculously designer dogs." A tear rolls down my cheek and I wipe it away.

Kenzie scooches closer. "Riley, do you even hear yourself right now?" She takes my hand in hers. "Look, I know you're scared and Sam's life comes with its own challenges, but please don't make a decision you're going to regret."

Regret. The only thing I regret is ever letting the cement wall around my heart crack. Because now it's always going to hurt. Knowing I could have had Samuel Hong. Knowing I let him go. And if I let him go, I may never see him again. And if I do, things will never be the same. My chin trembles and I bite back a sob.

"Ri." Kenzie pulls me close and rubs my back. "We'll all support you, no matter what. But whatever decision you make, promise me you won't make it out of fear. If you're going to give up on things with Sam, make sure it's because God closes the door, not because you're scared."

I clench my jaw and glare at the window.

"Kenzie, Alex is here," Lou-Lou hollers from downstairs.

I push away from my sister and swipe at my cheeks. "You should go."

She pinches her lips tight and looks between me and the door.

I nudge her knee. "Seriously, go. I'll be fine."

"If you're sure?" She squeezes my hand. "I love you, Ri."

"Love you too." I watch her leave, about to be swept onto her own romantic date.

And then I'm left alone, watching the boy I love argue with his manager.

Chapter 40

"I'm leaving." Sam drops the bomb as my dad and I finish cleaning the last of the dinner dishes. There's nothing as awkward as trying to eat your dinner while a celebrity and his management team argue on the other side of the sliding glass door.

I fumble the wet fork in my hand and it clatters to the tiles with a spray of droplets. "Leaving?" Of course, he is. Something hot and dangerous flares in my chest and I ball my hand on the edge of the sink.

Annabelle curls a hand over Sam's shoulder and I can't help but think her long, dark nails look like claws. "We decided it's for the best."

The best for who? I study Sam, but he won't meet my eyes. "Sam?"

"It's for the best, Riley." When Sam raises his gaze to mine, a world of pain flashes through his pupils.

Oh, Sam...

"Are you sure about that, son?" Dad crosses his arms and leans against the counter, studying the pair.

He nods. "We have some things to work out with my label."

Annabelle purses her lips. "Come on, Sammy. We've got a plane to catch."

"Are you sure?" Dad repeats his question without breaking his attention from Sam.

"Of course, he's sure," Annabelle snaps before softening her tone to a syrupy sweet version, "You've taken good care of him during this silly little escapade, but now it's time for Sammy Hong to go back to his real life."

Ah, the façade does have cracks.

Dad's expression hardens. "No offense, Miss Smith, but I was talking to Sam."

Annabelle purses her lips, but retreats to sulk near the door, the ever-silent Steve waiting beside her.

Sam steps forward, hand extended toward my dad. "I'm sure. Thank you for everything." His focus slides toward me. "It's...it's for the best, really."

No. Hot liquid blurs my vision and I resist the urge to stomp my foot. How I wish time had a rewind button. That we could go back to the conversation on the driveway. Before Dad opened the door. Before Annabelle ruined everything. Really, before *I* ruined everything.

My dad uses the handshake to pull Sam into a hug. "You come see us anytime you need, son."

When Sam pulls away, he swallows hard and a sheen washes over his eyes. "Thank you, sir." He looks around and spies Lou-Lou steaming on the living room couch. "See you, minion." He crosses to her and bumps his knuckles against her shoulder.

She raises her chin and has a staring contest with the wall. "If you leave, I will never forgive you."

He mutters something which may or may not be, "you and me both, minion." I can't have heard right, because next thing I know he's reaching for the door, Annabelle on his heels.

I don't get a goodbye?

He turns then. "You'll watch the old place for me, right, Ri?" His gaze flicks over mine, like he's searching for something…begging. But for what?

"Of course." I jerk my chin in the general direction of his house. "She'll be in good hands like always." I deserve an acting award because I get through my line without crying.

"Come on, Sammy." Annabelle taps around on her phone as a black car pulls into the driveway. "Our driver is here."

Sam's eyes stay locked on mine. "I—"

"Let's go." Miss Manager tugs on his arm.

A tear spills down my cheek and I wipe it away while Sam's attention is turned toward her. "Have a safe trip." My voice is thick with unshed tears.

It brings Sam's stare back to me. "It's not going to be like last time. We could still…" he trails off as if becoming aware of the others around us.

I shake my head, arms wrapped tight around me like a shield.

"What are you so afraid of?"

What am I afraid of? Mom's face flashes before my eyes, ashen, oxygen tube under her nose. Days before she died, when she wasn't fully there. Sam's face, round with baby fat he no longer has, his eyes bright as he set out to begin his career. When goodbye wasn't supposed to last four years.

And me.

Standing alone at my window. Mom gone, my friend's house empty.

I take a step back. "You leave, Sam. It's what you do. And when you do, the cameras will be there to capture it all." I do the only thing left to protect myself. I turn away. I leave first. Except it still hurts.

"Listen to the song, Riley." His words trail me. And then Sammy Hong turns and walks away. Out of my life.

Chapter 41

"What song?" Ugh. I wrench my tear-drenched pillow off my bed and hurl it to the floor. I've wracked my brain for the last two days, but I can't for the life of me figure out what Sam's talking about.

A knock sounds on the door and Lou-Lou pokes her head inside. "Stop moping and let's watch a movie."

Moping? "I'm not moping." I flop onto the edge of my bed and cross my arms.

"We're going to forget Sammy Hong ever existed." Lou-Lou marches over, snags my arm, and drags me downstairs.

"Lou—"

"Sit." She shoves me onto the couch and snatches the remote.

"I really don't feel like—"

She snaps her hand closed in front of my face. "Enough. I won't hear of it. We're forgetting that stupid boy—"

"Lou-Lou! Don't talk like that." I snatch one of the throw pillows and hug it to my middle. "Sam's not stupid."

"Then why did he leave?"

"Lou-Lou—"

"Can he not see what a good thing he had in front of him?" She gestures to me.

I snag her wrist and pull her down beside me. "Easy. He told me how he felt about me right before *she* showed up."

She crosses her arms and scowls so hard Sarge tucks his tail between his legs and scuttles over to me, looking around like he thinks he's in trouble.

I rub his head. The poor baby has sensed our dark moods for the last two days. "I turned him down, Lou-Lou."

She blinks at me so hard I'm surprised there's no sound effect. "You what?"

"It wouldn't work between us."

She smacks me with another pillow. "Why would you do that?"

I raise an arm to ward her off. "Would you stop?"

She bounces on her knees beside me. "Riley, Sam told you he loved you and you let him go?"

Does she have to make me sound like the bad guy? I pick at the tassel on my pillow. "You wouldn't understand."

"Riley!"

"Lou-Lou, please. Stop." I swallow hard.

She blinks. Studies me. "Okay."

"Okay." I nod and flutter my lashes to keep another bout of tears at bay. "You're right. It's time to let this all go. Grab your phone and we'll see what movies are showing today."

"We can't. That stu—ahem, I mean, *Sam* stole that from us too."

I stare at her. "What are you talking about?"

"You haven't seen the news today, have you?" She taps around on her phone and passes it to me.

I press play on the clip she's loaded.

Sam is caught outside his record label, surrounded by a group of reporters and paparazzi. Fan girls scream his name in a blocked off section of the parking lot. "No comment on who this girl is?"

A picture of me flashes across the screen.

My stomach drops and sweat dampens my palms.

It's from the zoo. Before the stingray incident. Someone saw us and put two and two together. More shots come from when we left his parents' house, before I shielded my face.

Sam's face goes hard. "That's none of your bison or your biscuits." He turns and walks into the building.

The whole world, or at least a good chunk of it, just saw my picture. And Sam, bless his heart, protected me.

Lou-Lou pries the phone from my grip. "Yeah, better stay home until people forget your face." She clicks the tv on and shuffles through movie options. Picks one. It could be the best movie ever or the worst. I don't know. Even though my eyes are focused on the tv, my mind replays Sam's last words to me over and over and over again.

"Listen to the song, Riley."

What if I'd run after him? Told him all the things I've held trapped inside this summer instead of pushing him away. Told him I lo—

"Riley, you have to see this." Lou-Lou scrambles close and pushes her phone into my hand.

"What..." my words die as I take in the image on the screen.

It's a post on Sam's social media page apologizing for his recent disappearance and announcing upcoming tour dates. I guess a part of me was hoping things had changed. Hoped Sam would get back to his label and realize he couldn't go back to the celebrity lifestyle. But no. He's back to being Sammy Hong. Just. Like. Last. Time.

"Riley?" Lou-Lou's hand is on my shoulder.

I don't feel it.

"You okay?"

No. I'm not okay at all. "Yeah. Fine." I all but toss her phone at her.

Lou-Lou eyes me. "You're pale. You sure you're okay?"

I bump my hand against my nose. "Of course. I've never had any claims on Sam. If he wants to tour the country, that's his business."

Why, God?

"But I thought—"

"In fact, I've always sworn I would never fall in love with Sammy Hong, so it's all good." I snatch my tablet as a hot sheen burns across my vision. "Now, if you'll excuse me, I need to get this logo finished." With a long, long apology for being late. After all, it seems as if I've wasted my entire summer. For nothing.

Chapter 42

D oes nobody else see that something's wrong?

Our Sammy doesn't look happy.

#wewillprotectSammyHong

For the next week, I can't use my phone without all of social media blowing up over Sam's tour announcement and a whole flurry of promotional photos. In fact, my picture going viral quickly becomes old news under the onslaught of tour buzz. He's doing it though, and I'm so, so proud of him. In almost every interview he finds a way to give the glory to God and share his faith. He's announced that at least a portion of his new album will include old hymn covers and he's put out a daily Bible verse on each of his social media platforms. Unapologetically.

But his fans aren't wrong. There's underlying pain in Sam's eyes in every photo. Every interview.

Oh, Sam...

I swipe to the picture of Sam I use as his photo in my contacts list. Dimple popping, hair his natural black though his stylists have already changed it to a midnight blue. "Why? Why would you do something so utterly ridiculous?" I ask the pixelated boy.

It's too soon.

He should have eased back into things. Instead, he's thrown himself in full throttle.

My Sam's not so foolish, is he? Well, there's one way to find out. I've spent the better part of the week balling my eyes out and feeling sorry for myself. No more. Sam needs me to stage an intervention. One I should have implemented the moment his manager stepped onto my front porch. I jab the phone icon with my thumb and watch my screen as I wait for him to answer.

He doesn't.

"C'mon, Sam." I dial again.

Once more he lets it ring.

Again.

Again.

Again.

Finally, I leave a message. "Sam, it's me. Riley. I just—what's going on? Why would you throw yourself into the deep end? I get going back to Hollywood. I do. But this?" I swipe a finger under my eye, catching a rebellious drop of moisture. Force myself to breathe. "Sam, are you okay?" I let the question dangle for a long heartbeat before I hang up and shoot him a text.

Call me.

I wait a good ten minutes, but nothing happens. But then again, I shouldn't be surprised. I was the one who called things off. The one who hurt him. A shiver sweeps through me. Am I the source of pain in his eyes? Ugh, why do things have to be so complicated? Why can't life be easy? If only we could be Riley and Sam with no outside influences coming between us.

With disgust, I shove my phone into the couch cushions.

It's time to get focused on what I can control.

An hour passes as I fill out the last details on the bakery design and hit send with an apology and partial refund for my late turn around. Then I check my phone. No messages. No missed calls. Nothing.

A sharp pang stabs my heart and I blink rapidly and shove my phone under a couch cushion.

Sarge looks up from where he's been drooling on the rug.

"Don't judge me." I wag a finger at him. "I can't do this. Not again. I watched him cut me out of his celebrity life once." I push down on the couch cushion, making sure my phone is good and buried. "I can't do it again." I won't. Except that nagging feeling hits again. This time I'm the one shutting him out.

Sarge huffs a weary sigh like listening to my problems is the biggest stress on his canine life. Maybe it is, poor baby.

Buzz.

I dig out my phone quick as lightning only to find an email notification waiting for me. From Aunt Auggie. For half a second, I contemplate chucking the thing back into the dark recesses of the sofa, but curiosity wins out.

Cheers darling,

I was recently on a cruise with my girlfriends and low and behold one of them showed me some preliminary designs of her grand-daughter's new bakery logo. Guess who the artist was?

I'm afraid I misjudged you, Riley.

You truly are a talented artist and I was wrong to ever discourage you in any way. Build your business, darling, and take your gap year. In fact, why don't we visit my villa together next summer?

With sincerest apologies,

Aunt Augustine

"Wow." It's the only word that comes to mind. In all of my recollections, Aunt Auggie has never once admitted to being wrong even in the slightest. And while I wish she could have said all of this without needing proof of success, none of us are perfect and I'll take what I can get. I shoot her a quick email assuring her there's no hard feelings and some tentative dates for France. Finished, I tuck my phone into the safety of the couch cushions to block out the world at least for a while.

"You want to go for a walk, buddy?" I crouch and rub Sarge's head. "I think we could both use one."

He thumps his tail against the floor.

"I'll take that as a yes." I pause at the foot of the stairs on my way to the door. "Lou-Lou, I'm taking Sarge for a walk. Want to come?"

"Nope. I'm getting in my last day of Kenzie's personal spa before my parents drag me back home."

Right, because their luxury town house is the worst place to be. But who am I to deprive her of her last day of pampering? "All right, I'll be back."

She responds by cranking up the volume on her spa playlist.

All righty then, I can take a hint. I hook Sarge's leash in place and duck outside, letting him lead as I kick pebbles.

Why, Lord? Why let him come back into my life just to rip him away again?

I bite my lip. Not exactly fair.

Okay, a different angle.

Thank You, Lord for the time You blessed me with Sam. Thank You for this summer.

Sarge pauses to snuffle a mailbox.

"Yoohoo, Riley!"

I swivel, painting on a smile. "Mrs. Brown."

She hurries over as best she can in her wedged sandals. "Riley, honey. My granddaughter has been texting me all week. Is it true? Has that nice boy I met this summer really gone and left you?"

I raise my eyebrows.

"Well, that's how it appears to me." She points two fingers at her eyes and then swings them toward mine.

"Um..." I step back to keep from getting jabbed in the eye by her coral colored fingernails.

"You have to tell me the truth, Riley. Is he gone for good?"

This is not the conversation I want to be having. I tuck my hair behind my ear and try to smile. "Yeah. It seems like it."

Mrs. Brown deflates. "But I could have sworn..." her words trail off and she shakes her head.

"Could have sworn what?" I adjust my hold on Sarge's leash, encouraging him to finish up so we can start moving again.

"Well, that there was something between the two of you."

The two of—I twist Sarge's leash around my fingers and lock my gaze on the ground. "No. No, not us. We...no."

Mrs. Brown leans close and touches my arm. "It's none of my business, but are you sure? For a no, that was tinged with a lot of question marks and longing."

"He's my best friend." I shake my head. "Maybe it's better if things stay that way."

"Honey, I married my best friend. And it's one of the best decisions I've ever made."

"I—" But really, what denials do I have left?

"Call him."

I throw out a hand. "I tried. He's not answering."

"Oh, sweetie." The woman who I only truly know through her dogs and her love of all things Sammy Hong, pulls me into a hug. "I'm sorry."

I melt into her unfamiliar, yet not unwelcome hold. Sarge nuzzles my leg, trying to get in on the hug.

"Let me tell you this. If he's worth it to you, fight." She steps back and looks me in the eyes. "Don't let him get away that easily. Especially if you haven't told him how you feel."

I bump a hand against my nose. "How did you know?"

She winks. "Us older ladies can pick up on such things. You know that song of his that topped the charts a while back? The one where he's talking about an unrequited love? I don't know, I always thought he was talking to someone special."

"I know what you mean," I say. "I think pretty much the whole country did."

"Well, the heart is a puzzle, that's for sure."

Puzzle.

I go still. "What did you say?"

She arches a brow. "The heart is a puzzle?"

"When was the last time you did a puzzle, Ri? Any kind of puzzle?"

And...

"Listen to the song, Riley."

Cheese and crackers. What were you trying to tell me, Sam? "Um, I actually have to go." I jerk a thumb behind me. "But thanks for your kind words." I back away.

"Fight for him, Riley Anderson!" Mrs. Brown whoops and raises a fist high.

Chapter 43

The shutter of cameras alerts me to something being wrong. It's enough to jerk me from my frantic Olympic style walking and pull my attention away from the sidewalk. What must be fifty photographers and news anchors are stationed outside Sam's house, spinning whatever tale they think will sell.

Can't they let the whole thing die off?

Sarge jerks toward the crowd as if they are his adoring fans, but I hold him back. "Leave it, buddy."

The last thing I need is to get caught up in—

"Hey, doesn't that girl look like the one from the photo?"

Cheese and crackers.

I whip up a hand to shield my face as several of the photographers swivel to catch me in their lenses.

"Lou-Lou!" I increase my speed walk, cutting through the grass to reach my property all the quicker.

"Do you know Sammy Hong?"

"Are you the girl from the picture?"

"Are you Sammy's discarded summer fling?"

My ears burn and I pull my shoulders up to block as much of my face as I can. Sarge pulls against the leash, trying to greet those he thinks are our new best friends.

"Can we get a comment?"

"Hey, back off!" Lou-Lou scampers down the porch steps and makes a beeline for the garden hose. Good girl.

One of the reporters steps onto our driveway. "Easy there. We just want to ask a few harmless questions."

"Harmless for who?" Lou-Lou narrows her eyes and aims the hose nozzle at his chest.

With the guy distracted, I jog the last few feet to the front porch.

"Come on, one comment."

I swivel to look him in the eye. "It's none of your business."

"You heard her. Now get off our property before we call the cops." Lou-Lou turns the hose on, sending a spurt of water to the ground inches from the man's feet. "That was a warning shot."

"All right, all right." He backs off, hands raised.

"Get in here," I hiss to Lou-Lou.

She hurries over and slams the door behind us.

I lock it and scooch a dining room chair under the handle for good measure. Lou-Lou runs around the house, pulling the curtains tight.

"You okay?" She throws the question over her shoulder as she heads for the stairs.

"I'm fine." I pat myself down to assure myself of it, and for a fleeting moment I'm tempted to throw out my whole mission, but some things are worth fighting for.

The moment I kick off my shoes in the entryway and set Sarge free, I race for the couch and rip off the cushion. Sarge bounds up snuffling like we're on a treasure hunt. I dodge his thrashing tail and reach around his girth to fish my phone from where it's gone down the crack where the armrest is.

"Riley, what in the world are you doing?" Lou-Lou calls over the rainforest soundtrack coming from my sister's room.

"Nothing." I snag my Bible and trot down to the basement and find the card table I haven't touched in…years. My energy deflates as I take in the almost finished aquatic puzzle Mom and I worked on together. Once upon a time, I would have had the pieces in place in an instant. Now my feet stall on the carpet.

Breathe.

I make myself inhale and exhale slowly until my breathing goes from shaky to controlled.

Then I slip into a chair and gather the loose pieces one by one. *Help me, God.* My chest aches, but somehow it doesn't hurt as much to put them into place as I thought it would. Instead, with the picture complete, the world doesn't change.

Instead of pain, all I can think of is Mom bent over one puzzle or another, twisting one of her curls around her finger as she thought. Her laugh as she finally got it and found the next right piece. Her hands guiding my small ones and then later joining mine in work as we knocked out puzzles in half the time it would have taken either of us individually.

I should never have stopped doing these. I thumb through a stack of word puzzles balanced on one corner of the table. Her favorite kind of puzzle. Mine too.

Why did I stop?

My phone buzzes with notifications. More guesses as to my identity from the one viral picture. A handful of girls have even come forward claiming to be me. I've got to give them credit, all except for the red-head, they actually look somewhat similar.

A few posts scroll across the screen with the photo from the zoo.

Who does this girl think she is?

It looks like our Sammy loves her doesn't it? Like if you agree.
#whodoessammylove?

And here I was hoping this whole thing had died off. If only the world could forget.

"Listen to the song."

Right. Sam didn't ask me to come down here and get lost in a world of puzzles or internet gossip. Well, he kind of did, but not exactly.

First thing first though.

I open my Bible and read through several Psalms, letting the scripture soothe my heart.

What have I done, God? I've been so wrong. I should have been seeking You first. Kenzie's right. I've been letting fear control me. Forgive me. Forgive me for letting my fear get in the way. For allowing the what-ifs to outshine the could-be. Help me to trust You and the path you've set before me. Help me to let go of the fear. Your will, Your way. Amen.

After letting repentance soak through my soul, I finally reach for my phone.

I swipe away the social media posts and find the song Mrs. Brown talked about. Bopping along to the beat, I listen. It's a song of unrequited love, one the whole world decided he'd written for his first Hollywood girlfriend after they broke up. Sam never denied it.

I tap my fingers against my knee, waiting for some magic spark, but there's nothing specifically *us* about it. For a song that's supposed to unlock some secret, it's disappointingly un-personal. Is he trying to tell me he loves me? Why not just tell me? Why point me to a song he wrote for some other girl?

With a sigh, I pull up the lyrics, hoping it'll change something.

Remember that time

I said you looked pretty

Laughed it off like something silly

Everyone always said we'd be perfect together

Yeah, I think I can see it now

And baby, oh my

I wish you could see it too

Cause it hurts every time I see you with someone new

And now I'mma spend the whole night wish'n I was dancing with you

And baby, oh my

You look pretty 'n blue

My heart stops

When I'm looking at you

Laughing, smiling,

Oh

Vibrance and sunshine

Everything that makes you, you

Yes, everything I love

Only hope you see me too.

Until time stops, I'll be waiting for you

And baby, oh my

Just tell me you can see me too

Wait a minute…if I tilt my head when I look at the first five lines, it almost looks like…oh, I need my laptop. I scramble upstairs, load up my laptop and print off the lyrics.

I snag a pen and flop on my bed, circling the first letters in the first five lines of the song.

Riley.

Cheese and crackers.

Sweat dampens my palms as I scan the lyrics again. Maybe it's a coincidence. Maybe I'm crazy. Or maybe he didn't write this song for Hollywood girlfriend number one.

"Riley?" Lou-Lou pokes her head inside. "What are you doing?"

"Huh?" I trail my fingers down the song.

"You're running around like a squirrel trapped in a house. Aunt V's going to be here any minute and you're freaking me out."

I pop my head up. "Vanessa's coming?"

"For dinner." Lou-Lou raises her eyebrows like I should totally know this.

Maybe it was discussed. I haven't exactly been paying much attention the last couple days. "Oh."

My cousin flops down beside me. "Hey, that's one of Sam's songs, isn't it?" She crosses her arms. "Riley, we talked about—"

"No, look." I sit up and point out my name before she can dive into a lecture. "Sam told me to listen to the song. He's trying to tell me something."

Lou-Lou frowns and takes the lyrics from me. "But this is an old song."

"I know, but look." I jab a finger at my circled name. "I'm not crazy." A shiver sweeps over me. "What if Sam's been trying to tell me something for a very long time?"

Lou-Lou purses her lips before slapping the paper. "So, you found your name. Now what?"

Right. That's the question. "Keep looking."

"For?"

"Words. Clues. It's a puzzle, Lou-Lou."

"A puzzle?"

"I used to do them all the time. Sam knew that."

"*Okay.*" She eyes me like she thinks I might have lost my mind before her attention snags on the paper. "Hey, isn't this the song he wrote for that one ex?"

"No, that's who everyone else decided he wrote it for." I run my finger down the length of the song. "Wait...here." I circle *yes, only,* and *until.*

"Y-O-U." Lou-Lou bounces beside me. "You're right, he's trying to tell you something."

"But what?"

"I don't know, keep looking."

"But it's been a week. I was supposed to do this a week ago."

"Riley, this song is old. You were supposed to do this years ago."

Oh my word, she's right. "But, Lou-Lou...I already turned him down."

"He wouldn't have told you to dig up this old relic if he wasn't trying to reach out again." She flicks the paper. "Now come on."

A few false starts, and then I find it. *Laughing, oh, vibrance, everything.* L-O-V-E.

Lou-Lou taps an *I.* "Look." She snatches the pen from my hand, and scratches out everything but the circled letters, leaving *Riley I Love You* in bold, circled strokes.

Sammy Hong has been trying to tell me for years. And if I hadn't stopped doing puzzles when my mom died, I probably would have figured out his message sooner.

Oh, Sam.

Lou-Lou flops onto her back, kicking the air. "Ah, this is huge!"

Sammy Hong loves me.

"Wow, what's going on in here?" Kenzie steps into my room, her work bag still slung over one shoulder. "Lou-Lou, you're going to rupture my eardrums."

My cousin flips over, snatches the paper from my hand, and shoves the lyrics at my sister.

Kenzie's eyes go round as she skims the paper and then she's running in place, squealing and I throw my hands over my ears to protect them.

"Wow, simmer down." Lou-Lou snags Kenzie's arm and pulls her onto the bed with us.

"Riley, this is huge. What are you going to do?"

My phone buzzes with an unknown number and I silence it. "I don't know. I've tried calling him, but I can't get through."

"Try again."

"I've tried. He won't pick up even if I call for an hour. I even texted and he didn't reply."

"I bet it's his manager. She's probably got his phone under lock and key." Lou-Lou slams a fist against her thigh.

Right. I take the paper from Kenzie and swallow hard. "It doesn't matter anyway. I'm too late. Not only did I throw his declaration back in his face, but I was supposed to do this last week. Now he's going on tour."

Kenzie's eyes narrow. "A mistake you and Sam are going to have to work through, but you still have a chance. Do you want to take it?"

"I—"

The doorbell rings.

"Oh, that should be Aunt V." Lou-Lou scrambles off the bed and thunders down the stairs to answer.

"You want to take it, right?" Kenzie squeezes my knee.

I play with the corner of the paper. Last chance. I take it or I don't. And if I don't, I have the sneaking suspicion I'll regret it for the rest of my life. "Okay." *Help me to set all fear aside, Lord. If this is the path you've set before me, let me walk it bravely.*

"Okay?"

"Yes, I'll take it. I...I love him, too." Admitting it aloud sends my heart pounding. But it's the truth. I can't help but picture him the day we drove to the lake, his dimple popping in the way that makes my stomach do a funny little flip. The paparazzi and limelight are still a concern, but it's a battle I'll face when I get there. Other celebrities have gotten with normal people and made it work. It might mean adjusting to a new normal, but maybe, just maybe, it will be worth it.

"Yes!" Kenzie throws her arms around me and squeezes so tight I can't breathe.

I pat her back as a reminder not to smother me.

She pulls away. "Oh, this is a good thing. Trust me. You guys are perfect together."

"Okay, but how am I going to see him? Kenzie, he's going to be surrounded by security now, not to mention a billion rabid fangirls."

She purses her lips and taps her chin.

"Excuse the intrusion, but I think I might be able to help." Vanessa knocks on the doorjamb, her other arm thrown around Lou-Lou's shoulders. "Lou-Lou filled me in."

Great. Regular old girl party in here, my love life up in flames around us.

She joins us, perching on the edge of my comforter. "Sam posted the destinations for his fall tour. And look where he's coming." She passes her phone to Kenzie

My sister gasps. "That's only like two hours from here."

Lou-Lou bounces on the foot of the bed. "You have to go."

I shake my head. "They won't let me see him. It's not like I can jump up on stage and kiss him in front of everybody."

Lou-Lou swats my arm. "Why not? Live a little."

I dodge her next strike. "Um, hello? Security. He's not the boy next door anymore."

"The important thing is that you'll be there. You never know what can happen." Vanessa squeezes my knee.

"Okay. Okay." I tuck my hair behind my ears. "Are there any tickets left?"

Vanessa taps around on her phone. "A few."

I nod. Swallow hard. And then I spring off the bed, scamper to my tea tin, and before I know it, I'm extending my life savings toward Lou-Lou's aunt. "Will you help me? Please?" It may mean doubling up on my commission intake and working until my fingers go numb, or worse, it might mean an extra year of saving until Europe, but all I know is if I don't do this now, then I will regret it for the rest of my life.

"And done." Vanessa's thumbs tap across her phone screen. "You now have tickets to the concert." She flattens her phone against her chest. "Assuming your dad says it's okay. I don't want to step on any toes. I'll resell the tickets if it's an issue and give you your money back."

Lou-Lou throws her arms around her aunt. "You're the best."

"You really are." The words fumble out, dry and awkward, but so true. "Thank you."

"Psh." She waves away my words, but a happy little smile graces her mouth along with twin spots of blush.

Kenzie claps her hands. "Oh my goodness, this is so exciting. Four weeks, Riley."

Simultaneously forever and yet somehow right around the corner. "But wait." I rub my forehead. "I still can't just jump up on stage. I do not want to end up in jail or something. And there's going to be thousands of people there. Sam won't even notice me."

Vanessa holds up one of her bedazzled fingernails. "Not at the show maybe, but if you go to the sound check before...at least you have a chance."

Right. A chance. And if Sam told me to listen to this song he wrote so many years ago, then his feelings are far from fickle. In four weeks, I'll know one way or the other if Sam is willing to give us a try. Whatever happens, happens. Why is that so terrifying?

Chapter 44

Four weeks later...

Do you know what day it is?

I wake to the text message from Lou-Lou on my screen.

The day before the concert. Just typing the words sends butterflies dancing through my stomach. I need to wash my hair. Find some clean clothes, plan an outfit for tomorrow, figure out what in the world I'm going to say to my best friend. If I even manage to see him. Funny, I had four weeks to prepare, and I still don't have any of this planned out.

No, silly. It's Sam's birthday.

Cheese and crackers, how did I forget? But no, it can't be. Except a quick internet search confirms, yes, the boy I love was indeed born today. Great. Some wannabe girlfriend I am.

What are you going to do about it? Comes Lou-Lou's next text.

Do about it? Nothing.

That's not very romantic.

I stick my tongue out, wishing she could see the action. *What do you want me to do?*

Bake a cake in his honor.

I roll my eyes. *That's ridiculous.*

Riley...

Lou-Lou…

Do it. And save him a piece. Bring it with you tomorrow.

So it can decompose in the car? We don't even know if I'll get to see him.

Don't chicken out now. Or over think. You do that a lot, you know.

Of all the… *Fine.*

Excellent. Bring me a piece after school.

When exactly do you expect me to bake this thing?

No reply, suggesting my cousin has moved on with her life.

Ugh.

I slide my legs out from Sarge's dead weight, interrupting him mid snore. He peeks at me long enough to decide I'm not on my deathbed or in a hazardous situation requiring his intervention, and rolls over with a huff.

Oh to be a dog.

"Let's go, lazybones." I rub his side, and he rolls onto his back to give me a better view of his belly. "I have to get to school and you have an appointment with the backyard before I go."

His tail beats a sleepy thump against my comforter.

I get dressed, throw my hair into a messy bun and coax Sarge out to the backyard. From there, it's a quick pour of coffee, a dash of creamer, and I'm out the door, pulling into the closest grocery store parking lot before heading to school.

I sit, hands on the steering wheel. This is ridiculous. I haven't celebrated Sam's birthday in pretty much forever. I don't even know what kind of cake he likes!

But somehow…

It also feels right.

I climb out of the car and head for the baking aisle. Or try to anyway. Apparently, everyone and their grandmother is shopping today. After almost getting run over twice by shopping carts, I come to a stop in front of the boxed cake mixes. How come there are so many flavors of cake? Confetti, vanilla, chocolate...

I step back and find a woman browsing pie fillings. "Excuse me, if you could have any kind of cake, what would it be?"

She blinks a few times like maybe she thinks I'm crazy, but then she offers a wide smile. "I'm pretty partial to chocolate myself. You can never go wrong there."

Perfect. "Thanks!" I snatch a box of chocolate cake mix and power walk to the self-checkout like someone's lit a fire under me.

From there it's a quick thing to throw my bag in the backseat for after school.

My phone vibrates with a new message from Lou-Lou.

Pick me up after school. I want in on this cake-making business. I'll need all the help I can get. *Okay.*

Lou-Lou licks chocolate icing off her finger and cocks her head to the side, studying the finished product. "Maybe we should have waited for Kenzie."

I squint at the sprinkle-covered creation. The directions were easy enough to follow, but somehow with the addition of the icing, it looks lopsided. I'll never be the picture-perfect chef my sister is, but I did my best. Too bad I can't pretty it up with a few strokes of my stylus. "Oh well. It only matters what it tastes like."

Lou-Lou snaps her fingers. "That's the spirit."

We share a look. "Get the forks."

She slides off the counter and goes to the silverware drawer and I snag a knife. The cake cuts beautifully even though the sprinkles scatter around the plate. And it's cooked through. Always a bonus. At least we managed to get one thing right.

Lou-Lou bounces on her toes. "Doesn't look half bad if you ask me."

I extend my fork to her. "Cheers."

We clink tines and dig in.

I moan as chocolate coats my taste buds. Our icing job may be wonky, but man, does this cake taste good. The lady at the grocery store was right. You can never go wrong with chocolate.

Lou-Lou nods her approval around chipmunk-full cheeks.

I point my fork at her. "Chew. I am not in a Heimlich maneuver mood." Not to mention her parents will kill me if something happens to their precious angel on my watch.

She offers a sloppy salute and downs her mouthful with a guzzle of milk. "I still say it's not fair." She slumps against the island, chin in her hand.

"What's not fair?" I carefully cut off a generous piece of cake and deposit it in a travel container. I still haven't worked out exactly how I'm going to get it to Sam, but I guess I'll add it to the list of all the things we're going to be winging.

"That you and Kenzie get to go see Sam." She pouts her lips.

"*Maybe*. We maybe get to see Sam." But what are the odds he'll even know we're there?

Make a way, please Lord.

Lou-Lou straightens. "Enough of that, Riley Alyne Anderson. You need to start thinking positively." She pokes my shoulder. "Get it together, woman."

"Easy." I raise my hands in surrender.

Her glare doesn't diminish. "You will see Sam, and don't come home until you do. Got it?"

It's my turn to salute. "Yes, ma'am."

"That's what I like to hear. You're all in?"

"All in." I nod. "Got it." And suddenly, I know what I'm going to wear tomorrow. Because she's right. If I'm going to do this, then I need to be all in. I grab some markers from the drawer by the fridge and scamper upstairs to my closet. It takes some digging, but I unearth one of my few plain white t-shirts.

"What are you doing?" Lou-Lou pants behind me.

"Something I should have done a long time ago." With steady strokes, I pen my message.

I heart Sammy Hong.

It's bold. Gaudy. Looks totally homemade. But I'm not sure I've ever worn a shirt with a truer message.

"Nice." Lou-Lou holds out a fist.

I tap my knuckles against hers before sitting back on my heels and blowing out a breath. "I guess I'm doing this."

"You've got this."

Chapter 45

I've got this. Completely. One hundred percent. Got this.

So why can't I make myself unbuckle my seatbelt?

"Nervous?" Kenzie brushes her hair out of her eyes and studies me across the console.

I mean, I've only been trying not to hyperventilate for the last two hours. But we're here. Sitting in the parking lot of the venue. Surrounded by cars. No turning back now.

Oh, help me God, please, because I'm terrified!

"You've got this." Kenzie nudges my arm.

Then why do I suddenly feel ridiculous? I tug at the hem of my t-shirt.

"Get out of the car, Ri."

I shoot my sister a pleading look.

Her face hardens. "Out. Now."

I moan and squirm deeper into my seat.

"Riley, I did not drive two hours for you to chicken out now. Get out, or you will regret this for the rest of your life."

Ugh. Why do big sisters always have to be right? I unbuckle and shove my car door open, almost banging the car beside us. Thankfully, I stop the trajectory before any collision can take place. That's the last thing we need to deal with right now.

Kenzie rounds the car from her side and takes me by the shoulders. "Just breathe. Everything's going to be fine. You've got this."

"And if Sam doesn't respond?"

"Then at least you know. At least you *tried*. But Sam's been in love with you for years. He's not about to stop now. Trust me."

"All right." I shove my hands into the pockets of my jeans. Okay. I can do this.

I *will* do this.

"Let's go." Kenzie hooks her arm through mine and I allow her to drag me inside the venue and time blurs as my heart races. Somehow Kenzie gets us to our seats. Or well, not seats. I guess we're in the standing room only section near the base of the stage. Kenzie keeps a death grip on my arm as she elbows her way through the tightly packed fans who have already gathered. And we got here early.

My stomach twists as I take in the fans around me. What are the chances Sam will even see me?

I bend close to Kenzie's ear. "I thought soundcheck was supposed to be limited?"

"Yeah, to like two hundred people. Don't worry. Everyone will calm down once Sam gets here."

I straighten and bump against a girl on my left.

"Watch it." She's decked out in a shirt with Sam's face on it and her skirt appears to be made out of art inspired by the covers of each of his albums.

"Sorry, I—" but it's all I have time to get out before Kenzie pulls me onward.

We push through until we're at the front of the pressing bodies.

"Hold your ground," my sister hisses in my ear.

Right. I plant my feet even as an elbow collides with my ribs on one side and a foot smashes over mine on the other.

A girl with hair dyed blue to match Sam's latest style shoots me a scowl.

I adjust my weight, cementing my feet to the floor, sending her the clearest message I can. I will not be moved.

Lightning sparks in her eyes and for a moment I'm worried she's going to wrestle me off the spot, but then a man with SECURITY marked across his shoulders moves into our line of sight, his gaze sweeping over us as if assessing the situation.

Right. No brawling.

The other girl seems to decide it's not worth it and starts texting or writing a post or something on her phone. Brave considering they have a no recording policy for this soundcheck. I wouldn't touch my phone on the off chance of getting kicked out. But, I guess she's probably not here to make an overdue declaration to the boy she loves.

I exhale. I may love Sammy Hong, but I'm not sure I'm ready to get into an ugly cat-fight at a concert over floor position. I shift closer to Kenzie, giving the blue-haired girl a peace offering of at least a little more breathing room.

And then everyone starts screaming and I cover my ears with my hands, flinching toward my sister. The shrieking and jumping can only mean one thing...

Sam is here.

Chapter 46

He's wearing ripped jeans and an oversized t-shirt, his hair disheveled, presenting a more relaxed mood than the stylized version he'll display during the actual concert. His earpieces dangle over his shoulders and he waves with one hand, microphone cupped in the other.

Girls scream and raise their glowing cell phones, proclaiming their ultimate fan status. More than one girl holds a homemade sign declaring her undying love for Sammy Hong. A few even include marriage proposals.

I study my shirt. Maybe the jagged letters and the lopsided heart were the wrong way to go. I blend in with everyone around me.

Kenzie cups her hands around her mouth. "Sam!"

But what is her call compared to anyone else's?

Sam starts in on one of his chart-topping songs and everyone screams their delight. Blue-haired girl shoves against me, trying to worm in front of me, but I stick out my elbow, nudging her back. She *will not* steal my chance.

"Sam!" Kenzie bounces up and down, waving her arms over her head.

The action seems to give a sign to the other girls and they start cheering and jumping to the song beat.

I lock my knees and shout, "Sam!"

But he turns his back and waves to the section of the crowd on the left side of the stage.

I grab Kenzie's arm, pulling her to a standstill. "This isn't working."

"What?" She frowns.

"Not. Working." I mouth each word slowly and deliberately.

She purses her lips and looks around.

I run a hand through my hair, watching Sam. The stage lights reflect off the blue tones in his hair. He smiles. Acting like he's having the time of his life. But I want to know if it's true. Is he happy? Why hasn't he returned my texts or calls?

Somehow in the time it's taken me to think all of this, the crowd has shifted and Blue-hair has somehow maneuvered forward with a handful of others.

"I need to get up there." I point to the barricade and security guards keeping fans from hurtling themselves onto the stage.

My sister nods her approval and without any further verbal exchange, she takes me by the shoulders and shoves me forward. I collide with someone's shoulder, mutter an apology even while stepping around them, a well-placed elbow there, and then a good old-fashioned lunge, until the barricade is right in front of me. I thrust myself forward and death grip the divider, holding on for all I'm worth. Bodies press against my back, but I use my grip on the barricade to shove myself back against them until they get the hint and stop trying to get past me.

"Excuse me, can I borrow this?" Kenzie asks and the next thing I know, she's got someone's sign and is twirling it over her head like one of those sales people who stand on street corners. Which considering that was her first job, she's got the moves down.

Sam circles our way.

It's now or never.

I fill my lungs with air and bellow for all I'm worth, "Sam!"

He trips to a stop, stumbling over his words even as the music pumps on without him. He scans the crowd.

"Sam!" I release my death grip on the barricade and wave my arms over my head like a mad woman, almost smacking the girls on either side of me.

"Over here," Kenzie shouts, the air whooshing behind me, so no doubt she's doing something with the sign to get his attention.

Sam looks our way and our gazes connect. "Riley?"

A hush falls over the crowd as the entire floor stares at me.

My cheeks warm and I'm sure they're as red as tomatoes, but I don't look away from the boy on stage. "Sam."

He's in motion then, scrambling off the stage and then he's on the other side of the barricade.

Blue-haired girl makes a grab for him, but a security guard blocks her. Another steps in, protecting Sam's other side, and I can feel Kenzie pressed up behind me, my own personal guardian.

"Riley, what are you doing here?" Sam passes his microphone to a stage hand who jogs up to him.

"I listened to the song. I got your message. I'm sorry it took me so long."

"You did?" His eyes search mine.

How do I explain to this boy how much I care? I wave a hand toward my shirt. "It's official. I'm in love with you, Sammy Hong."

He shifts closer, pressing against the barrier. "Are you sure? Because, Riley, as much as I love you, this life comes with obstacles and—"

I step as close as I can with the barrier between us. "I'm sure. I love all of you, Samuel Hong."

He frowns. "Don't call me that, you sound like my mother."

I lace my fingers around his neck and he must give some kind of signal, because no security guards tackle me to the ground. "How about my Sam?"

His mouth quirks in a smile, showcasing his dimple. "I could get used to that."

If I tip up on my toes...but I pause, toying with the hair at the nape of his neck.

"All the rest? We'll figure it out. Together."

His grin widens. "I love you, Riley Anderson."

"I love you, Sam Hong." I beam so widely my face hurts.

"You know, it's a shame we never finished the list."

"Fireworks can wait." Goodness knows there's enough shooting through me right now to last a life time.

"That was *your* version of the list."

I raise an eyebrow. "Oh, yeah? What was on yours?"

His focus flicks to my lips. Someone pushes against me and I use the momentum to tilt up on my toes. Sam meets me, lowering his lips to mine. The crowd shrieks, whether in support or protest, I don't know. It doesn't matter if we never got to watch fireworks. A million are shooting through my system right now.

Because...

I'm finally ready to shout it to the world.

I love Sammy Hong.

Epilogue

"Riley Alyne, open this door." Lou-Lou rattles the bathroom door handle.

Goodness, someone needs to teach the girl some patience. I cap my mascara and shove the tube into the drawer, give my hair one final fluff, and yank the door open.

Lou-Lou almost punches me in the face in her attempt to knock on the now open door.

"Woah." I lean back.

She pushes her glasses up on her nose. "Well, it's your own fault. Come on, Sam is waiting."

"All right, all right." I let her pull me down the stairs, after all, it's not every day my boyfriend manages to sneak into town. So far there hasn't been a whiff of paparazzi.

We weave through well-wishers gathered all throughout the main floor of the house. Streamers of silver and blue twist across the ceiling and a sign declares what we've all said half a dozen times 'CONGRATULATIONS.' A pair of chairs positioned in front of the fireplace bear signs of *future Mr. and Mrs.* for a game later.

Aunt Auggie grills poor Kenzie near the window. Bless Kenzie's heart. I hesitate. Maybe I should go rescue her. Sure, Aunt Auggie's mellowed out some due to frequent email updates, but

I'm sure every detail of my sister's life is under scrutiny. But then Alex steps up to her, planting a hand at her back, supporting her through whatever third degree our aunt is dishing out.

Outside the window, I catch sight of the yellow house next door and the newly moved in young family who play with their little girl on the driveway. How alive the little house looks. Full of love and joy. It's about time. Every house deserves to be made into a home.

Lou-Lou tugs me past all of that and we duck low behind the couch while Aunt Auggie's back is turned.

"There you are." Vanessa darts out of the kitchen and snags my arm, her newly installed engagement ring sparkling in the light. She wraps an arm around my shoulders and guides me through the onslaught of well-wishers calling out their congratulations. She may not be my mom, but that's okay. Because over the last few months we've developed a relationship all our own. I wrap my own arm around her waist and give her a small hug.

Finally, we make it to the kitchen where a guy in a hoodie, ball cap, and sunglasses leans against the counter, chatting with my dad.

I snag a glittery cupcake and sidle up to the pair. "I thought we agreed that this," I poke the brim of Sam's ball cap, "is a terrible disguise?"

"Maybe I'm not hiding." He pulls me close and kisses my cheek.

"Then why are you in here?" I weave my free hand through his and take a bite of my cupcake.

"It's a strategic position." He points to the sugary confection in my hand.

I snort and break off a piece and feed it to him.

He accepts and chews. "You've got something…" He lifts a thumb and swipes at the corner of my mouth. A smudge of blue icing comes off.

"As sickeningly sweet as you two are, we're actually celebrating another couple today, so please keep the PDA to a minimum." Lou-Lou wags a finger at us before snagging my dad's arm. "C'mon, Uncle Gavin. Aunt V is waiting."

"Right, right, coming." He pops a baby carrot in his mouth and allows himself to be dragged away.

I move to follow, but Sam tugs on my hand, pausing me.

"Hmm?" I lift an eyebrow.

"You okay with this?" He steps close and wraps his arms around my middle. Together we watch from the kitchen as Dad and Vanessa take their respective seats and each remove a shoe.

I sigh, but not because I'm bothered. More because everything is so, so right. "Yes, I'm good. This is good."

He presses a kiss to my temple. "I'm proud of you."

"Thanks for coming."

"Anytime, Ri-boo."

I elbow him. "Do not call me that."

He laughs.

"Ugh, will you two knock it off?" Lou-Lou breaks us apart. "Remind me never to fall in love." She shudders and gives an exaggerated gag.

Sam chuckles and tucks his hands into his hoodie pocket. "Sure thing, minion."

"*Please.*" Someday she'll be saying the exact opposite.

She hooks an arm through each of ours and herds us toward the party game. "So...Christmas break is coming up. We should make a list of all the things we want to do."

Sam and I make eye contact over her head.

"We'll see," he says.

I laugh.

"Fine, fine, think it over. There's plenty of time for that later." Lou-Lou yanks us into the living room and we join Alex and Kenzie on the couch as Vanessa and Dad dive into engagement party gifts and games.

Sam drapes his arm over my shoulders and I weave my fingers through his. Yeah, I love this boy and there's nothing about this day I'd change.

Acknowledgements

As always, thank you first and foremost to my Lord and Savior. Thank You for opening the doors for this story and helping me every step of the way. I'm forever grateful for the dreams You've allowed to come true, even the ones I didn't know to dream about.

To my family. Thank you from the bottom of my heart. Your constant support means the world to me. In many ways, this story is a love letter to each of you and if you look at the little details, there's easter eggs pointing to our family.

Special thanks to Aly for cheering me on and encouraging me to write this story even when I never thought I would. You loved this story first and your enthusiasm made the writing all the easier. Thank you for being my Lou-Lou.

Thank you to Gunner who inspired Sarge. Now you and Bernie are even. But let's be honest Bernie, your personality slipped in too. ;)

Huge thank you to AJ, Brittany, and Amanda for falling in love with *Riley + Sam* and saying yes! It's been an honor to work with each of you and the entire Quill and Flame team!

Thank you to Peggy Young for your proofreading skills!

To any typos that made it through the many rounds of edits, give yourselves a pat on the back. You did it!

And to my fellow Q&F authors, our group chat is one of the highlights of my day. I've loved getting to know each of you, and look forward to continuing to do so.

Big thank you to the members of my street team. You've made sharing about this story such a joy and I greatly appreciate every one of you.

To my friends and extended family for cheering me on and asking about all the bookish things. Your support means so much.

To you, the reader, for joining me on this adventure. For cheering Riley and Sam on. Thank you! If you enjoyed your read through, would you take a moment to leave a review and tell a friend? Even one sentence helps authors so much and I would be so grateful.

About the Author

Ashley Schaller is an award winning author who prefers tea over coffee, will never say no to puppy snuggles, and proudly wears the title of "Dog Mom". When not writing, she can often be found reading her next favorite book, taking long walks, baking, obsessing over owls (but only the cute cartoon ones), or learning new crochet patterns. As a writer, she seeks to create stories that glorify God. Stories that entertain, but you never have to worry about the content. To connect with Ashley and stay updated on all things books and writing, follow her on Instagram @ashleyschallerauthor or find her at https://ashleyschaller.wordpress.com

Find Ashley on Instagram at: @ashleyschallerauthor

Spread the Word

Do you know two other readers who would enjoy this story? A friend, daughter, niece? If they need a little cheering up or just something fun to read, I'd love it if you would consider passing this story along. Thank you so much for reading and trusting me with your time, it means more to me than words can say.

-Ashley